THE IMMORTAL HUN

A Novel

With my compliments

Tibor Farkas

ISBN: 978-1-5356-1477-1

To my grandsons, Carter and Hunter,
to whom I hope to pass on my thirst for
knowledge and imagination.

Table of Contents

Acknowledgements

This book would not have been written without a life lived as a Hungarian-American born into the horrors of World War II, living under Communism and experiencing the excitement of the Hungarian Revolution of 1956, followed by the exhilaration of escape and acceptance by the United States of America as a new citizen. It is through events, family, community, and friendships that I reached the point at which I realized that this story was born and needed to be told.

I must give credit to my dear wife Judith, who put up with my moods during the creative process, the excuses for postponing important chores around the house, skipping Sunday Masses, grumbling when reminded that salvation is so much more important than publishing.

Also, thanks for all the hard and meticulous work by my good friend Marilyn Borosdy and Barbara Scanlon of BookFuel. Thank you both, from the bottom of my heart.

Prologue

There was never a better time to talk about these things.

In January of 1983, on an exceptionally rainy evening when there was nothing better to do, they came together again. Four friends who immensely enjoyed each other's company, a chance for lively conversation, ideas to kick around, brainstorm a little. This by now had become a regular ritual, though quite not on a scheduled basis, only as their otherwise busy schedules allowed it to happen. But it was fun and they made sure that there were no restrictions, no limits put on the imagination, no taboos concerning topics. Well, almost none.

On many previous occasions the four had talked by the fireplace or by the poolside, whatever the circumstances permitted, their conversation often lasting into the wee hours, consuming topic after topic and bottle after bottle of fruity, spicy, delicious California riesling. They were a small, tightly knit group of middle-aged Hungarian immigrants interested more in conversation than in action. A sign of age, possibly. They came from widely differing professional backgrounds, which probably made their reunions more interesting. Very few words were wasted on the day-to-day worries and details of their occupations. The traits shared by them all were a sentimental love for the old country, an unquenchable thirst for new knowledge, and an insatiable desire for a good story.

This time it was the rocket engineer Tibor's turn to contribute the topic of discussion for the evening. Not that there were any rules to stick with a single topic; they let their minds roam where they would take them. Their lively imagination and boundless curiosity sometimes took them off on unpredictable tangents. But that was OK.

"What do you guys think of last summer's expedition to scale Mount Ararat in search of Noah's Ark?" Tibor asked, looking at their faces for telltale signs of disapproval. Tibor was the only one inclined toward topics on religion, which in the past had caused some friction among them. The other three had steered away from these topics any chance they got unless Tibor insisted.

"Another one? How many times do they have to try to finally get some positive results?" Paul, an expert computer-software engineer, asked indignantly, a predictable reaction. He was perhaps the most skeptical on issues bordering on religion.

"None of them were exactly completely fruitless," retorted Tibor. "If you recall, the Frenchman Navarra, he brought back some samples of wood on his third expedition in 1955 that he had Carbon-14 dated and found to be over forty-eight hundred years old. Which put the age of the wood right about the suspected time of the flood. I personally believe the wood came from the Ark; to me the references to the flood in the Gilgamesh Epic and the Bible are sufficient explanations."

"Isn't it amazing though that with all the all the proof or hard evidence collected by so many expeditions over the past few decades, not one properly planned, staffed, and financed expedition has been launched? Even for Noah's Ark? What then can you expect for lesser objects of interest?" commented Les, a marketing manager, in tacit agreement with Paul and hoping to keep the subject strictly on scientific and archeological grounds.

Tibor took the bait. "What lesser objects of interest? Give me a for-instance."

"Well," Les maneuvered carefully, "take for example the burial place, the legendary triple metal casket, of Attila the Hun. Tell me, has there recently been any attention paid to locating it? Don't you think he deserves a bit of interest from the archeological community? He is no Noah's Ark, but he would come in a close second to any other major find in this century, I would say."

George, a wealthy dentist, watched his friends carefully and poured another round of wine into their glasses. He suspected that his friends were onto something worthwhile to pursue into the late hours of the night. He was not one, however, to exercise his mind without proper lubrication, so he took another drink before joining in the conversation.

"Listen, guys, haven't the historians given up on that subject long ago? Is there a single piece of hard evidence on record even to suggest that the legend of Attila's burial had one ounce of truth in it?"

"Now wait a minute!" Paul perked up. "You're talking about a huge area when you consider that his burial supposedly took place along the banks of the Tisza River in Hungary. That region is subjected to severe annual flooding. How do you propose they would go about finding it? It would be an immense undertaking to probe every square foot of an area perhaps hundreds of square miles in size."

Something in Tibor's mind suddenly lit up. His background was in space vehicles. Currently he worked on the Space Shuttle and previously he'd helped build the Apollo and Skylab. Though not in intimate contact with the subject, he often heard discussions on the topic of radar imaging. Until now it had meant nothing significant to him, but just recently he'd read articles about reconnaissance flights over Ararat by US Air Force pilots stationed in Turkey and investigations of the same by Space Shuttle astronauts. He excitedly raised his hand.

"Hey! Stop. Let me tell you about something I just saw in the papers, very interesting article. It said something about radar imaging having been tested aboard the shuttle *Columbia* with great success, and that the scientific community now considers it to be a new and very useful tool for all kinds of underground research, including archeology. The stuff really works. They can locate metallic objects with it buried over fifteen feet underground. Don't you think it's fantastic?"

"Well, if it works as well as you suggest, it is fantastic!" enthused Les. "Why don't you find out as much as you can about it and we will kick the subject around some the next time we get together. Maybe we'll even suggest it to the Hungarian Archeological Institute to review the matter. It would be a great opportunity for mutual cooperation of the scientific communities."

"OK. You've got a deal. Next time I'll give you a full report!" Tibor picked up his glass and emptied it. The others quickly followed suit.

Well, the story will unfold during the next few weeks, irritating those who would have preferred to relegate such matters to the archives of the CIA.

Chapter 1:
The Scythian Blade

Ekhe, the youngest son of Utigur the Hunnic warrior, had been very busy today. Considering the condition of the sandy and rocky soil on this spring day, he herded his oxen a fair distance along the creek. It was a windy and cool day, the ground still soggy after last night's terrible storm. The shamans of his tribe could not remember a storm of this fierceness in their entire lifetime, although some of them had long and white beards reaching down to their waists. Thunder and lightning was everywhere, as if the Lord of Hosts had been angered against the people of these vast plains. Ekhe especially remembered the last blinding flash that lit up the whole camp as if it were daylight. He could see horses running wildly, dogs howling, all the girls cowering under their mothers' tunics. He would never forget that streak of lightning, that horrendous thunderbolt, which was thrown to earth by an angry God.

All the people knew that God spoke. Only time would tell of the meaning of his word.

The sun settled over the vast reaches of the plains, setting the world afire, casting long shadows of oxen walking slowly along the narrow, winding path, their horns glittering as if wrought of pure gold. The plains seemed endless, broken only by occasional clusters of leathery domes of rounded yurts in the distance.

This land was part of the wonderful place the Romans referred to as Pannonia, which only recently - in Ekhe's lifetime – had been wrested from the Roman garrisons by Hunnic tribes that swooped down the plains from the mountains in the east. Nothing could stop these horsemen from taking the land for themselves and their horses. It now all belonged to them.

This was home for young Ekhe and his father, Utigur, and his mother and brothers and sisters. His father and his older brothers rode their swift horses from here to the distant West to fight their battles with Romans and Visigoths and Germanic people who were misfortunate enough to cross paths with the Huns. These were glorious days. Days of victory and celebration, of rich booty from distant and strange lands.

Ekhe would glowingly recall the greatest day of his life when he'd first had a glimpse of Attila, his king, leading his warriors into battle to faraway places. What a man Attila was! A real king. Just to see him from a distance made his heart jump with joy. Though not a tall man, Attila had an aura of authority. He sat erect in the saddle, his clean-cut features sharply etched against the sky. He had black, shiny, piercing eyes that commanded whole armies in a flash. His countenance radiated confidence, restraint, and wisdom, reminding Ekhe of the graceful motion of the great cats his father told him about, in his tales of strange lands.

When he rode, Attila's long dark-brown hair would flow in the wind, occasionally resting on his muscular and broad shoulders. Unlike some of his captains, Attila dressed simply. Were it not for his personal appearance, one would not guess that he was conqueror of the world, the Whip of God, before whom all nations fled in panic or bowed down in servitude. Unlike the dress of his captains, Attila's clothes lacked the flash of gold and precious stones. His dress was that of a warrior, lightweight and permitting freedom of movement on a charging stallion in pursuit of a fleeing enemy.

He was protected only by a scaled leather breastplate, shin guards, and a pointed cap. What a contrast he made with the Roman and German warriors who could hardly move under the tremendous weight of their protective armor. No wonder he and his Huns were victorious. They would charge their foes with lightning speed and kill them with their deadly accurate arrows before they knew what hit them.

Ekhe admired Attila not just for his prowess on the battlefield but also for his widespread fame as a concerned leader and a just king. Though worshipped by his own people and called by some flowery-tongued Easterners the Sun God, Attila humbly considered himself well born at best. Standing in his plain clothes in front of his wooden mansion, or his tent when he was on a campaign, he would listen to his beloved Huns tell of their troubles and arbitrate their grievances and quarrels. At meals, he would eat sparsely from a simple wooden plate. His meal would consist mainly of meat and bread and he drank fresh spring water from a simple wooden goblet. When the occasion demanded, he would share with his captains or guests a drink called Kumys, a fermented mare's milk, the favorite beverage of the Huns. For all his simplicity of manner, he was both loved and respected. No Hun would think twice about giving his life for the beloved leader who was appointed by God himself for the glory of the Huns and the punishment of other peoples.

Ekhe was slowly considering these thoughts, turning them over in his young mind, thinking how wonderful it would soon be to come of age and become a warrior like his father and brothers, and ride into battle alongside Attila. How he envied his brothers for their glowing tales of victorious campaigns in the far lands where the sun set. Occasionally he would cast a careful eye over the small herd in his charge. One never knew in these parts. It would not be unusual to encounter a pack of hungry wolves trying to snatch a young calf out of the herd. For now, there were no wolves to be seen, but his quick eye noticed a young heifer limping heavily as she tried to keep up with the rest. Upon closer examination, he found that one leg of the animal was badly wounded, as there was blood running down her leg; the cut had apparently been caused by a sharp branch or a rock along the way.

He decided to investigate and follow the trail of fresh blood for a considerable distance. He did not want his animals to get hurt, since he felt responsible for them and cared for their welfare. He was walking along the trail when suddenly his searching eyes fell upon an object that did not belong. It took him a while to recognize it, but when he finally did, his heart started to beat wildly. With his skinny knees knocking and his cold hands shaking, he found himself staring at a sword of immense proportions. It was stuck into the ground as if thrown from a great height by some giant or perhaps an angry god.

He inched closer to get a better look.

"Oh, my Lord! Who in this world would possess such a magnificent weapon?" It had a broad, two-edged blade, smooth and tapered. Its edges were sharp and polished beyond imagination. The intricate gold-and-silver handiwork on its handle and guard and partly down the center of the blade had been done by artisans with incredible skills, certainly not from these parts, he thought. The guard was made of a single piece of lapis lazuli. The bronze handiwork was inlaid with jade, turquoise, and agate, and the handle and guard sparkled with the colors of the rainbow. As the rays of the setting sun reflected off the blade, he had the distinct impression that the sword was ablaze. He dared not touch it until the sun sank below the horizon.

Mustering all his remaining courage and strength, and with a pounding heart and sweaty palms, he tugged and pulled until he managed to draw the sword out of the ground. Quickly he wiped the dirt from the blade and tried to hide it under his tunic. To his great disappointment, it would not fit. The sword was as tall as he. It was certainly a heavy cutting weapon. One blow with this to the collarbone and it would cut through the poor wretch as if he had no bones, he thought. With considerable apprehension and trepidation, he supported the sword on his shoulder and turned to catch up with his herd. He was thinking very hard. What would he do with this magnificent sword? Surely no boy of fifteen could own a sword such as this. His father would never let him keep it and Attila's chieftains would certainly claim it for themselves.

Then it occurred to him. "Attila! Attila! That's it! It is his sword. He alone deserves to have it. Yes, tonight I will get my father's permission to present it to him. Just imagine how impressed he will be. I, a mere boy of only fifteen, will present the king with such a magnificent gift. Oh, how my brothers will envy me!"

With this happy thought fast on his mind, Ekhe whistled to his puli dog to get the herd to move faster. Had it not been for the weight of his precious cargo, he would have run all the way home.

The word about Ekhe's find spread through the camp like wildfire. Simply everyone was talking about it. Everyone claimed to have seen it, and all had an accurate explanation for its magical appearance or origin. Even those who sheepishly admitted to themselves that they did not so much as get a peek at it confidently boasted to know all about it.

"I happen to know," said Kursik, looking about him with an air of authority that befitted a man of high position, "that this sword belonged to the poor King Theodoric whom we fought in battle only a full moon ago. It is said that he received it as a gift from Gudeoc, King of the Longobards. I saw it with my own eyes when he was badly wounded by one of our archers and dropped the sword as he fled on foot."

"I must object!" spoke up Rugila, the heavyset retired warrior with deep-set eyes and a great droopy mustache. "Everyone knows about the dream the mother of our leader had when she married Mundzucus, Attila's father, whom he calls Ata." Here he stopped as if trying hard to recall something from the obscure past and allowing those gathered around him to do likewise. "In this dream," he continued, "Attila's mother recalled the legend of the magic sword of the Scythians, which was lost long ago. According to this legend, whoever owns the sword will rule the world. In her dream God told her that she will bear a son. Then a young boy appeared to her and had a beautiful sword hanging from his belt. The sword was aflame and emitted golden rays and had magic powers. It was a mighty weapon thrown down to earth by God himself to give this boy to rule over all the peoples of the earth."

Looking around him, Rugila waited to see if anyone disagreed. No one did. They all nodded in perfect agreement, having heard it many times before themselves and earnestly waiting for the dream to be fulfilled. Attila had become their king; now he would receive his heavenly sword. It had finally happened.

"Ekhe will give his gift to Attila tonight. I predict that the future of the Hunnic nation is sealed. It shall be as foretold. We shall rule the earth and Attila shall be our king!" concluded Rugila loudly, with a grave look on his otherwise jovial face.

It has been said of the Huns that their bodies have been joined together with that of their horses, for they eat and sleep in the saddle. The Romans, who mounted their horses only to fight their battles, thought it uncivilized to conduct their daily affairs on horseback. Instead, they lived in stone houses, walked on paved streets, and conducted their businesses under the protection of the roofs of public buildings. To be a Hun meant not to be tied up in one place, to constantly move in pursuit of greener pastures or a fleeing enemy. The Hun's shelter was often his clothing on his back and his horse. Both of them withstood the elements with the characteristic tolerance of creatures of open spaces, conditioned to their surroundings. The civilized and heavily armed Roman soldier was slow and no match for the rugged Hun, who outran, outlasted, and outsmarted him on the battlefield. To the Hun, his horse meant survival; to the Roman it was just another convenience. It was a rare occasion indeed to see a Hun wobble along on the road with the distinctive gait of a man not used to walking.

On this sunny afternoon, all the men in the camp mounted their steeds and slowly converged toward the center. Their faces were stark, often disfigured by slashes they'd received in battle or self-inflicted when in mourning. They gathered in orderly groups behind their commanders, each carrying his lance and his shield. The sun's rays scattered from the gilded scales of their armor.

Subdued excitement and expectation spread through the air. Old men, women and children on foot, and warriors on their horses were all flocking in the direction of the golden yurt in the center. This yurt was rounded in shape, just like the rest, but it was much wider and it towered over the others. On top of it flew the familiar horsetail, and the canvas was covered with silk, which gave it a golden hue in the sun. Inside, it was blue. On the walls hung woolen carpets and silk sheets in a colorful arrangement, giving the appearance of wealth and comfort. It appeared to be spacious and clean. Tapestries divided it into two rooms and visible were chairs and a couch made of carved wood and inlaid with ivory and gold.

Women gathered to the left of the entrance to the tent. Dressed in colorful silk and woolen tunics, the wealthy among them wore intricate headdresses, diadems made of bronze, overlaid with gold and decorated with garnets and almandines. Some of them wore belts and bracelets made of silver and gold, studded with amber and mother-of-pearl. Altogether they painted a very colorful picture standing there in their typical proud and reserved fashion. The women of the Huns were loved and respected by their men and their composure showed it. Their children were standing among them, hanging on to their mothers' arms or hiding behind their backs, sticking just enough of their faces out to show big black eyes opened wide and filled with wonder and the expectation of things to come.

The dust in the air slowly settled, reflecting the reddish hue of the late-afternoon sun. An expectant hush fell over the crowd as Attila appeared in the entrance of his yurt. Horses and warriors snapped to attention and greeted their chief with a terrific cry. He raised his right hand high in response and slowly scanned his eyes over the crowd. Pausing for quiet, he motioned the guards to lead the waiting Ekhe and his father Utigur to him.

The pair walked slowly and silently toward the king. The sword glittered in the sun as Ekhe carried it laid atop a silk cushion, weighing heavy on his outstretched arms. Beads of perspiration rolled down his forehead and cheeks. His face, however, showed none of the strain. He was intensely proud, and so was his father. They both felt that today's events held much significance beyond their understanding.

Attila fixed his gaze on the approaching pair. In his eyes, one could see the fever of expectation and the satisfaction of a dream fulfilled. Upon reaching Attila, Ekhe slowly genuflected, lowering himself on his right knee. He held his back straight and his head high, for no Hun would bow his head to an earthly being.

A sudden cold breeze blew across the plain, chilling the spectators. A cloud that no one had noticed before suddenly covered the sun, casting a shadow of darkness over the camp. Everyone shivered and felt that something unnatural and mysterious was about to happen. High above them flashes of lightning flickered, followed by the deep rumblings of thunder. The air became supercharged with electricity and tension. Horses whined and reared, trying to unseat their masters. Dogs, with their hair standing straight on their back, scurried for the protection of tents, their tails pulled between their legs. Shamans and diviners and haruspices cast knowing glances at one another and the sky and carefully adjusted the burning twigs under the burnt offerings.

Attila prayed.

"Lord of Hosts, God of the Huns and of the World. Let me be worthy of this honor. Cleanse me of my weaknesses. Anoint me with your power and might that I may become the fulfillment of your will here on earth. Strengthen my arms that I may carry this Holy sword high above my people and lead them to victory, protect them from adversity, and punish the evil nations of this earth. Let it be according to thy mighty will."

With this he stepped forward and took hold of the sword and held it high above his head for all to see. Suddenly, with a terrific crack, a flash of lightning shot out of the tip of the sword to pierce the dark cloud hanging overhead. People froze in their positions from fright. None dared move for fear of getting struck by lightning. The blade glowed strangely, emanating flashes of orange and red and violet light, and all around sounds were heard as if the very angels of God were singing and shouting, "Glory to God and to his faithful servant, Attila!"

The memory of that glorious day lingered long in the minds and hearts of witnesses. Tales of the magical happenings traveled far and wide, and were recorded in the annals of history for the marvel of future generations. The campaigns of Attila were successful beyond belief, and he reached the peak of his power soon after that day.

Ekhe, as expected, received his just reward. He was appointed personal aide to the king, in charge of the safekeeping of the sword. In a few years thence, he became a mighty warrior, a captain in his own right, in charge of Attila's mightiest fighters.

Chapter 2:
Discovery from Space

"We have liftoff!"

The big white bird slowly and gracefully lifted off Launch Pad 39B at Cape Canaveral. The orange flame of its solid rocket boosters spread wide as the bird gained altitude and slowly turned to a white mist against the dark-blue sky. Only a round of scattered applause and a few shouts of cheer were heard at Houston's Mission Control; launches had become routine now and shuttles lifted off the pads on a regular basis.

"*Discovery*, this is Houston," the CAPCOM's voice crackled over the headsets.

"Everything looks OK. We have a nominal ascent, it's a good burn. We're watching the APU lube oil pressure, it is slightly high, we may run into the same problem we had on the last two flights. EECOM, if the temperature exceeds three hundred degrees, go to APU shutdown!"

"FLIGHT, this is EECOM. I will call the Mission Evaluation Room and check with Renee and Dwayne to get their assessment of the situation. They should consult the contractor's rep and give us a position. I don't think we have a serious problem, but we'll have to keep an eye on it."

At Mission Elapsed Time of forty-eight hours, *Discovery* had completed over thirty-two revolutions and was circling the earth every ninety minutes in a 150-mile circular orbit. The craft faced the earth top down with the payload bay doors open and the crew was busily conducting an onboard experiment monitoring the growth of Parifera in the weightlessness of space.

The pilot turned to one of the mission specialists. "It's about time to check your equipment, Al. We should soon be over Eastern Europe. Please set up the ground surveillance camera and target it. Confirm coordinates with Mission Control."

"OK, Mac. I'll get right on it."

Houston came over the cabin's speakers. "*Discovery*, this is CAPCOM, do you read me?"

"Houston, we read you loud and clear."

"Point the GSC. Take them down: 2513, 0998, 0011."

"Roger, copy."

Al, one of the mission specialists – there were two of them on this flight – was still a little nauseated. He did not acclimate to the zero-gravity environment as quickly as these veteran astronauts; Mac, the pilot, and Jim, the commander, had flown two or three earlier missions, and Mac, the older of the two, had spent fifty-six days in orbit with Skylab. The other mission specialist did not have previous spaceflight experience either but logged over three thousand hours of flight time in a variety of aircraft in the Services. Al was the rookie on this mission, and a civilian at that. He was representing the US Geological Survey.

Al prayed fervently that he would be spared falling victim to motion sickness. He fought the nausea with all his might, swallowed the prescribed medicine tablets on schedule. The flight surgeon in Mission Control checked on him regularly and monitored his condition with concern. Al was scheduled to perform an experiment in the payload bay, involving the demonstration of fuel transfer, sort of an example of an orbital service station servicing captured satellites. The successful completion of the experiment was extremely important to NASA headquarters as a proof of the shuttle's flexibility not only to place and retrieve payloads to and from space, but to show that they could be reserviced while in orbit. Much of the future business for the shuttle depended on the success of this experiment.

As part of this, Al was required to perform an extra-vehicular activity, or EVA, in the payload bay. Preparations for the EVA were elaborate and time-consuming. Suiting up, pre-breathing in the low-pressure suit to avoid the bends, time to transfer from the cabin into the payload bay - the whole process took three to four hours, not counting the experiment itself. Then the reverse process of reentering the cabin. Five to six hours were typically allocated for an EVA, a considerable impact to the already busy mission timeline.

What concerned Al more than anything else was the unthinkable possibility of getting sick in the EVA suit. The unthinkable had happened on one previous mission; the crewman on EVA suddenly became sick and vomited into the helmet. He was barely saved from suffocating in his own vomit. The life-support system was not designed, and realistically could not be designed, to eliminate solid waste. In the weightlessness of space, the vomit floated around in the helmet, flying up the crewman's nose and mouth every time he tried to draw breath.

Death seemed inevitable. Fortunately, this had happened while still in the airlock - the space between the cabin and the external vacuum of the payload bay used for acclimatizing prior to exiting and reentering the standard atmosphere of the cabin. His partners – thank God there were two of them suited up in the airlock at the time - did not panic and performed the necessary steps to reenter the cabin in a miraculously rapid sequence. The unconscious crewman had to be revived through pulmonary resuscitation, after the others had vacuumed the vomit out of his air passages. The whole thing was a nightmare and Al shuddered to think that his wooziness on his first flight might be an indication of the first step leading to the same thing.

He forced himself to put the whole affair out of his mind and returned to the task at hand.

This was his big chance, the day he had been waiting for. Today he realized his dream to fly aboard this magnificent machine and get a firsthand look at the mysteries and splendor of space. This was why he had waited and labored for so long and so hard. His doctorate in geology and those thousands of hours of training spent in the simulator were not to be wasted after all. This trip made worthwhile every minute of study and hardship.

Looking out the viewing port, he noticed California, his home state, swim by slowly under an ocean of white fluffy clouds. He thought of a poem he liked so much. He'd seen it posted in the MER during one of the early flights, written by one of the contractor mission-support analysts who had poetic leanings and tended to view the flight of the spacecraft in a more romantic light. He started to recite part of it to himself:

> *Black beak on a snow*
> *white swan, on your*
> *wings we fly along. Our*
> *hopes, dreams, wishes*
> *aboard, good luck,*
> *God's speed, Au Revoir.*

"Hey Jim, what do you think of this poem?" Al now repeated the stanza aloud.

"It's OK," Jim said, "but I'm not much for poems. I think they are too romantic, or something. I hope the guy who wrote it didn't sit in the MER while he was thinking about it. I don't want to depend on some guy down there for mission support while he is sitting there dreaming up a poem."

"Yeah, you're right. But I know the guy. He wrote it between shifts while staying in his motel room at the Holiday Inn. Those motel rooms will inspire you to anything to while away the time. Those support guys spend a lot of time between four walls, so they are entitled to get a little poetic. Besides, I like the message!"

"All right, suit yourself." Jim was a pragmatic fellow and was not impressed.

Al gave up and looked out the window again. "Hey, I'd better stop philosophizing or I'll miss the next opportunity to gather this intelligence data. If I don't do it on this pass, maybe the ground conditions will change for the worse by the time I get another opportunity on the next pass. Europe is coming up now, I'd better move it!"

Al aligned the camera to the coordinates specified by the ground and waited for the timer to signal the countdown.

"Three...two...one...Go!"

He pushed the starter and listened for the camera's motor to start purring. This model was made specifically for underground surveillance of large mineral deposits from orbit, but it was capable of detecting metallic objects down to the size of a motorcycle. With careful calibration, sometimes even the shape of the object would emerge with sufficient resolution to permit recognition. The microwave rays emitted by the radar-imaging camera would penetrate to subsurface depths of sixteen feet, depending on soil mineral and moisture content. A truly amazing tool, the camera was a recent product of technology developed for and through the aerospace and military industry. Archeologists were eagerly waiting to get their hands on one to demonstrate its capability to detect ancient artifacts as well.

In specific applications imaging radars have been used in the past to explore the subterranean features of vast and arid regions of the Sahara, long suspected by geologists to hide great geological unknowns like the equatorial waterways of the Blue and White Niles. These riverbeds had been captured by the Egyptians 10,000 years ago. Scientists who had examined radar images from the region verified the potential of the Spaceborne Radar as a useful tool in geological mapping and archeological and hydrological exploration. Articles on recent findings in Southern Egypt and Northern Sudan, one of them titled "Radar Images of Earth from Space," appeared in the scientific journals with encouraging comments from the US Geological Survey, arousing excitement among scientists who now felt they had a new way of exploring the deserts of the earth.

Since microwaves, which penetrate the earth's surface and rebound to make the images on film of subterranean features, are weakened by moisture, the technique was found useless for mapping in cloud-covered or generally wet areas. On the other hand, in the dry deserts of the Sahara, Gobi, and Mojave, it was used with excellent results. The geographical region between the Danube and Tisza rivers in Hungary was one such arid and desert-like area, and NASA scientists had high hopes for radar imaging there.

The spacecraft moved silently and resolutely over the surface of the earth. Countries, cities, mountains, and valleys would pass below in smooth and steady procession. With Germany and Austria behind, the ship now floated over Hungary.

The camera kept humming.

"Hungary is a tiny country," Al noted, looking at the map. "Shouldn't take but a few minutes to pass over it." He verified the settings on the control panel and satisfied himself that he had the ultimate conditions for best resolution. "Somebody really wants this data. I am not sure what they are looking for, but this is the fourth pass they requested to retake the shots. There really is something down there. I wonder what?

"There, I see the Danube," said Al, pointing to the map. "And to the east is the Tisza. From up here you can even tell how the rivers changed course over time.

"Hey, look, you guys! You can see the old riverbed. There; the land must be really flat down there, because the river couldn't have moved around like that if the ground had any gradient at all. It probably moves around even today, depending on the amount of rainfall. It is springtime and the Tisza appears swollen to twice its normal size. Very interesting!"

"Yeah," said Mac, "you're right. We'll take another look on the next pass, but it's too far to the West now." Al switched off the camera and pushed the rewind button. The whole pass from Austria to Rumania was now recorded on tape. He removed the cassette and locked it in a storage drawer marked "FILE 23. SECRET." With four cassettes already in the drawer, he was running out of room. "Those darned DOD guys, they won't even tell us what they're up to," he mused, floating back to join his buddies for a "space shake."

Chapter 3:
The Wonder Bomb

The air was filled with anticipation in the small but luxuriously furnished projection room. The room was dark except for the light reflected from the screen, where black-and-white images alternated in rapid succession. The clatter of the projector intermingled with the whining sound of diving aircraft, the sharp whistle of falling bombs, and the deep thunder of explosions. Stuka bombers appeared from nowhere and dove with breakneck speed toward their earthbound targets. After releasing their deadly cargo, they pulled up sharply to evade the fire of antiaircraft guns. The bombs, however, fell with deadly accuracy on ancient buildings and parks, on boulevards and factories, leaving total and indiscriminate destruction in their wake. Large, billowing black clouds raced upward toward the sky, covering everything below with the darkness of death. Flashes of exploding bombs increased steadily in number and frequency and merged into one great all-consuming fireball, reaching in all directions and devouring everything. Even the bombers encountered difficulty and labored visibly to pull out of their steep dive; such was the force of the fiery gales below. One of them apparently dove too low and caught on fire. With a continuing power dive it finally disappeared as if swallowed by the sea of flames. As the black-and-white film neared its end, the lens zoomed closer and closer, until all that could be seen was a vast ocean of flames glowing ever whiter, showing an inferno, a flaming funeral pyre, a vision of Dante's hell.

"Fantastisch!" cried Hitler, jumping to his feet. "Absolutely incredible! This is how to do it. Burn them! Destroy them! Annihilate the inferior, miserable slaves!" The Fuehrer gazed triumphantly at the high-ranking Nazi officials and officers standing in rapt attention. As the lights in the room were turned back on, he walked around to each of them, smiling, shaking each hand, congratulating, obviously deeply moved by what he saw. Tears gathered in the corners of his eyes.

"Give me that magic weapon, the ultimate bomb of yours, and I will have this war over in a week. In a day! You have just witnessed the incredible destruction our conventional bombs are capable of. Give me the Wonder Bomb and I shall be victorious right now. I shall eliminate all enemies of our Fatherland," he raved on enthusiastically. "Gentlemen! You have seen Warsaw in flames. Tomorrow you shall see Moscow and London wiped off the face of the earth. I promise you!"

Suddenly, Hitler grabbed an elegant, very intelligent-looking uniformed young man by the arm. "By the way, my dear Minister of Armaments! What is keeping you? Why are you not ready yet? Where is that miracle weapon your scientists have promised me? I demand to know!" He said this with feigned indignation, loud enough for everyone to hear. No one, of course, took his tone seriously, for it was common knowledge that if there stood among them one man the Fuehrer trusted - even loved - it was this young man. His protégé, the master builder of pompous Teutonic monuments and prolific producer of Germany's mighty war machinery.

"Mein Fuehrer. Forgive me for these unfortunate delays. Building a nuclear bomb is extremely difficult. We have no experience in this field. I have discussed this matter with our top scientists, who have assured me of their dedicated support. They have also told me, however, that unless we accelerate our efforts to build our own cyclotron and produce fissionable materials in greater quantities, we shall not have this Wonder Bomb in the foreseeable future."

"Well, go build your cyclo...whatever," said Hitler with obvious displeasure and embarrassment at being unable to pronounce that word, and feeling that the discussion could no doubt turn to detail which could rapidly exceed his intellectual capacity.

"What do you need to do it?"

"We must mobilize our scientific and financial resources. We need our best minds to develop the necessary technical expertise. Also, as the Portuguese imports have dried up, we must develop alternate resources for raw materials. I am told that Hungary has large fields of deposits rich in high-grade uranium. I beg your permission to build a plant out there and purify the ore before shipment to Germany. It would save much time and effort to accomplish that task at the site, rather than to ship the raw ore for refinement here."

"Don't just talk about it. Go do it! You not only have my permission. It is my command!

"Gentlemen." Hitler looked around the room again. "Behold the only man in the world who can make building the Wonder Bomb a distinct possibility." He affectionately put his hand on Speer's shoulder and beamed proudly, as a father would for his talented son.

Albert Speer, the young and talented Minister of Armaments, went to work immediately, as he was accustomed to doing. He arranged for a series of meetings with General Frohe and Nobel Prize-winner physicists Otto Haupt and Werner Altenberg. He met them in the secluded chambers of the elegant restaurant owned and operated by one Herr Harcher. In these meetings Speer learned of the status of German nuclear research. He came to find that the miracle weapon was still only a dream in the eyes of the academic world; that it would take the redirection of enormous financial and scientific resources to create the technology necessary to put the existing theories into practice. He also learned that the Americans were making rapid advances in the field; in fact they'd overtaken the initial advantage the Germans had developed in the thirties. The potential of the nuclear bomb was already greatly appreciated. Groups of scientists realized the enormity of the weapon's destructive powers. They knew that it could destroy entire cities, annihilate entire populations, and were concerned that the winner of this race was to be virtually guaranteed dominion over the world. Speer was deeply impressed, but being more pragmatic than the others, he felt that there was little chance for rapid development.

"General Frohe. I must admit that I have yet to realize all the implications of what you gentlemen have shown me here. We must not lose time. The Fuehrer is impatient. Your American counterparts" – he turned to the physicists – "have the attention and support of the highest governmental authorities. They have the funds, the materials, but more importantly the desire to beat us in this race. If we want Germany to overcome its enemies, as I am sure you do, we must act immediately! Now tell me what our next move should be."

Dr. Altenberg answered somewhat pessimistically. "My dear Speer," he said, wiping his thick glasses very carefully and examining them closely before he continued. "Europe has one small cyclotron. And it is located in Paris. A most unfortunate location for obvious security reasons."

"All right. I will guarantee you the means to build one right here in the Fatherland. One of sufficient size. It is within my authority as

Minister of Armaments to put all the required resources at your disposal. Tell me what you need and you shall have it."

"Thank you, Mein Herr. But you and the Fuehrer must realize that even if all these facilities and resources were available in this very moment, we would still lack the experience to build a nuclear bomb. We still need more time. I estimate that we need at least two years for deployment of an experimental nuclear weapon. Even that may be too optimistic. Don't you think, Dr. Haupt?"

"I believe your assessment is correct," Dr. Haupt answered, nodding his head.

"I shall release several hundred scientific assistants and technicians from the armed services. In the meantime, I ask you, Herr Speer, to arrange for the necessary appropriations and obtain the highest priority," said General Frohe, putting the emphasis on *highest*.

"You shall certainly have it," said Speer. He wondered, however, whether even an all-out effort would produce anything in time to affect the outcome of the war.

Soon after the meeting Speer authorized the plans for the cyclotron and the construction of a uranium-refining facility in eastern Hungary, adjacent to the already existing mining operations there. All projects, including the one in Hungary, were operated under the strictest security. With Goering as the head of the Reich Research Council, the importance of the project needed no further emphasis. Special SS task forces were deployed to protect the operations at all sites, within and outside Germany.

These meetings took place in 1942, when the Germans were still optimistic about the war's outcome. The research facilities were built and, the cyclotron was near completion and was just about to become operational when the end came in 1945. The first shipment of refined uranium was placed in a large protective lead-lined container and was to be transported back to Germany under the protection of a team of tanks and armored trucks, all with the utmost urgency. The situation for Germany became desperate, and the miracle weapon was sorely needed. Hitler's astronomers predicted victory and the top Nazis relied heavily on the occult to justify their unfounded optimism. As ridiculous as it may seem today, they stayed optimistic to the very end.

The race against time began.

The chilly winds of the unseasonably dreary autumn in 1944 had brought sudden and unpleasant changes in the lives of the inhabitants of the sleepy little village of Óhegy, hidden amongst the rugged peaks of the Carpathian Mountains in northeastern Hungary. Only two years earlier the German military occupied the area and with feverish pace had constructed a processing facility adjacent to the mine, which had already been in operation at a very subdued level for a number of years. The large quantities of water needed for the dewatering phase of the process were provided by the abundant lakes in the surrounding mountains. The mine and the refining plant were operated by the Germans under the supervision of Commandant Erich Mueller, who at a relatively young age had earned the enviable confidence of his superiors to let him manage the Wehrmacht's jealously guarded secret.

In the nearby secluded small village of whitewashed houses with thatched roofs, the natives gradually grew accustomed to the German presence. They tolerated it with a sheepish indulgence, as people do who have been disciplined for the worst twists of fate by merely living in this inhospitable corner of the world. Domination by foreign landlords was not exactly new to them. This countryside, this no-man's land, changed owners frequently throughout history. Whether the new landlords were of Czech, Polish, Hungarian, or German origin mattered little. At their level of poverty, for the mountains offered the minimum of opportunities for the improvement of their lot. Things could have hardly become any worse. On the contrary: the secret German operation actually provided the mountainfolk with regular income, however meager, and introduced into their humdrum existence a measure of mystery and excitement. Most of the men in the village were to be inducted into the Hungarian army and transported to the Front, but were saved by the top priority of the refining complex. Though they worked around the clock, as shifts typically ran twelve hours, meals were at least regularly provided, and with their earnings they could now afford luxuries heretofore considered unreachable.

The village's only connection with the outside world was through the German trucks delivering supplies and mail for the servicemen once a week. Curiously enough, the troops did not find it beneath their dignity to mingle with the locals on occasion; as a matter of fact, they even performed little favors for them, such as a ride into town, or a small shipment to stock the general store. Commandant Mueller did everything in his power to stay as innocuous as possible. Traffic on the roads and even the telephone contacts were kept to a minimum, and only the colonel in charge at the nearest army headquarters, over fifty kilometers away, had a vague idea that something clearly important was going on at Óhegy.

Mueller had four hundred men under his charge. In addition, a dozen tanks of the Panther type, as many armored trucks, and two Howitzers were hidden in bunkers and tunnels underneath the precipitous cliffs. The troops wore civilian clothes in the daytime and all equipment was cleverly camouflaged to ascertain that the enemy's curiosity was not aroused. Mueller's concerns were not entirely unfounded, since partisan activities against German installations were frequent in other areas. Until now, however, his good fortune had allowed him to remain undisturbed and without incident ever since the plant became operational. Uranium oxide, or yellowcake, as it was commonly called, was kept in lead-lined stainless-steel containers about four feet in length. One was readied for shipment to Berlin at the end of the month of November. Since the operation began, the total production amounted to only about a couple of hundred pounds; nevertheless, this was a significant achievement for a new operation. Further refinement in Berlin would reduce the useable quantity of uranium to ounces, but that capability was not available at the site, no matter how badly the Germans wanted to develop it in the beginning.

Winds of change started to blow as early as October. With the coming of winter, the cold winds from the northeast brought not only a taste of the icy weather to come, but also rumors of terrible German losses on the Russian front. The rumors told of the incredible defeat at Stalingrad, of losses numbering in the tens of thousands on both sides, of Russian advances across the Vistula, of refugees and starvation, of plunder and rape.

By early fall the ten Soviet armies of the second and third Ukrainian fronts, commanded by General Petrov, burst into Rumania and fanned out from there into Bulgaria, Yugoslavia, and Hungary. The Soviet High Command ordered the invasion of Hungary and directed its thrust with General Malinovsky's army toward Budapest. The village's only telephone line in Captain Mueller's office rang off the wall.

"Captain Mueller? Colonel Leipzig here. I understand the Russians broke through our defenses and have crossed the pass thirty miles north of you. They are advancing rapidly. You must leave tonight. We are relocating the headquarters to the west bank of the Tisza. Move your men and equipment immediately. We will consolidate our forces on the east bank by tomorrow night and attempt to cross the next day. Do not hesitate. You have no time to lose!"

"Can you estimate the Russian strength coming in our direction?" asked Mueller, fighting to control his agitation.

"The reconnaissance planes report a powerful offensive of about twenty thousand troops, two hundred tanks, and heavy artillery. Do not attempt resistance. You do not have a chance. Protect your men and be sure you leave nothing behind."

The faint sound of distant heavy artillery pounding the retreating German defenses convinced Mueller to act at once. He issued the orders for immediate evacuation of the facilities. The orderly evacuation was a real testimony to the preparedness of Mueller's troops. In less than two hours the mines were blown in and the plant was in flames from charges set from both within and outside. All equipment was totally destroyed and the convoy of panzers and armored vehicles stood ready for departure outside the burning gates. Troops huddled in canvas-covered transport trucks and the roar of the engines suppressed even the sounds of nearby explosions set off by the raging fire inside the compound. Mueller was pleased with the remarkable job they did to destroy all the evidence. He wanted to say goodbye to the villagers, whom he had grown fond of in the past two years, but none were in sight. All of them had disappeared into the mountains to hide in caves discovered by ancestors, hidden from uninitiated eyes for centuries. Taking their meager belongings, the animals and their newly acquired treasures, and memories of a rare gift of peace and tranquility, the villagers left without a trace. Not a soul was to be seen on the streets or in the houses. The village of Óhegy was swept clean by the cold winds rushing down the western slopes of the Carpathians. "Move out!" yelled Mueller to his driver, and the command vehicle, his heavy Ferdinand tank, lurched forward. Engines roared all around them and the convoy began its slow descent down the steep and winding mountain road.

Mueller took another look at the large, heavy metal container behind him and sighed, wondering if his precious cargo would ever reach its destination. The chances of crossing a partially frozen river before the Russians got there appeared slim. He thought of seeing his family, his wife and only son. How they would have changed. He smiled at the thought of his son and wondered if he'd joined the Hitler Jugend. Erich junior was always an aggressive little fellow, ever ready to engage in a brawl with his buddies. He would make a good soldier for the Fatherland. Mueller was extremely proud of his son, but at once concerned. He did not like the recent turn of events, the unexpected German retreat, the remote and unthinkable possibility of even losing the war. He hoped fervently that his shipment would reach Berlin and be used for whatever purpose to reverse the tide in the Fuehrer's favor. Mueller did not know why, but he felt sure that the metal container must arrive safely. There was so much invested into the production of the stuff inside, it had to be a very important strategic material, and it might just be used to successfully defeat the Fuehrer's enemies. As for the immediate future, he hoped his troops would be able to join forces with the panzer division under the command of General Rossler before encountering any Russians.

Captain Mueller's wishes were not to be fulfilled on this day. The Russians crossed the mountain passes much faster than Colonel Leipzig had estimated and, unbeknownst to Mueller and his men, they were in the process of cutting them off from joining up with General Rossler. It was a race against time and the Russians appeared to be winning. In the darkness of the following night, Mueller's convoy ran smack into the midst of a Soviet tank battalion of T-34s blocking the highway. Before he could formulate any plans, the Russians opened fire and the battle was on.

The heaviest German tanks, the Ferdinands, named after Ferdinand Porsche, the famed automobile designer, soon became useless. As they sluggishly waddled across the fields they broke down with mysterious mechanical failures. Others plowed on, but as the Russian riflemen picked off the German infantry riding on the Ferdinands, the tanks became victimized by screaming Russian soldiers jumping aboard and squirting through the engine ventilation slots with their flamethrowers. The tanks burned, then exploded in great balls of flames.

Mueller and the driver, a lieutenant, escaped from the fiery hell by the skin of their teeth. Their Ferdinand stopped in its tracks without getting hit and would not move. They jumped for safety behind a row of hedges and lay in a ditch for a while, hiding their precious cargo. Momentarily, the entire area lit up with the flames of burning tanks. When it became dark and quiet again, commands and curses in German as well as Russian could be heard in all directions followed by rapid bursts of machine-gun fire hitting unseen targets. Only the screams of those hit indicated whether the bullets scored or not.

In a flash of light, Mueller noticed another tank nearby, standing with its hatch open, apparently unattended. A dead soldier's body hung over its side, head down, evidently caught by gunfire in his frantic attempt to escape. Mueller shoved the body off and jumped in. Thank God, the tank was one of theirs. His lieutenant climbed in right behind him, but first dropped the metal container in, which landed with a terrific bang.

"Close the hatch!" yelled Mueller and started the engine, which to his joyful surprise started at once. With trembling hands, he shoved the engine into gear and the monstrous machine jumped forward with a tremendous jerk. Mueller had no idea which way to go. He did not know if there were any German survivors left, whether he would be hit by friendly or enemy fire, or if he would blindly drive into the midst of Russian positions. Beneath the pallid moon, he drove onto a highway littered with burned-out equipment, smashed guns, and tanks with their turrets blown off. Dead bodies were strewn everywhere. He saw Russian and German equipment intermingled, tanks standing so close to each other that he shuddered at the thought of the fate of their crews. With tanks firing at such close range, the thick armor plates provided no protection whatsoever. The shells easily pierced the side or penetrated the armor and fried the crew trapped inside, inflicting death through unimaginable agony. It occurred to him that the tremendous noise of the battle at least mercifully suppressed the cries of the dying. Mueller drove on, hoping that amidst the confusion he would be able to slip by unnoticed and get far enough to hide someplace before daybreak.

Much to his relief and amazement, as daylight broke he found himself surrounded by German tanks and troops. Under the blanket of darkness, he ran into General Rossler's panzer battalion, which had managed to withdraw from the battle scene with most of its forces intact. Rossler wasted no time. He ordered an abrupt turn west and raced for the river immediately. With the Russians not far behind, the Germans' chances of crossing diminished by the hour. Still, it was the only alternative to engaging the enemy, who vastly outnumbered them, possibly ten to one.

The withdrawal did not proceed in an orderly fashion by any stretch of the imagination. As individuals and motorized vehicles raced for the river, disregarding their own and each other's safety, the mechanized units found themselves entangled in a hopeless mass of steel and humanity, unable to move at but a snail's pace. Troops, heretofore hanging on the sides of vehicles as clusters of ripe grapes on the vine, jumped off and raced on foot to reach the water. On the hillside Russian tanks appeared, moving into firing positions. The retreat became utterly chaotic. Troops were frantically tearing their clothes off to enable themselves to swim in the freezing water, only to drown a few feet from shore. The Russians watched the horrible scene and commenced firing with a terrible vengeance, venting their rage bottled up inside with memories of slain families and friends, of atrocities, of burned-down homes and fields, of famine and starvation. On the bank of the river all discipline collapsed.

Units were completely intermixed and it was every man for himself. Thousands of troops crowded against the icy waters. The T-34s shelled the milling masses, inflicting instant injury and death upon thousands. Driven to desperation, thousands tried to swim across. Most of them did not succeed. With their energy sapped in a matter of minutes, they drowned almost instantly. Dead bodies of men intermingled with carcasses of horses drifted downstream, rolling and bobbing amidst chunks of ice, slowly disappearing into the grey mist suspended over the great river.

Mueller drove his tank right into the water and made it into the deep when the cursed engine stalled and the interior sprang a leak. It was hopeless to try to save the uranium container, and in final desperation the two of them struggled to throw it overboard into the bloody waves. They reasoned that if the enemy later salvaged the tanks, at least the uranium would not be so easy to find. Fate had other plans.

Gathering all his strength, Mueller dove into the icy waters and swam with all his might for the remaining distance. With superhuman effort he reached shore, where he collapsed and lost consciousness.

Captain Mueller's survival of the ordeal was nothing less than miraculous. Most of his fellow Germans were not so fortunate. General Rossler lost nearly all his men and his own life in the attempt to escape the wrath of the advancing Russians. All survivors were taken prisoner. The site of this tragic battle was strewn with frozen bodies for months, until the spring thaw permitted the cleanup crews to bury the dead in mass graves.

The Russian invasion encircled Budapest. General Tolbukhin's wide outflanking maneuver approached the capital from the south at the confluence of the Danube and the Drava. Pest fell by the eighteenth of January 1945 and Buda on the eighteenth of February. From Budapest, the road was clear all the way to Berlin. Times had changed not only for the natives of the village of Óhegy, but for all Hungarians as well.

The shipment of uranium never reached its destination. Sunk into the muddy waters of the Tisza, it waited patiently for discovery by another generation.

Captain Mueller fell captive to the Russians and spent the next six years as a prisoner of war in Siberia. He often pondered why he'd survived the ordeal at the river. Often, he wished he had not. Apparently born under a lucky star, however, he was one of the very few Germans allowed to return to his homeland. Finding his son killed in action, and his wife remarried, he emigrated to the US in 1952, where he lived a quiet and prosperous life as an electric engineer; something he always wanted to become before being called up to serve during the war.

In 1972, he was abruptly reminded of the fateful autumn of 1944.

At the Nuremberg trials, the ex-Nazi Minister of Armaments was also sentenced for war crimes, to life imprisonment. While in prison at Spandau, he wrote his memoirs, which were published in the US in 1971. Upon reading Speer's memoirs, Mueller found references to the making of the atom bomb. With nuclear bombs constantly in the press, Mueller finally realized what his cargo was intended for. He felt no remorse, however, for the failure of his mission.

One fine day, Captain Erich Mueller bought an airline ticket to Washington, DC. There he told his story to the CIA.

Chapter 4:
CIA Agent and Sword Collector

Steve yawned deeply and raised himself on his elbow, straining his eyes in the dim light of dawn to read the faint numerals on the phosphorescent face of the alarm clock.

"Six thirty! Damn it!" He popped out of bed, throwing the covers back to expose perfectly shaped buttocks attached to one June Carson, who was sprawled out on her stomach on the other side of the bed. She was sound asleep, breathing almost unnoticeably. Steve moved aside some loose strands of long blonde hair from her face and planted on it a light kiss while patting her fanny.

"June, dear. Wake up. I have to get ready. Hear me? Got to get up!"

"What? What time is it? God, it's so early! Can't you let me sleep a little longer?" She pouted her lips and stretched her arms out, eyes still shut.

"Come to mama, gimme a big hug."

"I'd love to, sweetie, but I really must get going. Why don't you be a good girl and fix breakfast while I shower, hmm?"

Steve disappeared into the bathroom and stepped into the steaming shower and began to wash with gusto, humming aloud and splashing mightily.

June yawned repeatedly and dragged herself out of bed without much conviction. She put on his short terrycloth robe.

"Breakfast. He wants breakfast. At this hour? What am I gonna fix for breakfast. I've got to find my glasses. I can't see a thing without my stupid glasses," she muttered, squinting her eyes and fumbling around in the semi dark room.

"Ah, that's better. At least I can tell that I am in the kitchen."

In spite of all her complaining and foot-dragging, she'd set the table and prepared ham and eggs and poured orange juice and hot, steaming coffee by the time Steve showed up from the shower, searching for his robe and prancing around in his shorts.

"Brrr! It's cold in here. What did you do with my robe?"

"Here it is," June said, slowly disrobing and handing the robe back to him. "You mean old man. What would you have me do, run around all day naked?"

"Ah, splendid idea! Why didn't I think of that? But go ahead, keep the robe if you want. I have to get dressed anyway."

"Oh, no, baby. You'll just end up undressing again." She snuggled up to him, purring like a big soft cat and running her fingers through the curly hairs on his chest.

Steve pushed her aside. "No, I told you. I can't miss my flight, this is the only one to Frankfurt today. It has a good connecting flight to Budapest. I can't miss it. Have mercy on me."

June gave up. "OK! But hurry back. I'll be waiting for you right here." She sat on the edge of the bed, clutching his robe against her chest. It did not cover all there was to cover.

"Hold that thought." He winked at her, walking over to the breakfast table.

"Why, look at this! Knew you could do it. Better than Denny's." He bit into the buttered toast with delight. His light-brown hair, cropped fairly short, was still messed up and wet after the shower, and his bluish-green eyes twinkled mischievously.

In everything Steve Buday did, in work or play or lovemaking, he exuded genuine enthusiasm, creating an aura of galvanic optimism that usually rubbed off sooner or later on others around him. His friends and his lady friends loved him not so much for his good looks, but for the positive outlook and uncomplicated, straightforward nature he maintained in all situations. Being around him was fun and secure. He waved at June, still sitting on the bed, pouting.

"Come here, you nut. Join me. You are a great cook, have I ever told you that? Hmmm. I love it!" he said, stuffing his mouth with a big slice of ham.

June sauntered over slowly and reluctantly sat down across from him.

"You know, before you leave, you should at least tell me something about yourself. I know almost nothing about you, and you were not very talkative last night." She giggled.

"Well, you didn't ask any questions, that's why. What do you want to know? There really isn't much to tell."

"Oh, come on! I am sure you are more than just a handsome guy from the beaches of California. If you came to see my boss, Baumgarten, you must be important. Tell me" – she leaned forward excitedly, her bare round breasts flattened against the table's edge – "are you a spy?" Her eyes were opened wide with anticipation. She wanted so much to have made love to an honest-to-goodness spy!

Steve laughed wholeheartedly.

"Not me! Not this guy! I am too exposed for that sort of thing. And too chicken to play that role. If you had paid any attention to the papers last year, you would have seen my picture splashed all over the magazines after a stupid incident when I ditched my plane into the drink taking off from a carrier. It made a helluva story. Don't you remember?"

June lowered her head, not recalling anything. But then again, she rarely did.

Steve continued. "No, I am sorry to disappoint you, but I am not a spy." He slipped his hand under the table and placed it on her bare knee and winked.

"I must admit, however, that given the rare opportunity, I have been known to do a bit of snooping around, on occasion."

"Take your hand off me, you brute!" she scoffed, her feelings hurt. "I am serious. I don't want to fall for some guy who won't show on the next date just because he happens to be rotting away in some filthy jail in some godforsaken country!" she shouted, grossly lying, covering up her disappointment.

"OK. OK. I am telling you the honest truth! I am sorry if I disappoint you, but I am not a spy. That's all there is to it." He shrugged and continued while pouring a second cup, "I may travel a lot, talk to a lot of people, look around a bit, and usually leave in a hurry before there is any trouble. Believe me, I do not like trouble. I value my life too much. Spying is not for me!" he went on in a more serious tone. "All I can tell you is that I am a graduate of the Naval Post-Graduate School and I love flying with a passion - as a matter of fact, I have flown over two hundred combat missions in Nam - and look at me! I am still here. In my earlier days, I got a degree in aeronautical and astronautical engineering, from Northrop Institute of Technology, a school in which women were a rarity, except for a girl from Alaska, who was a bush pilot and looked it. She gave me my first flying lessons, but we never developed a relationship because I wasn't burly enough, didn't have red hair, and did not sport an equally red foot-long beard, which, apparently, she preferred. Now that I am out of action, I teach Hungarian at the Defense Language School in Monterey. I ask you, is that so dangerous? Actually, I once had aspirations to become an astronaut, but on account of some minor health problem I was turned down. So here I am. Your boss asked me to help him out just this once, because I speak Hungarian, and I promise I will be back again. Unharmed!"

Steve got up and softly caressed her shoulders. "But now, my love, I must leave. You can expect me soon, then we'll continue with my résumé, OK?"

June also stood up; she had to get on her toes to reach his lips. They kissed all the way to the door.

"Hurry back. I'll be waiting."

"You better put some clothes on, you'll catch a cold."

And he closed the door behind him.

Chapter 5:
Steve's Visit to the CIA

Mr. Baumgarten sat up straight in his black Naugahyde chair and looked around the office once more. Everything seemed to be in order. His desk was cluttered enough to impress the most skeptical visitor that he was a very busy man. The blinds on the rather narrow windows were drawn halfway, letting in just enough diffused light to give the dark simulated-wood-paneled room an air of secrecy, in which the visitor's first impulse was to subdue his voice and carefully select his words before speaking.

Mr. Baumgarten had spent twenty-two years in this office. He worked hard at climbing the ladder of success, and not without results, as attested to by the fact that he had three telephones on his desk, one of which was colored red. In the darkest corner of the room stood a computer terminal with its television-like viewing screen faintly glowing in the darkness. On the screen, lines formed by green fluorescent letters would appear and disappear. Occasionally the terminal's printer would type something on an endless roll of white paper that would fall on the floor and neatly fold itself in layers. The clatter of the printer would be Baumgarten's clue to get out of his comfortable chair, stroll over to the terminal, read the display, mutter something in approval or with displeasure, then type something in response, which was then sent to some mysterious place where a CIA agent would receive it in code.

Mr. Baumgarten was Section Head of the CIA's Eastern European operations. Today he was especially anxious to start working. He'd just received some valuable and exciting information from the Office of Orbital Surveillance, a branch of NASA that supported the CIA's clandestine activities in foreign countries.

He pressed the buzzer. "Miss Carson, please tell Mr. Buday that I will see him now." He waited. Over a minute passed and he was losing his patience. The one thing he disliked was waiting. Adjusting his glasses, which were persistently sliding down his oily nose, he forcefully pressed the buzzer again.

"Miss Carson, I said I will see Mr. Buday, now!" As the door finally opened, he heard Miss Carson say something in a remarkably deep voice, something that sounded like "OK, I'll be ready at eight."

"Good morning, Mr. Buday. Please come in and make yourself comfortable," he said with as jovial a smile as he could muster, motioning toward the chair in front of his desk. "It's good to see you again."

"Thank you," said Buday curtly. He remained standing as one intending to make his visit short and to the point. "Hey, Baumy. You've given me twenty-four hours' notice. Maybe you forgot that I live on the West Coast! What's the panic, if I may ask?"

Baumgarten looked at Buday with poorly disguised distaste.

"Spoiled brat," he thought. "What do you know about panics! I've spent twenty years of my life in this hole, coordinating panics all over the globe. Sometimes I sleep in here." But he composed himself.

"It is a matter of utmost urgency. I am very happy that you could be here on time. Please forgive me for the unreasonable schedule, but I've received strict orders to proceed with this matter immediately. Now, please sit down, I have something very important to tell you."

Buday walked over to the window. With his hands in his pockets, he looked outside as if there were something interesting to view through these narrow and dirty windows. All he could see, of course, was stories upon stories of dirty windows with half-drawn blinds. It was not that he was interested in this drab view of Washington's bureaucracy, just that he enjoyed this little game with Baumgarten. He knew it upset the old bureaucrat to turn his back on him. Baumgarten enjoyed talking down to his visitors seated in the guest chair, which was a little lower than most regulation chairs.

Steven Buday was slightly taller than average, with a lean and muscular build. He was tanned and impeccably dressed, but in a casual California way. He struck a sharp contrast with Washington's potbellied clerks stuffed into pinstripes who as blind moles scurried around the city's concrete mazes. He always wore civilian clothes when summoned to the Capitol. Though an ex-Navy pilot with the rank of lieutenant commander, and more recently an instructor at the Defense Language School in Monterey, he knew that these excursions to Washington meant that his uniform would not be needed for quite some time.

"Dear Commander," Baumgarten said, his voice somewhat strained. "I think we've found the perfect assignment for you. You will finally have the opportunity to use your knowledge of Hungarian. I have heard that you speak it as a native. I presume you learned as a child?"

"Yes, as a matter of fact, I did. My parents were DPs. Displaced persons. They immigrated to this country shortly after the war. Somehow, they never learned to master English fluently. Too old for it, I suppose. Between them and my neighbors - we lived in Cleveland – I was lucky to learn English." Steve chuckled.

"Well, for a change, you'll be needing all the Hungarian you know," remarked Baumgarten wryly.

"Please go on," said Steve, trying to suppress his aroused curiosity.

Baumgarten walked over to the window. "Last week I received some very interesting data from the surveillance group at the NASA. Photographs taken from space with radar-imaging techniques. I think it is what we've been looking for." As he was talking, he pulled down the blinds. The room became quite dark and he felt his way around the wall to the cabinet and searched momentarily for some switches. He eventually found them and, pushing some buttons, he activated a mechanism that extended a projector out of the wall and lowered a screen on the opposite. He seemed quite content with his accomplishment.

"Let me show you a few slides, Mr. Buday! This first one was taken over southern Hungary, between the Danube and Tisza rivers. Both rivers are flowing south at this point. Notice the rivers on each vertical side of the screen. The land here is primarily alluvial deposit, mostly used for agriculture. A lot of it is just plain desert and very sparsely populated."

Steve thought to himself, "I wonder what this is leading up to... Truly, that part of the country contains nothing more interesting than a few archeological digs from the fourth and fifth centuries. The CIA could not be interested in that."

He motioned to Baumgarten to continue.

"All right, let me change the scale. Here we are looking at an area a few square miles in size. It is immediately adjacent to and lying on the east bank of the Tisza River. If you observe carefully, you'll notice the river has changed its course over time. It is now about two miles from its old bed."

"We're getting into a lot of details for no apparent reason! Would you mind getting to the point?" commented Steve, rather irritated.

"Oh yes, of course. In due time, my friend. In due time. Now let me go to the next level of detail, if you please... This is a very small area, only about a few hundred square yards. This is not an ordinary photo, mind you. The picture you see was reconstructed with the help of computers. Computer enhancement, they call it. It is actually showing underground objects or mineral deposits down to the depth of about fifteen feet. As you see, in addition to this elongated and rather rectangular shape in the southeast corner, there are other large shapes, reminiscent of tanks, trucks, guns, etc. All buried next to each other in deep sand." Baumgarten fidgeted with the controls and turned the projector off. He seemed excited. Then he suddenly blurted out, "If you haven't guessed yet, even though the other objects tell a story themselves, it is that rectangular shape that we're after!"

"Well, unless you tell me what it is, I can't get overly excited about it," Steve said sarcastically, knowing fully that he was in for a long afternoon. "Make yourself comfortable Mr. Buday. I'd offer you a drink, but regulations, you know how it is. What I have to tell you has everything with your being here!"

"All right, here it comes," Steve thought, and resigned himself to the inevitable. The shapely torso of Miss Carson sitting just outside the door flashed into his mind. But only for a moment.

Baumgarten really enjoyed playing a game with Steve.

"I do not for a moment forget that you are passionate about your sword collection. I have made some inquiries at the Library of Congress about a certain sword belonging to Attila the Hun, a sword with magic powers, if you can believe such utter nonsense. You would not be interested, would you? It so happens one of the archeologists in Hungary is digging for Attila very close to the site I am interested in. I think you might wish to look into it yourself. You never know." He chuckled, knowing he had Steve in his pocket. But I admit that an occasional reading of weak radiation could also be interesting.

Chapter 6:
Digging for Attila the Hun

D r. Ildikó Vértes was a full professor of archeology at the University of Budapest, specializing in conquests of the Hungarian plains in the third through the fifth centuries. Her main interest at the moment was the settlement of the Huns in central Hungary, an area from which they conducted their terrifying raids into Western Europe, all the way to the plains in France. Attila had built a wooden palace at Sycambria most likely located between the two great rivers, the Danube and the Tisza. A great wooden structure suited the Hunnic warrior nation, since their nomadic lifestyle did not agree with the use of permanent structures, like the fortresses built by the permanently settled societies of Europe.

Her primary source of historical information on the Huns came from a Greek traveler and contemporary reporter, Priscus, who visited Attila's palace and personally witnessed the king and reported on his demeanor, his visitors, and representatives of subjugated peoples. In her classes, she often quoted Priscus's report, which she disseminated among her students and asked them to memorize. The report is shown below. Readers of her publications often read it more than once.

The conventional account from Priscus says that at a feast celebrating Attila's latest marriage to the beautiful and young Ildikó, he suffered a severe nosebleed and choked to death in a stupor. An alternative theory was that he succumbed to internal bleeding after heavy drinking, or a condition called esophageal varices, where dilated veins in the lower part of the esophagus rupture, leading to death by hemorrhage.

Per Jordanes the Goth's account: "On the following day, when a great part of the morning was spent, the royal attendants suspected some ill and, after a great uproar, smashed in the doors. There they found the death of Attila accomplished by an effusion of blood, without any wound, and the girl with downcast face weeping beneath her veil. Then, as is the custom of that race, they plucked out the hair of their heads and made their faces hideous with deep wounds, that the renowned warrior might be mourned, not by effeminate wailings and tears, but by the blood of men. Moreover, a wondrous thing has taken place in connection with Attila's death. For in a dream some god stood at the side of Marcian, Emperor of the East, while he was disquieted about his fierce foe, and showed him the bow of Attila cracked in that same night, as if to intimate that the race of Huns owed much to that weapon. This account the historian Priscus says he accepts upon truthful evidence. For so terrible was Attila thought to be to great empires that the gods announced his death to rulers as a special boon.

"His body was placed in the midst of a plain and lay in state in a silken tent as a sight for men's admiration. The best horsemen of the entire tribe of the Huns rode around in circles, after the manner of circus games, in the place to which he had been brought, and told of his deeds in a funeral dirge in the following manner: 'The chief of the Huns, King Attila, born of his sire Mundiuch, lord of bravest tribes, sole possessor of the Scythian and German realms — powers unknown before — captured cities and terrified both empires of the Roman world and, appeased by their prayers, taken annual tribute to save the rest from plunder. And when he had accomplished all this by the favor of fortune, he fell, not by wound of the foe, nor by treachery of friends, but in the midst of his nation at peace, happy in his joy and without sense of pain. Who can rate this as death, when none believes it calls for vengeance?'

"When they had mourned him with such lamentations, a *strava*, as they call it, was celebrated over his tomb with great reveling. They gave way in turn to the extremes of feeling and displayed funereal grief alternating with joy. Then in the secrecy of night they buried his body in the earth. They bound his coffins, the first with gold, the second with silver, and the third with the strength of iron, showing by such means that these three things suited the mightiest of kings; iron because he subdued the nations, gold and silver because he received the honors of both empires. They also added the arms of foemen won in the fight, trappings of rare worth, sparkling with various gems, and ornaments of all sorts whereby princely state is maintained. And that so great riches might be kept from human curiosity, they slew those appointed to the work — a dreadful pay for their labor; and thus, sudden death was the lot of those who buried him as well as of he who was buried."

Following her lectures, Dr. Vértes usually jumped into her car and sped down to the dig, a trip taking several hours, to supervise the critical activities and continue her research at her favorite tent.

The supervisor in Dr. Vértes's absence, Sándor the husky foreman with the greying handlebar mustache, rang the large cast-iron gong.

"All right, you guys! That's enough for today. There will be more sand to shovel tomorrow. Go and get some rest." Young and old men in dirty coveralls and torn pants dropped their picks, shovels, and wheelbarrows and filed past Sándor, who was standing at the gate of the makeshift wire fence surrounding the site. Their faces, hair, and clothes were thickly covered by the fine dust stirred up by their digging, which forever hung suspended in the motionless air.

"Good night, see you tomorrow." "Good night, sir. Jó éjszakát."

The shabbily dressed men shuffled with slow but deliberate strides toward the old army truck waiting beyond the gate to transport them to the village. They were local peasants out to earn a few extra forints now that the harvest was gathered and there was little else to do. All day the hot sun beat on the backs of their necks without mercy. There was no relief, no escape from the infernal heat, no shade to hide under anywhere in sight. The only break came at noon, when the diggers would walk down to the river and roll up their trousers and soak their feet to cool off. The younger among them undressed to their underwear and dove in to frolic noisily in the muddy waters of the shallow, lazy giant.

Ildikó Vértes, the archeologist in charge of the site, had accelerated the pace in the last few days. She was electrified by the unexpected discovery of a mass grave in which scores of Hunnic warriors, archers and slaves, were buried under fifteen centuries of sand in peculiar disarray.

She found it curious, to say the least, that so many of the skeletons were lying on top of one another, bodies of warriors and slaves intertwined as if some cataclysmic force had created a mass grave and threw them in with savage force.

She took her time to painstakingly clear each of the skeletons and had them removed one by one, sketching and photographing the process every step of the way. There must have been fifty, maybe a hundred bodies, with arrows randomly piercing the necks, chests, and limbs of the victims. All her life she'd scorned superstition, believing all things had a logical explanation; it just took a matter of time to find it. But on this dig, she was overtaken by premonitions she could not shake. They made her shudder with discomfort. As a scholar, she wanted to know all she could about her new and exciting discovery. But something in the recesses of her subconscious resisted lifting the veil.

Dr Ildikó Vértes was in her late twenties, youthful and energetic, and, above all, totally dedicated to her work. Often, she would sit at the site until sundown, long after the workers left, and in the twilight examine the exposed items one by one, pick up a fragment or an iron helmet, or inspect for the tenth time the intricate construction of an archer's bow. She could totally absorb herself in the atmosphere the excavation created, which seemingly only she would sense, only she would understand. She felt mysteriously linked with the story of this site.

Ildikó not only liked her job, but was totally fascinated by it and truly loved it. Already at her young age her superiors had noted her bright and logical mind, trusted her clear judgment, and were amazed at her uncanny understanding of life in earlier ages and her tireless drive and discipline under harsh conditions. Her articles appeared in the prestigious *Archeological Bulletin* and she participated in excavations with erudite scholars, both domestic and foreign, at important Hunnic sites in Hungary, such as the Valley of the Moon, Törtel, and Bántapuszta. Professionally, she was noticed and on the way up.

Ildikó stood up and repeatedly attempted to brush off the sticky fine dust hanging to her khaki shorts and blouse. Soon she resigned herself to the futility of it all.

"I need a bath," she said aloud. "It's dark enough already."

She strolled slowly toward the river, following the narrow footpath winding its way among once-tall mounds and deep holes created along the sandy shores by intense shelling of the area during the big war. For hundreds of yards the riverbank was a veritable graveyard of burned-out and rusty German and Russian war equipment that had almost made it across the swollen and frozen river a quarter century ago. Trucks, jeeps, and tanks, rusted and mangled almost beyond recognition, were strewn about, their wheels and axles and turrets sticking out of the sand pointing an accusing finger toward an indifferent sky. They were the silent reminders of the horrors of war, appearing into view, then disappearing again with the seasonal changes in the size of the river. They were a real hindrance to progress for excavating in the area and she wished the government would for once keep their promise and clear the bothersome and ghostly junk away. Fortunately, the grave under excavation, and so far the only one discovered, was a hundred yards further to the south along the ancient riverbed somehow spared by the annual flooding in modern times. The river moved far enough to cover up the junk left by the war each springtime and uncover it again each summer. Just to be on the safe side, Ildikó ordered sandbagging of the easterly border of the excavation. The semicircular mound created by the bags and the sand blown up against them by the westerly winds formed a formidable barricade against any possible onslaught on the area by the worst floods expected.

She'd almost reached the water when the slight vibrations caused by her footsteps suddenly released a gush of sand to flow out of the cabin of a nearby half-buried army transport truck. In the cabin, the still-sitting skeleton of the driver emerged. Sand flowed out of his mouth, eyes, and ears. He wore a rusty German helmet. She gasped in surprise. Though she had worked with skulls and skeletons for many years, she was still startled by the ones that popped out of the sands unexpectedly. These skeletons were somehow different from the ones she excavated. So much more recent, so much more real to remind her of her own mortality.

By the time she reached the shore she was fully relaxed.

She felt completely at ease to wash in the river. Though alone, she knew that Sándor was somewhere nearby, probably fishing at the bend. It gave her confidence to know she would be protected from unwelcome intruders. Sándor was a trusted old friend, a family man with grown children, and he was more like a father or a big brother to her. He was an excellent fisherman and he used to catch some of the biggest catfish the Tisza offered, and for supper he prepared fish stew that would be the envy of the finest restaurants in Szeged, which was reputedly the hometown of this famous delicacy. The saliva in her mouth flowed at the prospect of tonight's supper.

"He'll make it hotter than blazes with that red paprika of his" – she smiled – "but I'll love it."

The narrow crescent moon was already climbing above the horizon, and the world assumed the nondescript color of dusk, undisturbed, peaceful, and quiet. An occasional swallow zigzagged with lightning speed just above the surface of the calm water, in search of flying insects, gathering food and strength for the coming sojourn to the south. The giant river gently rolled in its shallow bed. The afternoon breeze died down and there were no waves or even ripples to splash its banks. The water's surface was polished to a mirror finish, reflecting the silver bridge of the faint moon.

She undressed.

"Oh God, it feels good," she sighed as she lowered herself into the wonderful, refreshing, wet coolness. Like silvery scales on fish, the myriad beads of water sprinkled on the white skin of her slender and shapely body sparkled in the moonlight. She felt beautiful, safe, and completely united with her surroundings. With steady strokes, she swam out into the darkness.

By the time she returned, a small patch of cloud covered the moon and the night had turned pitch black. "Oops," she mumbled, slipping on a rock. Uneasily, she searched for the spot where she'd left her clothes. She could not find them and she began to panic.

"Good evening, Miss Ildikó," she heard a man's voice. It sounded so close that she thought she could touch him. It startled her and she let out a small shriek.

"Who...who is this?"

"Don't worry, miss, it is I," she heard the voice again, which she now recognized as Sándor's.

"What on earth are you doing here," she snapped, trying to swallow the lump in her throat. "You scared the devil out of me!"

"I am sorry, but I heard you go swimming out there. It was dark and I worried about you. Besides, you left your clothes up there, about a hundred yards upstream. I figured you would float down a bit. I think you need them." She thought she could detect a slight hint of teasing in his deep, mellow voice.

Suddenly she felt a bundle of clothes being pushed into her arms. She just stood there, dripping and shivering, feeling quite foolish. Her nakedness never crossed her mind.

"Thanks, Sándor, you're a good friend."

Later, the two of them sat by the fire and gazed into the flames, each lost in their own private world. The warmth of the glowing embers and the hot fish stew took their toll and soon Ildikó felt her head and eyelids grow heavy with sleep.

"Good night, Sándor. I've had it!" She disappeared in her tent.

"Good night, missy. Sleep well," said Sándor, but his voice came from very far away.

Chapter 7:
A Haunting Dream

No sooner had her head touched the pillow than she was sound asleep. With each successive breath, she sank deeper into a dark, bottomless abyss, as if passing through space and time, where between worlds, familiar and unknown, nothing existed. She was totally relaxed now, breathing deeply and rhythmically.

From what might have been an eternity spent in limbo, a place or state best described by the total absence of awareness of being, of time and place, her consciousness gradually returned. Recalling nothing of her previous state, she slowly and with trepidation opened her eyes. Little by little she came to realize that she was standing, standing ankle-deep on a soft and luxurious fur carpet. Looking down, she noticed her bare feet. Raising her gaze slowly upward, unsure of what she might discover, her eyes caught a glimpse of her reflection in a brilliantly polished full-length mirror standing against the wall, which was richly covered with silk the colors of the sunny sky and the azure of the southern seas.

She saw her image as that of a strange but strangely familiar person, dressed in a beautiful, luminescent white gown made of translucent silk and finely embroidered lace.

The gown was draped over her smooth ivory shoulders and cascaded over her full and round breasts in graceful folds down to her bare feet, at once revealing and concealing.

Reminiscent of the darkness of the night embracing its queen, the silvery moon, her profuse raven-black hair framed her alabaster face and fell in a torrent of abundant and exotic and unruly waves down to her slender waist. She was desirable beyond human endurance, an apparition too ethereal to feel and touch, but unbearably painful not to. She recalled now that this was the day of her wedding.

It all happened today. Thousands of people lined the path of the royal procession, hundreds of illustrious guests attended the reception after the ceremony, the tables were laden with sumptuous foods and delicious wines...but best of all, there was the handsome, youthful groom whose commanding appearance made her tremble with anticipation and pleasure and happiness. The glorious wedding was over now and she was alone with him, at last.

Ildikó quietly approached the royal nuptial bed in the center, where amidst luxurious pillows and furs lay the princely groom, Attila, resting peacefully. She approached him with anticipation, anxious to see his surprised face when he opened his eyes and for the first time saw her in all her splendor. As he apparently did not hear her approaching, she gently touched his hand hanging over the side.

"My king...my love," she whispered. "It is I." She lifted his hand to her lips and kissed it. "My lord, my sweet, open your eyes."

His hand felt strangely cold. She carefully brushed his hair fallen over his brow. His brow was cold. An icy chill shuddered through her body and she started to tremble uncontrollably. She violently shook his shoulders, but to no avail. He gave no response, no sign of life. Just lay there in frozen, unbearable silence. She screamed:

"My prince. My dearest! It is not true! It cannot be! Please awaken, my darling, please!"

Suddenly darkness enveloped her. She fainted.

Brought to her senses by the stinging rays of the hot midday sun and the roar of an angry mob, Ildikó found herself crouching on the floor of a shamefully ugly and dirty wooden cage placed on display in the center of the camp. The white gown she'd worn on her wedding night with which she wanted so much to surprise her lover was now hanging on her body in shreds. Stained, soiled, and torn beyond recognition. Her cheeks were swollen and wet with tears intermingling with streams of partially dried blood running down from awful bruises on her forehead. Strands of her long black hair were stuck to the wounds on her face and arms, and they were too painful to remove or brush aside. Her whole body ached as if she had been severely beaten and kicked.

Streams of tears welled up in her eyes as she remembered the events of the night before. Great sobs shook her body in uncontrollable and painful spasms. Burying her face in her hands, trying to block out her surroundings, she rocked to and fro, sobbing and praying.

"God of my fathers, why have you permitted these horrible things to happen? Why have I lost my beloved one before he even knew me? Why, why did I not die in his stead, or at least accompany him on his dark journey? Now we shall be forever separated!"

Ugly and bloody scarred faces surrounded her cage, screaming with vindictive hatred and violent rage. Hysterical men and women of the market rabble wrestled with the guards, struggling to get closer and tear her to shreds. Seeing her sobbing infuriated them even more. Her tears were like adding fuel to an already raging fire. They demanded a sacrifice."

"Kill her!" they shouted. "Murderer," they shrieked.

"Punish the guilty wretch. She is the cause of our grief and sorrow!"

"The king is dead. Our nation is dead. We are lost!" they shouted and slashed their faces to a bloody mess, beyond recognition.

Ildikó just sat there stupefied, trying to grasp the meaning of it all.

"How could they be accusing me of his death? I loved him. I adored him. I would be willing to die a thousand deaths for him, if I could just restore him to life." She cried silently. For a moment she even felt sorry for her enraged accusers, knowing how much these people loved their king. She understood their grief, their deep sense of loss. But they were mistaken to accuse her of a heinous crime she did not commit. Even the thought was unbearable. All the bottled-up emotions welled up in her suddenly with great force and she let out a violent, bloodcurling scream, momentarily startling everyone around:

"No! No! No! I did not do it. I am innocent. Please believe it. Please." And she again lost consciousness.

Her fervent pleas had no effect on the angry mob, which continued jeering and shouting: "A thousand deaths upon the murderess of our beloved king!"

Only Rugila, the wise one, shook his head in disbelief and murmured to himself, confiding only in his wife in the privacy of his tent.

"This makes no sense to me at all! What has happened to these people? Have they gone mad? This is unbelievable," he said gravely. "I know that Ildikó is the daughter of Theoderic, the defeated and captured king. I realize that she would be fully justified in avenging her father's shame. But were you not at the wedding yesterday? Did you not see her with your own eyes? Was she not the embodiment of sweetness and innocence and gentleness? Did her eyes not glow with fervent love and admiration for him? No! I tell you, she is not a murderer!"

Rugila looked around and peeked outside the tent to make sure no one would hear what he now had to say.

"I have my firmly grounded suspicions that it was the king's nephew, the son of Buda, who committed the crime," he whispered. "He had the real motive to kill him. He had to prove his manhood, he had to avenge his father's death, though I believe the king's action was justified when he put his brother to death for rebellion. That's right...he must be the one. But be careful. Not a word to anyone. Even the walls have ears now. We could be executed just for thinking such things."

The rest of the day the Huns spent with quiet preparations for the funeral. The royal corpse was laid in state under a silken canopy for viewing. Thousands of mourning warriors and weeping women and children filed by in slow procession. The best horsemen of the tribe mounted their steeds and rode in circles around the tent. A group of haruspices chanted a funeral dirge in a monotonous voice which was underscored by the dull sound of drums and the thumping of the horses' hooves:

"Here lies the king, the great king of the Huns, the son of Mundzucus, the ruler of the most courageous tribes; enjoying such powers as had been unheard of before him, he possessed the Scythian and the Germanic empires alone and terrorized both empires of the Roman world after conquering their cities, and placated by their entireties that the rest might not be laid to plunder he accepted an annual tribute.

"After he had achieved all this with great success he died, not by an enemy's wound, not betrayed by friends, in the midst of his unscathed people, happy and gay, without any feeling of pain.

"Who therefore would think that this was death which nobody considers to demand revenge?"

Rugila drew his wife aside and murmured in her ear something to the effect that the words of the dirge cleverly disguised the real murderer's role in the king's death. The manner in which he was suspected to have died had to be kept secret. Fratricide had already tarnished the king's reputation once before; there was no need to bring the old ghosts out of the closet again. Therefore, the chieftains conspired to cover up the truth and spread the rumor that he died a natural and peaceful death.

None of this, unfortunately, altered Ildikó's fate. The grieving masses refused to believe the chieftains' story and turned violently against Theoderic's daughter.

Attila's death demanded a sacrifice to appease the angry Lord of Hosts. And who were the chieftains to stop the masses from sacrificing Theoderic's daughter, anyway?

Later, when dusk turned to night, Rugila silently crept up to Ildikó's cage.

"Pssst. It is I, your friend, Rugila." His voice quivered with the strain of repressed emotions. She raised her eyes in amazement. She thought she had not a friend left in the world. But as she recognized Rugila's voice, she whispered back.

"Dear friend, dear trusted old friend, Rugila. Please be careful. If they find you here speaking with me, they will have you executed. Tell me, what brings you here in this darkest hour?"

"I just want to tell you how terrible I feel about all this. I know that you are innocent. I know how much you loved our Lord. But the ignorant crowd wants a sacrifice. Don't they always? And the chiefs cannot blame it on the true murderer, Buda's son. Not publicly, anyway. He is in extremely high esteem. Of noble birth. He is a potential future leader of our nation. But I know he is the guilty one. Oh, if I could just get him at the sharp end of my arrow!" he cursed silently.

"Be quiet! Someone is approaching," she gasped.

Both of them froze motionless with fright, holding their breath until the sound of the steps abated into the distance.

"What can I do for you, my princess? If I could just offer my own old and useless life to save yours. If I could only make you comfortable in this despicable contraption, not fit for even an animal, let alone for the bride of our Lord," he cried into his hands.

"Nothing, nothing, my friend. I am ready to go. Just hold my hand for a moment. I just want to touch someone human. Here, take this. It is something for you to remember me by. And please keep me in your prayers and remember that I am innocent. I am no more capable of having killed my loved one than a gentle doe is capable of killing her mate the mighty stag." She stopped for a moment as if thinking or catching her breath.

"Take this and keep it with you always, it will bring you recognition someday."

Rugila felt something cold and smooth between his fingers and he clutched it tightly, careful not to drop it. He was deeply moved and tears were unashamedly streaming down his wrinkled face. An old, retired warrior, to be worthy of receiving a gift of remembrance from his beautiful princess. He was overcome by grief and wept silently as he kissed her outstretched hand.

Suddenly, he became aware of approaching steps again. There were two of them this time. They were talking and sounded very close. He squeezed her hand for the last time and as quietly as a cat withdrew into the darkness and disappeared.

Later that night Rugila was commanded to join a select group of elderly archers to accompany the royal casket to the gravesite. He was wearing Ildikó's gift on a chain about his neck. It was a gold pendant, wrought in the form of a stag. A fugitive stag, with his head turned backward as he fled some unseen but terrible pursuer.

Ildikó sat dazed in her cage and watched the preparations for the burial as if through colored glass. Everything seemed to move in slow motion and to be strangely distorted into grotesque proportions. She saw everchanging images of orange- and red- and yellow-colored warriors and horses; dark, elongated shadows dancing and fluttering against the ocher grounds and melting into the darkness of the all-engulfing night. The shapes moved about in absolute silence, or at least she was unaware of sounds. Images suddenly flared up at random, then just as suddenly disappeared into darkness. Her senses alternated with them and she sometimes felt consumed by heat; at others she shivered uncontrollably with bone-chilling cold.

The Huns built a terrific bonfire near the tent where the king's body was laid in state. All around, somber-faced priests and shamans with long white beards and colorful robes busily tended the corpse, putting on finishing touches to place him into the waiting and open sarcophagus placed on an adjoining platform. The coffin, at first glance, was simplicity itself. Humble, unostentatious lines, with none of the ornate frills covering the exterior as one would have expected. Closer, however, it became evident that it was three coffins in one. The first was bound with gold, the second with silver, and the third, the outermost, with iron. These were made to signify that Attila was the mightiest of kings: iron because he subdued all the nations, silver and gold because he received tribute from his mighty enemies.

The priests carefully laid the corpse into the coffin and added trappings of rare worth: gems, ornaments, and arms he took in battle. On his chest, they laid his favorite sword, a lifeless steel, once the glittering gift of the Lord of Hosts that gained him power and fame in life.

The shamans sealed the coffin closed. His bride watched him disappear in silence. She had no more tears left to cry, no more emotions to surface. She was physically alive, but unaware of her existence, already united in spiritual death with her lover.

A sluggish procession of forty archers began to move into the night. In their midst, occasionally illuminated by the pale light of a river of flames of the thousand torches, floated the coffin and the cage, bobbing up and down in harmony with the steps of the pallbearers. It was as if they were carried atop the waves of a gentle river; up and down, up and down.

While the gloomy procession was winding its way into the impenetrable darkness, a contingent of slaves was digging furiously near the river. A canal was dug with incredible speed, apparently intended to flood a huge pit, the grave, with water from the river. By the meager light of a few torches the canal was fast approaching the bank. Only a few more feet to go and the water would break through. Beads of sweat were pouring down the tortured faces, glistening for a moment before dropping on the soggy ground. The only sounds that could be heard were the clanking of the shovels and picks against the rocks, and the soft thumping of the soil thrown high from the canal over its sides. Occasionally the muffled voice of a guard, the sound of a curt command, would break the monotony, prodding the slaves to work faster.

Suddenly a slave jumped out of the hole and made a mad dash for the darkness, attempting to escape from this devilish scene - but to no avail. A sharp twang of the bow, the whoosh of a discharged arrow, a cry and the thud of a body falling. Then deadly silence. The rest of the slaves hung their heads a little lower and continued their labor as if nothing had happened. And nothing escaped the eyes and arrows of the guards. Those dark men were the sons of the devil himself. Their eyes penetrated the darkness and they shot their target with cruel and deadly accuracy.

As the slaves were ready to lay down their tools, for the water had started seeping through the thin remaining wall, the grim procession reached the gravesite. The bobbing motion of the casket and the cage finally ceased. A captain issued a sharp command and the pallbearers lowered their cargo, the now covered coffin, and placed it on the ground.

The archers stood at attention, then turned abruptly and divided into two groups marching up the mounds on both sides of the grave, lining up facing each other, man for man. Next, the slaves picked up the casket and carefully carried it down into the dark pit. As they descended, they sang a song reminiscent of prayer, monotonous and sad; a song of mystery, of human suffering, of beginning and of the end. It was a song of the unchangeable course of history, of events that were greater than the strength of men, a song of death. Dark, inevitable death.

"Attention!" snapped the hoarse voice of the captain standing at the head of the grave. Archers slowly raised their drawn bows, saluted the dark heavens with arrows pointing to the sky, then suddenly lowered them and discharged them into the dark belly of the pit. Screams and cries filled the silence of the night. The archers reloaded and discharged again. And again. Then finally there was silence.

Ildikó was shaken to the depths of her soul with terror. Her teeth chattered audibly, her feet and hands were icy cold, her body shook uncontrollably, as if convulsing. Her mind was no longer capable of grasping these events; she just rocked to and fro and mumbled something unintelligible over and over again. Her captors suddenly picked up her cage and carried it down to a spot near the foot of the casket, now covered with dark, writhing masses of limbs and bodies. As she gazed up she saw the archers once again pointing to the sky with their arrows.

"Finally," she thought, "this is the end." She waited for the sharp pain of arrowheads to pierce her skin, her back, chest and arms and legs...but nothing happened.

As she opened her eyes and looked up again, she saw the flash of the flurry of arrows piercing the night, across the grave into the chests of a multitude of men. All soldiers.

"Oh...God..." she moaned. "What next?"

Bodies were crashing everywhere. She could hear the cries and moans of the mortally wounded, the gurgling of blood spurting up in their throats, filling their mouths and nostrils and muffling their voices. It seemed to take an eternity for the awful sounds to abate, and as they did an eerie, deathly silence settled over the grisly, bloody scene. In the breeze, the flames of the torches flickered and danced undaunted against the dark curtain of the night. "Why did you leave me here?" she yelled out in panic. "What will happen to me now?" she sobbed when no one answered. Then she started to tear frantically at the leather straps binding her cage together. She tugged and pulled and clawed until she could bear the pain no longer. Her hands were bleeding profusely.

Suddenly she stopped.

She heard a sound. A strange, gurgling sound.

It was the sound of water. Rushing, cascading water.

Then she screamed:

"No! Oh my God. Nooo!" The flames were extinguished one by one by the rising water, just a series of hissing sounds, followed by dead silence and pitch darkness.

Next morning the sun rose over a peaceful scene, a field flooded with water, showing no signs of the previous terrible night. Attila's grave was hidden forever and there were no surviving witnesses to tell of its whereabouts.

"Missy! Wake up! Ildikó. What's the matter?"

She felt a pair of strong hands shaking her shoulders, then the sharp sting of a slap across her face. She came to, shaking and crying and clutching herself in defense against some dark and evil terror. Her clothes were soaked with perspiration, sticking cold and clammy against her skin, as if she had just surfaced from under water.

She gasped for air.

"Ildikó! Missy! Calm down. It's all right. Don't worry, I am here. It was just a nightmare. Please, just lie still. Here, I will cover you," she heard a voice she slowly recognized. It was Sándor's. Clutching his hands, she cried and sobbed.

"Please believe me. I did not do it. I am innocent. I loved him."

Calmly, Sándor just patted her back and comforted her, at a total loss to understand the mystery of her terrible nightmare.

Chapter 8:
Germans, Arabs, and Dirty Bombs

Captain Mueller's story was buried in top-secret CIA files for decades, until a scheduled periodic effort to declassify them resulted in its accidental discovery. By this time the idea of a dirty bomb had surfaced. It had the clear advantage of doing maximum damage in a confined area and did not destroy buildings, and its effects were limited to poisoning people in large numbers. It was small in size, fit in an average-size briefcase, and could be shielded from detection by the limited capabilities airports employed even in the eighties. Efforts to develop them by potential terrorists of many ill-willed groups were already in process, hidden in remote facilities yet to be discovered by the CIA.

Leaking of secret information was ever-present in the Washington, DC, environment, even at the risk of empowering the enemy to do harm to the United States of America. The leakers were not all spies, either. Sadly, Captain Mueller's secret also found a path to WOILA, which wasted no time putting into practice the designing and building of a dirty bomb. All they needed was the uranium lost in the Tisza in 1945.

In a remote Middle Eastern country, WOILA has built a facility to construct the bomb. A dirty bomb! Considering its remote location and difficult accessibility, it proved to be a wonder of new technology, design and machining capability, nuclear safe storage, and all that is desired for such a purpose. Some experts on the subject advised the White House that the mountains of Iran might be a good bet for its location.

As we now follow one of our Arabic terrorists inside the Assembly Room, we see white-smocked technicians in the process of electronically checking out the systems of a dirty bomb in a guarded and spectacularly equipped laboratory. Glistening in the test stand, a bomb lies next to a foil-lined common leather briefcase which has switches, timers, and gadgets for remote control. A label in Arabic scribble is visible on the inside.

In a stockpile on the floor there are dozens of bombs and briefcases ready for use. Technicians are standing at attention as the blond Germanic-looking chief scientist and his entourage, an odd mixture of Middle Eastern and Far Eastern nationalities, gather around the bomb. They all know that exploding such a device in a populated area, like any large city in America, would cause widespread panic and would poison by radiation thousands or even tens of thousands of people. The effect would be devastating. They worried how the person delivering it would escape the effects himself. So far, the only workable solution seemed finding a person willing to commit suicide for a much higher cause. These persons seemed to be in ample supply in the Arab world.

A scientist demonstrates the last test to the raptly attentive group. He turns off the power switch. He announces, "That's it! All systems go!"

The chief is as happy as a lark. "Excellent! Excellent!"

One scientist carefully inquires, "Begging your pardon, sir. When do we get the fuel? We are ready to fuel the bomb."

The chief brushes him off. "Soon, very soon. In a matter of days, actually. I am working on it! Ausgezeichnet!" he says as he leaves.

The chief gone, the others bombard the scientist with questions about the bomb as he gingerly puts it into a briefcase. He is musing to himself, "Chicago! Chicago! This ought to light you up at night!"

An Arab enters the room in a hurry and whispers something into the chief's ear. He exclaims, "Holy shit! Steve Buday! Sir Lawrence of Afghanistan!" He dashes off to report it to his higher-ups.

Chapter 9:
Budapest and the Secret Police

Malev Flight 123 banked sharply and started its final approach into the Ferihegyi Airport near Budapest. As the pilot lowered the flaps, the Russian made Tupolev 54 shuddered noisily. Passengers nervously tightened their seatbelts in fearful anticipation of a bumpy landing. Some of them complained loudly about the pilot's rough handling of the plane, as if the damned thing were a fighter and not a commercial passenger aircraft. All had unpleasant memories of the noisy, roller-coaster-like takeoff from Frankfurt am Main, then the slalom-like flight over the Alps. Only the breathtaking scenery over the Bavarian and Austrian fairylands and the delectable meal served on board placated the grumbling Western European and American passengers who were deeply depressed by the rough ride and the drab grey, uncarpeted, and scantily upholstered interior. The remaining passengers, obviously Hungarian, other Eastern Europeans, and a couple of Middle Eastern types, noisily enjoyed the food and the wine and carried on heated discussions accompanied by loud laughter and wild gestures.

Steve put down his magazine as the aircraft jerked again and gazed out to see where they were. To his pleasant surprise, he saw the great bend of the Danube, about thirty miles north of Budapest, where the river takes a ninety degree turn south. The pastoral scenery impressed him deeply. He saw densely forested green hills along both banks, interrupted by fields and villages and small towns scattered in a haphazard display of color and occasional haze.

In the midst of this profusion of color was the majestic silver ribbon of the mighty river, the highway of nations, the waters of the not-so-blue Danube. Steve thought of his parents and their fervent love for their homeland. He thought of the bitter-cold winters in Cleveland, of the times he would sit in front of the fireplace with his family, and his dad would dust off old and worn albums with faded photos and picture postcards of Hungary, and would tell loving tales about his youth spent near here in the countryside. Tales about Visegrád, once the seat of Hungary's kings; the ancient Castle of King Matthias flashed into his mind. He remembered that it was located near here just above the bend. He looked frantically, until he found a clearing and some ruins on top of some of the hills on the south shore. He strained his eyes and thought he recognized it from the pictures and his heart beat a little faster with satisfaction and with the pleasure of seeing an old, forgotten friend. The long-abandoned castle stood silently and defiantly above the bank of the river. He let his mind wander a bit into the past and fell under the spell of centuries gone by, suspended as mist over the ancient river.

He was brought back out of his daydreaming by the smiling face of a pretty blonde stewardess who tapped him on the shoulder to remind him to fasten his seatbelt and straighten up his seat. Letting her hand linger on his shoulder a bit longer than necessary to accomplish her task, she sweetly whispered a reminder to be sure to call her during his stay at the capital. Her accent sounded a bit harsh, as most Eastern European accents in English do, but now her voice and words were like music to his ears. He was finally here, on an important and perhaps dangerous mission to be sure, but here at last in the land he'd heard so much about but never visited. A country he was so strangely drawn to and fascinated by even though he was never confused about where his loyalties were. He was first and foremost an American.

The plane touched down, if it could be called a touchdown, because Steve wondered if the landing gear had collapsed. The big bird lifted off the runway again and settled down shortly amidst a flurry of loud complaints in a variety of languages, some in Hungarian, which he understood and which were not at all complimentary to the pilot. He was still trying to figure out what one of the passengers meant when he sent the pilot to warmer climates when the doors were opened and the mad rush to disembark began.

The passengers walked off the plane and over to some people movers waiting a short distance away from the plane. Soldiers with submachine guns patrolled the whole affair, the boredom on their faces evident even from a distance. Passengers were ushered into a waiting room and told to queue up at one of two windows to get their new entry visas issued, or have their old ones reprocessed. This procedure took a bit longer than Steve anticipated.

Again, the Eastern Europeans had the advantage. Being accustomed to red tape, long lines, and endless hours of waiting in front of shops offering whatever happened to be available on a given day, they easily resigned themselves and spent the time sleeping, talking, or playing cards. Steve, along with the rest of the Western visitors, found it difficult to sit and wait, and thought it incredible that a terminal of this size, handling thousands of tourists each day, would provide only two clerks for the task. It was also obvious that each passenger was thoroughly screened prior to gaining entry, and each case had taken a long time.

Just before his turn came at the window, a tall, mustachioed man in military uniform approached him.

"This way, Mr. Buday. Please follow me. We will go to my office for a brief chat. It won't take but a minute. Please, do not be concerned, your papers are in perfect order," he said in fluent English with only a slight accent that could have easily been taken for British. He seemed reserved but very courteous.

"Please, sit down, Mr. Buday. I am Captain Kutas," he said, smiling. "Won't you have a cigarette? Marlboros, my favorite brand. We make this brand here under license, but it is every bit as good as those you can get back home."

"No, thank you. I don't smoke. What is it you want from me?" said Steve curtly, declining the cigarettes. He was a little tense and that made him angry at himself. He knew how important it was to keep his cool with these masters of interrogation.

Captain Kutas smiled obligingly, allowing generously that under the circumstances a little tension was perfectly forgivable.

"Mr. Buday, please relax. As I said, only a few questions. I just wish to chat with you for a short while. One has so few opportunities to practice his English these days. Even though the number of visitors to this country has swelled to an unbelievable twelve million annually, more than the population of Hungary, they are mostly German-speaking, or Italians, Polish, Czechs. Few Americans venture this far, though they are pleasantly surprised when they do. But now" – he puffed on his Marlboro with pleasure – "may I ask you the purpose of your visit?"

"It's all on the visa," answered Steve, still unfriendly.

"Oh, yes, I know. But I would very much like for you to tell me. Please try again."

"I am an amateur archeologist. I am here on vacation, and I plan to visit some of the excavations sites, with your government's permission."

"Ah, an archeologist. How wonderful. Hungary has many sites: Celtic, Hunnic, Turkish, and Roman sites. You name it, we have it. You'll find Hungary a veritable treasure trove of prehistoric and historic archeological digs. But I thought you said you are an amateur archeologist. What then is your full-time profession?"

"I am a teacher. High school. I teach history and languages," answered Steve calmly.

"Languages? What kind of languages?"

"I teach German and Hungarian."

"Hungarian? That's odd! I didn't know that the United States has any need for Hungarian language instructors. We are such a small and insignificant nation, and our language is so unique. No one but us has any use for it," the captain said, gesturing as if excusing himself. Steve, however, thought he noticed a flash of aroused interest and a large dose of irony in his voice.

"Well, it is true that there is no overwhelming and universal demand for Hungarian in the States, but there are some large concentrations of immigrants in metropolitan areas, where second-generation parents would like their children to receive some rudimentary knowledge of their language beyond that which the kids learn in the home."

"A very commendable effort, to be sure. Still, one can't make a very good living teaching Hungarian even in this country, let alone in yours, however affluent it may be. Surely you must have other interests, Mr. Buday," he pressed on.

"No. That is all. I have more than enough to occupy myself, teaching history and German during the week and Hungarian on weekends. I admit, it's not a great living, but I am satisfied. How about you?"

"Certainly, Mr. Buday. I realize that teaching can be a very rewarding profession. Much more so than mine. I ask you how much satisfaction can one get out of questioning visitors at the airport. Especially when it's such a useless and bothersome formality. Old habits die slowly, even if we are in the eighties. Hungary has come a long way in welcoming visitors, but I and my superiors are still of the old guard. Please forgive me for being so nosy." Kutas smiled, but was obviously annoyed with Steve's responses.

He continued. "I must assume, then, that you are fluent in Hungarian and won't be needing the assistance of a guide to get around. Am I correct?"

"That's true. I think I can get along without one."

Kutas said, "On the other hand, would it not be much easier for you, Mr. Buday, to employ the services of a professional guide who could introduce to you the most interesting sites in Hungary? Someone intimately familiar with them all? You know, many of these sites are extremely remotely located. We would not want you to lose your way, would we now? We have an eminently qualified person in mind to prevent that from happening," said Kutas with a touch of sarcasm.

"No, thank you! It is very kind of you to offer, but please don't bother. Really. I don't need anyone," Steve said and stood up abruptly.

"You will be contacted by your official guide at your hotel, the Hilton. Tomorrow morning. Please do not leave the hotel grounds until then. Good day, Mr. Buday. Please be careful and enjoy your stay." He angrily answers the phone.

"Hal, Captain Kutas here. Give me Colonel Fehér, immediately!"

"Colonel Fehér. Sir, I have just interrogated the American passenger at the airport. He says his name is Buday. Just like the picture in Newsweek magazine. Hasn't changed a bit. He says he is a high school teacher. History and languages. And an amateur archeologist. Hah! We'll show him a site or two. He may just become a relic himself, if he is not careful."

"Calm down, Kutas. Don't blow it! Let him do what he wants. Just keep an eye on him. I want Dr. Vértes assigned to him. You know, the archeologist? I want her to report his every move... Again, remember, the Americans are no dummies. Don't ever make that assumption. If there were not a good reason for his being here, he would stay in Monterey and train more spies, if that's what he really does. Or didn't he mention that? Listen. He may be our lead to something big. Stay on him. I want to find out why he is here! Furthermore, I am telling you, Kutas, if you blow this one, you'd better apply for a job on a collective farm, because there won't be any room for you around here. I guarantee you. And stop objecting to using Miss Vértes for the job. We need a professional to allay his suspicions."

"Yes sir! Whatever you say, sir!" Kutas hung up, thoroughly disgusted with himself and the HSP. It seemed that his career as a secret police officer was coming to an end. The last few years were a series of blunders, though not all of his own making. If he failed to deliver on this one, he was finished... He thought of what he might be forced to do. Work on a collective? Or worse!

"That goddamn Fehér hates me, and on top of it all forcing me to use a woman. You just wait, Fehér! I'll have your job yet!" Kutas was talking to himself aloud as he stormed out of the airport terminal and threw himself into a big black Mercedes waiting for him in front. To an astute observer it would have seemed odd to see all those black Mercedes with state license plates lining up waiting for government officials. Why, one might ask, is the distinction, the capitalistic symbol of affluence, necessary in a classless society?

As the black official car pulled away, a dark-green Mercedes pulled into the vacated spot and two well-dressed Mid-Eastern types wearing three-piece suits and dark sunglasses got in.

It seemed that everyone in Budapest traveled in style today. Except Steve Buday. He took a taxi.

Chapter 10:
The Assassins

The 4.5-liter engine roared to life as the big green sedan pulled away from the curb. Hassan leaned back and collapsed with a frown on his round jovial face. He breathed heavily and wiped the sweat from his brow and balding head with a huge white handkerchief and smoothed back some of the unruly hairs of his enormous handlebar mustache.

"Phew! It's hot today, and humid. I wish it would cool off before we get to work. You know, I should be used to this muggy weather, but I just can't stand it. I would honestly rather be assigned to the North Pole. How in the hell, my friend, can you stand it and stay so calm and cool?" He was continually fanning himself and clumsily started to unbutton his vest and collar around his size-eighteen neck. He was a big guy, not tall, just husky. Broad shoulders, thick and heavy muscular arms and legs. With every move, his expensive tailored suit stretched to its limit.

Sahir just sat there motionless, gazing out the car's window, seemingly watching the scenery passing by. The sedan rolled smoothly along the Danube for awhile, then turned onto the graceful old suspension bridge, which terminated just short of the steep hill rising precipitously out of the east bank. The car disappeared into a long tunnel passing under the Castle Hill. Sahir still did not speak. His beady black eyes were fixed at some distant point in space and he was obviously unaware of the beauty of the surrounding cityscape.

"Come on, Sahir! What are you thinking of? We have nothing to do but wait for our next set of instructions. Let's enjoy a little time off, OK? Everything will go like clockwork, you'll see. You worry too much."

The skin on Sahir's bony face was taut with tension. He impatiently raised his hand to shut Hassan up.

"Listen, no wisecracks! We're not in Paris or Munich. Everyone is under suspicion here. Did you notice how long the clerk was looking at our passports at the airport? Then us? She didn't say a word, just looked, then handed them back. I tell you, she suspected something. Next time I want better passport photos. Damn it, if it were not for the Bulgarian entry stamp and the exit visa, we could be on our way to the dunes of Sudan.

Sahir had good reason to be worried. The assignment came as a sudden surprise and the counterfeit passports were prepared hastily. They'd received them the night before departure. Someone must have done them in Germany. He knew WOILA had agents in Germany, but he did not know who. Along with the passports came twenty thousand Deutsche Marks and a brief order to fly to Budapest immediately under the guise of wealthy businessmen, set up residence at the Hilton, and await further instructions. He was glad to leave Frankfurt, since Interpol was hot on his trail and it was time to relocate anyway. What bothered him more than anything was that the whole affair had been conducted in such a hurry that it was unlikely that all the important details had been worked out. He'd almost fallen victim to poor planning once before, which could have netted him a life term in Italy. He liked clear and concise instructions and sufficient time to work out contingency plans in case something should go haywire.

Jumping over the railing was not part of Steve's plans

As far as his appearance, Sahir was the exact opposite of Hassan. Tall and gaunt, he had deep-set dark-brown eyes and dense black closely cropped hair. The oily dark-brown skin was always tightly drawn on his high cheekbones, giving him the appearance of nervous intensity. Even freshly shaven, his dark facial hair, a dark five o'clock shadow. He never smiled. Never found a reason to. Always under the influence of some mysterious inner pressure, he loved to live on the brink of disaster. He had never loved anyone and was convinced that no one had ever loved him. Occasionally, he would feel temporary relief from this incessant inner drive, but only following the accomplishment of an important mission. Especially if it involved the assassination of some important public figure. The sight of blood never failed to trigger a release of tension in him, but only temporarily. Soon, he would itch for renewed action.

He was born in the early fifties in a backwater village at the southern foothills of the Caucasus Mountains. His parents lived in abject poverty. What little money they earned his father would drink away on weekends; and if his mother dared complain, he would beat her mercilessly. Fortunately, his father died while Sahir was still young, but still, he had enough bitter memories to keep him eternally rebellious against any father figure in his life. This included his older brother, his uncle, a teacher, local policeman, or even public figures who, in his mind, exercised undue influence over the lives of others. All his life he rebelled against authority of any form and on more than one occasion, even in his early youth, he often ran into trouble with the law and ended up in jail or in a juvenile correction facility. No degree of physical suffering ever deterred him from his goal of establishing a name for himself. He often dreamed of seeing his name in the headlines, perhaps his photo, too. This was a prize worth struggling for, even if it meant the assassination of someone important, even if it meant he would be hanged for it. Even death would be more tolerable than this nameless, faceless existence with everyone in the whole world dictating his every move. No, he could no longer bear living under this terrible burden, he must be free...he must make his break. The sooner the better.

Early in his youth Sahir had been noticed for his rebellious attitude and reckless courage. He fit none of the typical revolutionary molds. He was no religious fanatic, though many of his contemporaries were. He did not embrace communist or fascist doctrine, or become a mercenary. He had no ideals, even though he was intelligent and surprisingly well read; and most importantly, he wanted to serve no masters. All he wanted to do was vent his rage at the rotten humanity that caused him to be here and be so miserable. He lived in close kinship with madness, sort of on the periphery of society, and felt that everyday life was only an illusion in the twisted reality of his dreams.

Though he busily served a multitude of strange and violent causes, always violent in nature, it was not until recently that he'd found a group whose goals he could fully identify with. He did not pick them. They picked him. It was an international terrorist group, one of a new breed emerging its ugly head all over the globe. Active in Ireland, Palestine, or other unlikely places, the group acted seemingly independently, but mysteriously connected into a great, ugly octopus stretching its arms to embrace the world, capitalist or communist, no matter which; and with its tentacles of fear and terror strangle and poison and paralyze the nations into a palpitating, gory mass of writhing human cowardice. They certainly seemed to be successful at it. Their campaigns of violence, urban terrorism, kidnapping, and assassination left victims everywhere and rarely resulted in apprehension, arrest, and conviction of any of their members. The group was called WOILA, which stood for World Organization of Independent Liberation Armies.

Just whom they planned to liberate, nobody knew.

Sahir had very little respect for Hassan. Especially for his mental capacity. But he knew that, despite Hassan's jovial and fatherly appearance, he was capable of the most brutal and cold-blooded murder. This was their first assignment together. Until now they'd only heard of each other through the grapevine. Sahir had also heard of Hassan's total and unquestioning dedication to the cause, and knew that he would not hesitate to cut his throat here and now if he suspected him of some independent thinking. Neither of them had any idea whom they worked for. To meet the leaders was impossible and also very undesirable. On the other hand, the group's invisible leadership already amply demonstrated to the worldwide membership that membership in the club was lifelong. Guaranteed by the management to be lifelong.

The car passed through the tunnel and followed the great curving Kristina Boulevard along the back side of the hill via Blood Field and up the grade, through the Viennese Gate and up to the plateau of Castle Hill. It came to a stop in front of the tall, classic, modern glass building of the Budapest Hilton.

Chapter 11:
WOILA and the Dirty Bomb

Inspector Kroeger of the Frankfurter Kriminal Polizei was feeling quite miserable and repeatedly tried to get rid of the sharp pain in his stomach by exerting pressure on his diaphragm with his hand. The persistent pain had woken him up this morning, driving him mad with a savage desire to plunge a knife into the middle of it to stop it. His hiatal hernia had flared up again, as it always did when tensions on the job mounted and especially when, against his doctor's strict advice, he regrettably broke his diet with rich and greasy Bavarian bratwurst, lots of hot mustard, and spicy German potato salad. Not to mention beer. Lots of beer.

He stood up from his chair and mixed a heaping teaspoonful of bicarbonate of soda in a glass of tepid water and gulped it down hastily, grimacing with disgust. A couple of loud belches followed as he patted his protruding belly and sighed with relief. Why the soda would relieve his pain, what it had to do with hiatal hernia, he did not know, also did not care. It did the job every time. He was continually amazed that the German Food and Drug Administration did not regulate the stuff as a prescription drug, if for no other reason that it could he sold for three to four marks, instead of a few pfennigs, making a bundle of money for the already filthy rich doctors and drug companies, who were not generally known for passing up such moneymaking opportunities. He'd tried all sorts of over-the-counter remedies, flavored and unflavored – sometimes he felt he was chewing pure chalk – but he finally came to the conclusion that none of them outperformed the lowly bicarbonate of soda, in spite of the presumptuous claims on their labels. In fact, as a side benefit, the soda tended to neutralize his system as well, reducing to a considerable degree his allergic reactions to foods; though, to his chagrin, drinking the awful-tasting stuff caused his nose to run profusely, resulting each time in a five-minute nose-blowing ritual.

Adding to his misery was the late evening telegram he'd received from Interpol, advising his office of the sorry fact that one member of the special task force formed to track down and recover Speer's uranium had defected and joined WOILA. Secret plans and all.

Kroeger looked up through the folds of his bath-towel-sized handkerchief and between loud blows cursed at the blond curly-haired lieutenant standing before him. "It's not enough that I wake up with excruciating stomach pains, that I freeze my butt off in this lousy weather to change a flat tire on the way to the office, that my boss chews me out for not apprehending those Turkish sonsabitches before they skipped the country. To top it all, you have to come here and ask for a raise. Do you realize," he yelled at the unfortunate subordinate, his face turning crimson, "that the department just cut my budget? Do you understand" – he stopped to blow his nose into the supersaturated cloth – "that unless we come up with a significant breakthrough on this idiotic case, my group will be assigned to apprehending petty thieves at the October Beer Festival? Don't talk to me about a raise, for God's sake. Not now!"

The young man cast a bewildered expression at his raging superior and backed off a few steps and shrugged, realizing the futility of another attempt to discuss his pressing financial problem. He turned, dejected, and started to leave.

"Ernst! Warten Sie! I am sorry. Please don't take this outbreak of hysteria personally. We'll talk about your raise shortly. I promise. But not right now. I've got something very urgent and important to do. On your way out tell Helga to call the Hungarian Embassy in Bad Godesberg. I have no choice but to alert those guys about the situation and advise them about the terrorists' attempt to capture the cache. I think WOILA is desperately trying to get their hands on some uranium and terrorize the world with a homemade atom bomb. They've got to be stopped!"

Kroeger wiped the sweat off his brow with his woolen necktie – the oft-used and nondescript-colored rag shined like silk in some spots – and pressed his hand against his stomach again, his face contorting with pain as he cursed. "Goddamn it, Ernst, hand me a cup of water. Hurry!"

After gulping down the white, effervescent liquid he sat down, searching for paper napkins in his desk drawers. There were none, so in desperation he retrieved the saturated kerchief from the wastebasket where he'd thrown it just a minute ago.

In the meanwhile, the phone rang.

"Hallo. Your Excellency, Herr Ambassador? Good morning to you, sir! Yes, I am Inspector Kroeger of the Frankfurter KrimPol. If you can spare a moment, Ambassador, I have something very interesting to tell you."

In another scene, the incredibly high-tech Communications Center buzzes with activity. Two controllers, Comtec1 and Comtec2, on the computer screens intently follow *Iron Chef*, the popular food channel. Comtec1 seems bored. "Last week it was wiener schnitzel, today it is Texas-style chili. One more chili recipe and I will literally blow up! Goddamn Mexicans, beans, beans, nothing but beans." Comtec2 warns him to switch channels and watch closely, reminding him that messages in code may translate to something important. Sure enough, Comtec1 notices something odd and calls his supervisor. The supervisor loads the garbled text into the decoding software, and soon the following running text shows on screen: steve buday agent warfare specialist malev flight 107 from frankfurt to budapest lv 1100 hrs arr 1330 hrs copy. The supervisor dashes off to report to Mohammed.

The supervisor dashes off to report to Mohammed.

Chapter 12:
The Vérteses

"For God's sake, shut that radio off already! How many times do I have to tell you? It is driving me insane! That insufferable noise gives me a headache. You call that music? I call it trash! Hooligans; they won't leave you in peace, even on Sunday! Where is that boy? I will break his neck!"

The loud complaints from the kitchen proceeded the plump, ruddy-cheeked elderly matron who appeared fuming at the kitchen door, her cheeks flushed and eyes flashing with fury.

"All right, Mother! All right!" A young man in his early twenties jumped out of his lounge chair and darted across the veranda in the direction of the infernal noise. Soon the sweet melodies of the Merry Widow floated out to the sunlit veranda and waltzed into the tiny fruit orchard in the rear of the cottage.

"That is what I call music. Oh, the lovely melodies. Why can't you enjoy something civilized just once? Why do I have to remind you constantly? You naughty boy." As the young man returned, he was received into his mother's ample arms and squeezed with a hug that left him breathless.

"I know, Mother. You don't care for my taste in music. In fact, you hate it. How can I forget? You keep reminding me constantly. I promise not to listen to it again in your presence." And he squeezed back valiantly, only to run completely out of breath again. "Mother," he whispered. "Let me go, I am choking to death."

After having recovered, he winked at his sister. "What do you think, Ildikó? Am I not an agreeable chap? An obedient son?"

"Yes, Árpi. You are so obedient, but I would dare say that your stereo would have been in dire danger had you not immediately obeyed Mother's command." She laughed gaily, gazing at the two of them still standing there locked in embrace. What a contrast they made. Her mother, bursting with vitality and energy, full of mischief in spite of her fifty-six years. Her abundant chestnut-brown hair, with only a sprinkle of grey at the temples, combed back tightly around her head and tied into a prominent bun, crowning her round and happy face, which showed ageless beauty and refinement. Her figure, though plumped by accumulation of excess cells over the years, was still attractive if somewhat generous in proportions. Her big brown eyes sparkled with inner strength and tenacity in spite of a life filled with memories of depression, near starvation, war, and revolution; brief periods of peace followed by long periods of despair for the safety of her loved ones. At long last they were together in safety and good health, their last decade uninterrupted by major calamities.

Árpád, or Árpi by his nickname, on the other hand, took after her father, in looks as well as character. Tall and slender, with blond hair and handsome but slightly delicate facial features, he struck a marked contrast with his mother and sister. Ildikó often wondered how his fair complexion had burst into her family's typically dark and Hungarian features. She was told of ancestors on her father's side that were German, which could have explained his looks. But the real contrast was not so much in his looks as in his brooding nature, given to periods of intense unhappiness and anxiety over things Ildikó considered too early for him to be so deeply concerned about. She wanted him to have a carefree and happy youth, different from her own, which was spent in the serious pursuit of her career with little or no time left for the lighter side of life.

"Come on, children, let's sit down to eat. Árpi, go get your father. I wonder where he is hiding again? He always manages to busy himself with something trifling when I need him to help set the table.

"István! Where are you? Lunch is ready!" she called out loudly. Momentarily, the haggard figure of Mr Somogyi appeared at the top of the staircase leading up from the wine cellar. He was carrying a decanter of golden-colored wine and walked with considerable difficulty.

Mother lamented loudly as the children rushed to help their father up the stairs to the veranda. "Just look at him! You'd think he would take care of himself. No, not for me, not for anybody. He is like a scarecrow. He will not eat, refuses to exercise, won't see anyone. All he wants to do is hide in the cellar!"

"Oh, woman. Stop your eternal complaining. A man cannot find peace in his own house. I am all right. I just like to have some peace and quiet. Especially if I can find it in the cellar." The old man attempted to smile feebly but the bristly, leathery skin on his face drew into a thousand wrinkles, turning his smile into a grotesque grimace.

"Here, kids. Taste this wine. It is the best. Young and full of life and fire!" And he proceeded to pour the wine into small clear wineglasses with shaky hands, but with obvious pride and enjoyment.

"God has brought you here. To your health!" he said while ceremoniously lifting his own glass to toast and clink it against the raised glasses of others. They all drank slowly, tasting the wine, swishing the golden nectar around in their mouths to enjoy its full bouquet and nodding their heads in wholehearted approval and smiling happily as they sat down to table. Mother, in the meanwhile, was not going to let herself be outdone by mere wine and started to bring out her magnificent creations from the kitchen. The gentle aroma of freshly drawn wine was abruptly and mercilessly swept away by the powerful smell of seasoned and brightly colored foods.

"Eat, my beloved. Eat. Árpikám, do not take it so sparingly, my son. No wonder you are so skinny!" Mother grabbed the big spoon out of Árpád's hand and measured out generous portions of dumplings and chicken swimming in a golden-red paprika and sour cream sauce.

Soon a hush fell over the veranda. Everyone busily occupied themselves with devouring the delicious food in reverent silence, as was customary among Hungarians at table. You eat first, then you talk. Mrs. Vértes's eyes scanned the situation quickly and her hand moved silently to refill any empty space that might have shown up on her children's plate.

"Mother, have mercy, I can't eat anymore." Árpi groaned and gazed at her beseechingly to stop this wonderful torture.

"I am so happy that you like it, Árpád. I know it is your favorite dish. That is why I made it. Just rest awhile, then you can eat some more. I will go and fix coffee in the meanwhile." She stood up, her cheeks glowing red with pride, and disappeared into the kitchen to perform some more of her magic for her beloved family. Outside, only sighs and groans could be heard; music to her ears. Blackie, the hairy puli with no discernible beginning and end, sat with disciplined restraint, hoping for a tasty morsel or even a scrumptious bone. It was Sunday, after all, and he expected his share in this wonderful feast. It took a while for thoughts to be set in motion again.

Father lit up and leaned back to enjoy the fine, strong flavor of a Camel cigarette that his son brought for him on his last trip abroad. He was a heavy smoker in spite of his persistent cough and usual banishment from the house.

His hoarse voice finally broke the silence.

"You are unusually quiet today, Ildikó. What is the matter? Is something bothering you?" he asked, gently laying his bony hand on Ildikó's.

"No, Father. I feel fine. Just tired, I guess. I have been working hard recently. It is hot and dusty at the dig and it is so good to be back here for a while."

"My daughter, I can tell when there is something wrong. I know you better than that. Out with it! Is it Ottó, your friend? How is he?"

"Oh, no," laughed Ildikó. "I have not seen him in ages. We don't see each other any longer, except as friends; and even as such, very rarely. He is away on a business trip again, they sent him to Yemen, of all places. No, it is something else, Father. I received a call from Colonel Fehér of the Secret Police."

"You what?" Mr. Vértes sat up straight in his chair, his forehead furrowed with wrinkles of anxiety. "What do they have to do with you?"

"An American, an amateur archeologist, I think, arrived here yesterday. The police suspect him of espionage. They want me to accompany him wherever he goes and report on his activities."

"You'll do no such thing. You spying on an American? How utterly ridiculous! It is outrageous. Tell them you'll have none of it. You are an archeologist, not a snoop!" The old man trembled with indignation and gestured wildly as he shouted.

"Calm down, Apa. The whole neighborhood can hear you. Quiet down, please," Mrs. Vértes cautioned him warily as she returned with a pot of steaming espresso.

"I can't refuse them, Father. I could lose my job, you know that. What should I do? I am so afraid. It is against my principles to spy on somebody; besides, I am completely inexperienced at such things." Ildikó covered her face with her hands to hide the tears in her eyes.

Árpi touched her hand. "Hey, sister. Don't worry. I will help you. Leave it to me. I will call Fehér tomorrow and tell him to lay off and find somebody else. Those rats should not involve an innocent woman in their dirty work!" he said bitterly.

"You'd just better not get involved!" Mrs. Vértes protested and grabbed him by the arm protectively. "Stay away from the HSP as far as you can. Look at your father. Was five years in prison not enough for him? Do you want the same thing to happen to you? You are too hotheaded to be involved in something like this. Your sister is a smart girl, I trust her judgment better in these matters."

Mr. Vértes sat motionless in his chair, staring into space. The rays of the setting sun penetrated the shield of giant green grape leaves suspended on the weathered rafters of the patio and turned his snow-white hair to pure gold. He recalled the time he'd spent in prison, charged with espionage. Thirty years ago, the new communist regime indiscriminately imprisoned its real and imaginary foes alike. There were more of the latter in the beginning; the ratio changed steadily with the passing of time. Admittedly, he was both. With his aristocratic family ties and military background in the Horthy regime before the war, he was the embodiment of opposition to everything the communists stood for. On the other hand, he was a peace-loving, timid person; he hated to serve in the armed forces and never progressed beyond a desk job shuffling papers, and never did anything to invoke the government's charges against him. Nevertheless, he was accused of and convicted of espionage for the United States and received a life sentence later commuted to ten years. Following his sentencing he worked five years in a coal mine, which ruined his health completely. He was released early, only a bitter and broken man. He came home to die, and had it not been for the loving care of his wife, he would have long ago. And now they wanted to use his daughter. Wouldn't they ever let up? There must be others willing to serve in hopes of gaining something for themselves. There were so many of those around; why would they pick on somebody innocent, like his daughter? He threw up his hand in a helpless gesture.

Ildikó spoke beseechingly: "Don't worry, Father. I will be all right. I will report where he goes, what he does, whom he sees. I will do what is required of me, but no more. That's all. I will not get to know him personally, or to pry into his private life, into his thoughts and feelings. I will make a very reluctant spy. Perhaps they will tire of me soon and find someone else."

Evening had slipped upon them unnoticed when they finally said good bye. Ildikó and Árpi walked carefully down the steep and unlit street to the bus station. Their hearts were heavy with concern for their elderly parents, knowing full well that no amount of reassurance would help them sleep through the night. Ildikó felt saddened and angered at the same time, feeling sorry for the lonely old couple sitting up at night praying and worrying for the safety of their children.

"They should not have to go through this. Not anymore. They have had their share of misfortune," she said, clinging to Árpi's arm as their feet felt the way along the dark path.

Chapter 13:
Archeology Meets the CIA

Her vanity got the better of her when she rushed out at the last minute to buy a new dress, just for the occasion of her meeting the American stranger at the Hilton. With the argument that "first impressions are the most important and I need a new dress anyway," she stood before her mirror and tried to soothe her guilty conscience for grossly exceeding her budget. The dress was outrageously expensive, even for a post-Klára Rotschild design. "Why am I doing this? This is ridiculous," she mumbled, but put on the dress anyway and called a taxi.

Her pulse was slightly above normal when she inquired at the desk for Buday's whereabouts. The hotel clerk pointed him out as the clean-cut American gentleman sitting at the third table outside on the terrace.

She approached him.

"Excuse me, sir! Are you Mr. Buday?"

Steve got up, a little surprised by having been asked for by name.

"Yes, I am. How do you do?"

"May I introduce myself? My name is Dr. Ildikó Vértes and I will be your guide during your stay here. I do hope you will enjoy your visit in Hungary. May I sit down?"

Steve pulled a chair out for her. "Please do. Forgive me, so clumsy of me."

"Thank you," Ildikó said, seating herself.

"Miss, will you join me for a drink? Or perhaps an espresso? I must tell you that I enjoy sitting out here immensely and watching the people mill by. And the view is simply magnificent!" He gestured, aiming at the reflection of the pointed cupolas of the Fishermen's Bastion in the silvery glass walls of the hotel.

"I think it is too early for a drink. Coffee will do, thank you."

"Waiter, a cup of coffee for the lady, and bring along two glasses of soda, please."

A wall of silence fell between them as they both tried to think of polite conversation, but nothing seemed to pop into their minds. Her cheeks flushed slightly as she tried to get a better view of him without appearing interested. He did look very handsome, she noted, to her added discomfort.

The waiter finally showed up with the steaming black brew and mercifully broke the embarrassed silence by clumsily dropping a spoon. They both broke into a silly giggle.

"I am truly sorry, but I didn't get your name, Miss. Would you mind repeating it for a helpless foreigner, please?" Steve asked rather coyly.

"Doctor Ildikó Vértes."

"Thank you, Doctor Vértes. It is Miss, isn't it? And how is it possible that I am so fortunate to have such a lovely guide? I must retract a statement I made to someone just yesterday about not needing one. It was a statement made in ignorant haste, I assure you. Fortunately, in his infinite wisdom, this person insisted that I must have one."

Ildikó blushed and glanced aside to hide her embarrassment. In spite of her beauty, she had rarely received compliments. Working in the field, her attributes were covered by dust most of the time and few noticed. She answered coldly.

"My dealings with you, Mr. Buday, are strictly on the professional level. I have been requested by the authorities to provide you with guidance in your search for archeological sites. I hope that I can satisfy your curiosity quickly. I am a rather busy person and anxious to return to work. The bottom line is that I have very little time for tourists. What specifically are you looking for?" she asked, regaining her composure.

"She is beautiful, even when she gets angry," Steve was thinking, and sized her up one more time. He watched her drop a sugar cube into her espresso and stir it carefully. Her hands were slender and graceful but showing telltale signs that exposure to work and the sun was not strange to them. Steve was also wary of guides, especially employed by the state. The less he was watched, the more quickly he would get his job done.

"Yes, the sites. Of course, I should think, or rather," Steve fumbled for words. "Why don't you tell me where to start? You are the expert! I will give you a clue, however. I have seen enough Roman relics to last me a lifetime. On the other hand, I have yet to see something out of a Hunnic grave. Can you show me one?"

Ildikó perked up. She was on home territory now. "Certainly. I have participated in some of the most important digs in this country. None of them are near Budapest, unfortunately. But I would like to make a suggestion, if I may. Before you visit the remote sites, why not get acclimated and get familiar with the better-known historic monuments around the Capital and develop a feel for the subject? If this should be your first visit here you owe it to yourself to play tourist for a day or two and visit the Castle next door, the Coronation Church, the Parliament; perhaps a boat ride up the Danube. How does that sound?"

"Wonderful. But only if you accompany me. I would most likely get lost alone," Steve continued to tease her. She tried to ignore it.

"Only if you promise not to take too long. I really should return to work in a few days. By the way, I noticed your last name is Hungarian? How many generations removed are you?"

"Only one. My parents emigrated after the Second World War. I was born right after the boat docked in New York harbor," he said, smiling.

"Well, then. You must have some knowledge of our language?"

"Not what you would call excellent, but I can get along with what I know. You won't be able to sell me easily, if that's what you are thinking of," he chuckled.

Ildikó retorted, "I must be careful then of what I say in your presence. Besides, I really don't make trade in foreigners. Apropos, where do you intend to stay? Here at the Hilton?"

"Well, I think I would prefer another place. I am not even sure why I checked in here. This is a wonderful place for tourists, but I prefer more modest accommodations and, if possible, mix with the local people. I may as well get to know them while I stay in your country."

"I thought as much," Ildikó agreed. "Give me a little time and I will find a suitable place for you. Would you object to staying with a family? Or is that a little too much togetherness? Many people in this city sublet their flats for short periods. It is really quite a comfortable arrangement and breakfast is usually included."

"You mean your apartment?" Steve wanted to joke but as soon as he said it he knew he was in trouble.

"Definitely not!" Her eyes sparkled angrily. "But I can provide you with a list through the Chamber of Commerce."

"I must think about it." Steve laughed, sorry for his impertinence. "In my country, we do very little of that. Perhaps it would be too drastic a change for me, initially. Why don't we start out with a separate, furnished apartment?"

"Because there is a drastic shortage of those. It must either be a hotel, and there are many of those, or a friendly family. Which will it be?"

The thought of sharing a flat with a strange family did not particularly appeal to Steve; on the other hand, he weighed it as a possibility to stay out of sight and blend into the scenery. Also, he did not wish to involve some unsuspecting hospitable family in any trouble with the authorities, in case he got caught.

"There is no rush. Give me a few choices in a couple of days and I will decide then. My room is paid up to Wednesday, actually. By the way, Dr. Vértes, may I ask a peculiar question?" Steve probed carefully. She nodded in agreement.

"I have heard from unofficial sources that King Attila possessed a sword, according to legend, a magic sword, sometimes referred to as the Scythian Blade. Well, do you think that if you find Attila's grave, it will have this sword in it? I mean, legends are what they are, but I am curious."

Ildikó frowned on subjects like this. They detracted from the main effort to locate the grave; irresponsible speculations only interfered with the real purpose of her research.

"Let me say this much about that subject, Mr. Buday: I find it surprising that a person of your credentials would fall for such stupid tales. I don't see how a grown man would pay any attention to magic swords, perhaps stuff of Hollywood movies, which set no limit to the imagination. I wish to separate facts from fiction, if you don't mind."

Steve was taken aback by her angry response. He retorted:

"Dear Doctor Vértes, did I just touch a sensitive spot? For all I know, the whole subject of Attila's burial is the stuff of legends, nothing found to date, after hundreds of years of search produced not one iota of results, a weapon, a wooden castle, a bow – let alone a sword? Tell me, honestly, what hope do you have to find Attila's grave? You are as much a hopeless dreamer as I am.

"In my defense, let me tell you, my father received a gift from a noted researcher of the Scythians, a Doctor Ligeti, who possessed a rare find, called the Golden Stag, and gave it to the Museum of History in Vienna, it is still there, I am certain you have seen it. Well, that stag was all but a legend until they found it not too far from the purported location of Attila's wooden castle, near the midpoint between the two rivers, the Duna and the Tisza. So the sword is not out of the question, don't you think?"

Before Ildikó had a chance to respond, Steve's voice turned a tad icy as he suggested:

"But now, Miss Vértes, if you are willing, let us start my familiarization tour. Why don't we stroll over to that magnificent building and learn something about it?" Steve stood up abruptly and pointed toward the thirteenth-century Neo-Gothic Mathias cathedral immediately adjacent to the Hilton.

Ildikó silently obliged and the two of them soon disappeared under the pointed arches of the elaborately decorated entrance.

Inside the cool and dim cathedral Steve found it increasingly difficult to pay attention to detailed descriptions of somber and stone-faced statues of kings and saints, and of candle-lit side altars and endless rows of historic battle flags and colorful heraldry; or of subterranean burial grounds for kings and princesses hidden in dark and musty chambers. He found himself sneaking a peek or two at Ildikó's long black hair falling in sumptuous waves over her chic and colorful dress ending just above a pair of softly padded knees and shapely legs. Being near her in the dark recesses of the cathedral created in him an intense desire to smell her sweet and fragrant perfume and get a closeup view of her curving neckline; maybe nibble on her delicate ears. Preoccupied as he was with his attractive guide, he missed entire portions of her lectures delivered in flawless English and with apparently genuine enthusiasm.

Perhaps she was unaware of his attraction for her, but each time he moved too close she gracefully slipped away, exciting him even more. In the interest of future possibilities, however, he decided to act reserved and remain cool and aloof.

Steve vaguely sensed that underneath the facade of the erudite historian and enthusiastic guide, a sensitive and fragile, perhaps fearful person was trying awkwardly to hide her real and vulnerable self. This was not a typical assigned person in the service of the all-knowing, post-communist state.

Ildikó looked sullen as they were to part and Steve asked if anything was the matter. She mumbled something about not enjoying her role assigned to her by Captain Kutas, and Steve abruptly suggested that she should tell him to get lost, which Ildikó thought of as rude.

"Mr. Buday, you obviously have no experience with ex-communists, you don't talk to them like they were your neighbors in Kansas City. There are consequences. Keep your biased American opinion to yourself."

They parted company. Steve felt the effects of jetlag and wished to retire for a short rest. He didn't even attempt to appreciate Ildikó's last comment; he felt it was just a woman's emotional response to a non-problem. He shook it off.

Ildikó also felt she'd spent enough time with him for today and remembered the report she had to make to Captain Kutas by evening, who'd insolently suggested she get friendly with the American as soon as possible. She felt nothing but contempt for Kutas, that slithering snake of a man, and shuddered at the mere thought of having to report to him the details of their encounter.

Playing the snoop made her feel embarrassed and uncomfortable with Buday. His openness and naturally forward behavior she considered to be typically American and it confused her even more. Right now, she wanted to disappear and return to her job to be left alone with her work. She at once liked Steve, but was also suspicious of him, of all overly confident Americans, all too knowledgeable, pretending to be nice but carrying a big stick.

Chapter 14:
Dreams and Reality

Having returned to her small second-story apartment, Ildikó stood in front of the dresser for a long time, admiring her dress in the tall mirror, playfully spinning around a couple of times like she used to do when she was in college and in love with her paleography professor. Rarely did she permit herself to act this way; she thought it extravagant because of her serious work and concern over the well-being of her parents and Árpád; but secretly she enjoyed acting feminine like this, combing her hair and putting on makeup and looking at herself in the mirror and all that.

She caught herself humming a catchy tune she'd heard Árpád play at her parents' house, before mother blew her top, and she smiled; so rarely would she remember tunes, especially if they were of the new modern variety her brother listened to. His favorites ran along jazz and rock, especially the Beatles, whose popularity continued unabated among the young people. She felt a twinge of sadness, noting that her attitudes were becoming too conservative for no apparent reason, and worried that as time was slipping by she would age soon without ever having let her hair down, so to speak, and allowed herself the simple pleasures of life her uninhibited generation seemed to enjoy so fully. It seemed that the time had come to add a little spice and adventure to her emotionally dull and uneventful life.

For one thing, she'd never really had a man in her life; not someone serious, anyway. Oh, the men she dated were serious all right, but she never let them too close. Dinner, a night at the opera, a stroll arm in arm along the bank of the Danube, necking and petting a little on the bench in the park - but that was all. A man's apartment was off limits for her and her apartment was kept off limits for her dates. None of her past beaus appealed to her enough to tempt her beyond a good-night kiss, and she missed the embrace of a lover only rarely. For years on end she managed to avoid thinking about this and threw herself into her career. Most of her friends and colleagues admired her scholarly achievements but thought of her as somewhat aloof, unapproachable and perhaps even frigid. She did not like this image of herself at all and she wanted so much to change it, wishing that someone would finally appear who would earn her respect and love and break her out of the mostly boring pattern. But so far no one had. Mother tactfully inquired about her friends and plans to marry, but she would jokingly brush aside the subject as something not worth considering at this time.

It wasn't that she had never had any experience with a man, but the one she did have she would rather forget. Except today. For some reason, today she again remembered.

Just after graduation, her high school senior class threw a party on an excursion boat to Visegrád, sort of a last fling the class would do together. The kids had a blast during the boat ride, drinking pops - and an occasional swig out of a flask of pálinka hidden in somebody's oversized pocket – and dancing and generally raising hell as was expected of them. More than once the concerned captain of the boat threatened to turn around and begged the unruly passengers to stop favoring one side as the boat listed treacherously and threatened to overturn at any moment.

Ildikó spent all day in the company of a longtime classmate of hers who for the first time was paying any attention to her. He was a good-looking young man, of the athletic sort - he held great potential for the national rowing team – and extremely popular with the girls, whom he continually chased to build his already inflated ego. Many times she'd felt jealous seeing him run around with girls of tarnished reputation, but outwardly scorned his flirtations. Except on this day, when his attention was finally focused on her. Her excitement knew no bounds when they danced to the wild beat of the ear-splitting rock, and her heart pounded wildly while they danced close together, touching tightly with their bodies during the slow and romantic numbers.

Having disembarked at Visegrád, the couples scattered in all directions of the compass, clambering up the hillside, disappearing along narrow paths that led nowhere in particular among the trees and bushes except out of sight of the others. She followed him breathlessly and in silence and they climbed higher and higher in the blazing sun only to fall panting and exhausted under the merciful cool shade of a dense, flowering lilac bush. The scent of the purple and white lilac bunches hanging over their heads was devilishly intoxicating. Her partner wasted no time and began caressing and kissing her passionately, his hands roaming all over her body, feeling her breasts and thighs, giving her trembling and tense body a wonderful sensation she'd never experienced before. She feebly resisted, but her sense of embarrassment and guilt evaporated with each strange wave of excitement. As they wrestled, she fell to the ground, hitting her spine against a sharp rock, and she groaned with pain and covered her face. He instantly misinterpreted this involuntary signal and with trembling fingers undid her blouse and unclasped her bra.

Even today she refused to speculate in her own mind on the possible outcome of this escapade, but as fate would have it, it was interrupted by an inconsiderate couple who happened by, perhaps in search of a suitable spot of their own. She quickly dressed and with tears streaming down her flushed cheeks she ran down the hill to hide in the rear of the boat, noticing only later how spoiled her white blouse was and that one of her buttons was missing. To date she cannot remember how she explained the whole thing to her mother.

Ashamed and terribly upset, she avoided the others for the entire return leg of the trip, and would not come out of hiding even as the class resumed dancing on the moonlit deck of the graceful excursion boat gently floating down the romantic river, still visibly listing to one side.

She rummaged through the kitchen in search of a can of instant coffee but all she could find was leftovers from this morning. She lit the gas stove and reheated the uninviting brown tar and looked inside the tiny refrigerator for something to eat. Ecstasy was not what she felt when her search turned up the only edible item in there: a slice of layered chocolate cake her mother had hidden in her purse yesterday. "That's all I need," she grumbled, but it was better than nothing.

Her room smelled stuffy and she drew the lace curtains aside and opened the windows to let in some fresh air. Next, she switched on the shaded lamp standing on a small oval table adjacent to the window, and brought in the coffee and cake and sat down facing out so she could see the lights and the trees in the tiny park below. Her feet ached terribly and she kicked her shoes off and leaned back to relax, closing her eyes and stirring her coffee, slowly turning over the day's events in her mind. Her thoughts freely floated about in a confused pattern, forming a colorful kaleidoscope of undefined and shapeless images. She fell into a blissful state, unperturbed by memories of the past and anxieties of things to come. As she quieted down, she could hear her own blood pulsing in her ears. The small, cozy apartment was her "island in the Pacific," a pleasant refuge from the noise and tensions of this great metropolis. She decorated it as an extension of her personality with loving attention to every minute detail; from the white lace curtains to the hand-embroidered pillows with colorful flowery patterns put in prominent places on the couch and the bed; to prints of paintings by famous Hungarian and French masters like Rippl-Ronay and Renoir carefully arranged on the wall; to the graceful antique furniture and well-stocked bookcases. She loved the privacy of the bedroom where she spent endless hours couched upon her comfortable bed reading her favorite volumes, poetry from the idealist and revolutionary Petőfy; novels by the witty writer-caricaturist-sociographer Moldova, whose background she wished had been different, less socialist, but who dissected contemporary Hungarian life with the sharp knife of a surgeon. Her favorite music was famous operatic arias, mainly Puccini's bittersweet melodies; and the music of Bartók, the quiet and contradictory genius who collected ancient folk tunes and composed abstractions two generations ahead of his time.

The handsome face of the young American emerged out of the depths of her imagination as that of the deep sea diver emerges from the murky waters of the sea, and at last she painfully admitted her desperate need for someone to share her private little world; someone strong but compassionate and gentle who would enjoy the quiet times with her, reading, listening and discussing a variety of exciting topics; someone who understood her thoughts and ambitions and desires; and cared - most of all cared deeply for her. She wished to be totally and heedlessly in love, to discard those bothersome inhibitions, and for once experience that exquisitely painful state of barely controlled mania others had told her about.

She would have continued like this forever and would have stayed in this uncomfortable position had she not suddenly become aware of being watched. The breeze through the open window now chilled her and she stood up shivering to close it when she got a glimpse of the shadows of two men standing on the opposite sidewalk, marginally illuminated by the fringes of the cone of light cast by the tall streetlamp on the corner. The men were quietly talking and repeatedly glanced up in her direction. One appeared to be taller and thinner than the other. Hastily, she closed the Venetian blinds and drew the curtains, then turned off the lights. Through the slots in the blinds she peeked out to watch the two figures turn and walk away to be swallowed by dark shadows between streetlights.

She shuddered violently and wished that someone was there to keep her company.

That was all she needed. Forced to spy on the American, being spied on herself, worried about her brother, fighting the crew and the elements at her dig, preparing lectures to teach her ignorant and insolent students. When it rains, it pours – she remembered the American advertisement for the Morton table salt becoming more popular in Hungary.

Chapter 15:
Wine and Politics

Early next morning Ildikó promptly called Steve at the hotel.

"Good morning! How are you, Mr. Buday?"

"Fine. A little tired maybe. It will probably take me a day to recover from jetlag and get acclimatized to the time difference."

"Are you very tired?"

"Not really. Maybe it will hit me later today. I have been through this many times before and I know what to expect. It never fails. Tonight, I'll sleep like a log, by tomorrow I'll be as good as new. What do you have in mind for me? Shall we search for the Scythian blade?"

"No, definitely not that. Well, I thought that today we could do a bit of sightseeing – if you are interested, that is. If not, I have a backup plan."

"OK, let's hear the backup plan first."

Ildikó laughed at the other end. "Boy, it did not take you very long to decide against sightseeing. But anyway, I have some friends who own a vineyard near the Balaton. Out there the air is clear, the view is spectacular, the grapes are ready for harvesting, and you will find the food and the wine delectable, the conversation friendly and interesting, as long as we avoid legends. We could have a nice picnic and get back to town whenever you feel you have had enough. All we need is transportation."

"Sounds great to me. At least we'll have a chance to get to know each other better." Steve did not see Ildikó blush at the other end. "I love Hungarian food and I know the wine is great. And who are these friends of yours?"

"An old schoolmate of mine. We used to room together at the university. Her parents own the vineyard. Older folks, but full of life and good humor. I think you'll like them. I know they will like you."

"When do we leave? I can rent a car right here at the hotel."

"I hoped you would say that. Going by bus is a torture. I will be ready by ten and you could pick me up at my apartment. We should be out at the vineyard by noon. I'll phone ahead that we are coming."

"Excellent. I'll see you at ten. Thanks for the invitation."

Very reluctantly, Ildikó redialed as soon as she hung up and asked for Captain Kutas. She was afraid to leave the city without letting him know of their whereabouts. They talked for a few minutes and he made her promise that she would turn in a detailed report later that evening. After she hung up she felt slightly nauseated, but the feeling soon disappeared when she telephoned Mrs. Somogyi about her plans to visit her today.

"Sure...of course...we'd love to have you! You know how much we love you... Yes, bring him along, too... You mean he speaks Hungarian? How wonderful. István will just be tickled pink to have someone to talk to about politics. You know how he loves politic. Yes, yes, hurry up. And, just a minute," she asked, apparently speaking to her husband, who was somewhere in the background, "are you still there? OK, he wants you to pick up our daughter. She is in town and could use a lift to get here. We have not seen her for so long. Would you? Wonderful."

"Yes, Mrs. Somogyi. I will bring Lenke along. I haven't seen Lenke for ages. I had actually hoped that she could join us today. Well, great. We'll see you about noon."

"Bye."

Steve in the meanwhile arranged to rent a car. Filling out the multitude of forms, he got the feeling that they wanted him to purchase the thing, it was so complicated. While providing the necessary information to the inquisitive clerk, he made a couple of observations. One, that unless one is on an unlimited expense account, like he was, one could certainly not afford to stay at the Hilton at 125 dollars a day; second, he would never rent a car in Budapest, he would rent it somewhere else and drive it into Hungary. At fifty dollars per day, not including mileage, insurance and gasoline...well, he was not in the right income category to be able to personally afford these outrageous rates. Fortunately, Uncle Sam was footing the bill. Dear Uncle Sam! So good that he was so prosperous and generous with his money. Not that Steve was frugal, but with his background, he knew the value of the dollar.

At five minutes past ten he rang the bell on the intercom panel on the ground floor of Ildikó's apartment building.

"Hallo?" her sweet voice came on. "Hi, I am here. Are you ready?"

"Yes, Mr. Buday. I'll be down in just a second."

Ildikó and Lenke both turned up at Steve's car, to his surprise.

"Mr. Buday. This is Miss Lenke Somogyi, the person whose parents we will visit at the vineyard. She would like to come with us, would you mind?"

Steve appraised the slightly rounded figure and friendly smiling face of Lenke and extended his hand. "It will be my pleasure. Happy that you could come along." Then he turned to Ildikó.

"Miss Vértes! Good morning again. Gosh! You are beautiful! I thought we were going on a picnic," he remarked, scanning over Ildikó's pretty dress, a bit formal for the occasion. The two women glanced at each other and giggled gaily.

"Let's go," Ildikó said. "If we want to eat lunch, we'd better be there by twelve. Mrs. Somogyi expects us to be rather prompt, don't you think, Lenke?"

"Very much so. If there is one thing my mother expects, it is punctuality."

The car was a newly rented sky-blue Volvo sedan — Steve could have rented a Moszkvics for less, but upon seeing one he'd decided against it. He soon found his way onto the highway and the car quietly and effortlessly gobbled up the miles ahead. In a little over an hour the waters of the great lake Balaton sparkled before them in glorious multicolored aquatic visual splendor. They turned north and followed the road along the shore of the long and shallow inland sea, heading for the volcanic hills along the coast, which exposed the southern-facing slopes to the plentiful sunshine available to grow some of the finest grapes in Europe. Vineyards, great and small, lined up in orderly fashion along mile after mile of curving road and climbed up the mountain slopes as far as the eye could see.

The air was warm and they opened the car's windows to let it flow through. In some vineyards, the harvest had already begun and scores of pickers, men and women, were popping up among the rows, carrying great buckets on their backs, filled with freshly picked grapes destined for ignominious death in the crusher, only to be resurrected to a glorious life in the bottle.

They were all taken by the beauty of the pastoral scenery, a painter's paradise, and spoke sparingly except to point out the familiar landmarks to Steve, who found it difficult to see it all while driving. He offered to turn the wheel over to Ildikó, but she laughingly declined, saying that she had never driven a modern car in her entire life and it would not be a good idea for her to start just now. Steve insisted and she took over and drove like a teenager, thoroughly enjoying the experience. The others barely hung on. Steve tried to shout over the noise and waved to Ildikó to slow down.

"Hey, I not only got a guide, seems I got a Formula One racer." Ildikó smiled and accelerated.

Finally, after about five minutes of driving away from shore and climbing up a steep hill, the top of which was crowned by the ruins of an ancient, once mighty castle, they came up to the Somogyi vineyard. Hearing the commotion outside, the elderly couple rushed out excitedly to greet them all with welcoming hugs and kisses planted on both cheeks, Steve's notwithstanding.

"Welcome, my children. How wonderful to see you. Please come right in. What a wonderful surprise! Mr. Buday, please come here and have a seat. No, not there, over here. It will be better for you. Later on, it will get hot in the sun. There, don't you girls look lovely," she beamed, looking at the girls, still panting from the steep climb up from the gate to the house. "Let me see you. Ildikó! I always said you are the most beautiful girl in all of Budapest. And still not married! What a shame. Don't you think she is beautiful?" She turned to Steve, her arms open wide. "Someday she will make the right man very happy." She would have continued, but seeing her friend's discomfort, Lenke came to the rescue and cut her off.

"Mom! I can smell the food. What have you made for us? We are famished!"

"Ah, my word! I almost forgot! István, go and check if I burned something. Foolish of me. Of course you are hungry, my darlings." She looked at them one by one, beaming with glee. "A handsome young man, he is." She winked at Ildikó. "And he speaks Hungarian! Tell me, how lucky can you get! I wish Lenke should get that lucky."

Mr. Somogyi, or István by his first name, hustled off to carry out her order, not even getting a chance to get past the introductions. Soon, however, he was back, anxious to get a word in to the American and discuss with him the truly important things in this world. He pulled Steve aside at the first opportunity and whispered in his ear: "Do American women talk this much? I bet they don't. I bet they let their husbands talk whenever they wish to and as much as they wish to." Without pausing for a response from his captive, he quickly continued. "Tell me, is life really that wonderful in America? I mean, are you people really as well off as Americans claim? I read the papers, you know, and I know a lot about the world, but sometimes I fear that the papers don't tell me everything I should know. By the way, do you like wine? This is wonderful wine. Hárslevelü! The best on the hill!" He proceeded to fill the small wineglasses to the brim with the deep-golden, almost amber-colored, fragrant wine. "Egészségedre!" They greeted one another and took a hearty sip.

"Delicious!" Steve remarked, smacking his lips. The girls helped Mrs. Somogyi to set the great big stone table and served a "small" lunch, which left them breathless and slightly numb. Of course, the heady wine may have had something to do with the relaxed atmosphere, too.

There was peace out there. Real, down-to-earth, basic and fundamental peace. Nothing disturbed their meal and conversation, not even the few obstinate flies that returned to buzz over the food, causing Mrs. Somogyi to flail the flyswatter furiously. In the background, the voice of a cuckoo bird sounded and Steve could have sworn that he was in fairyland. Ildikó looked at Mrs. Somogyi, who reminded her of her own mother. The same vitality, the same bubbly love for life, family, and friends. These were the ingredients that formed the traditional basis for a contented life in rural Hungary. Steve enjoyed himself fully, grateful to

Ildikó for suggesting this outing and grateful to his parents for insisting that he learn to speak Hungarian. He managed to sit close to Ildikó, their knees touching occasionally. She pulled hers away repeatedly and after a while she gave up and moved away. In spite of her closeness exciting him again, the wine and the lack of sleep were catching up with him and Lenke mercifully suggested that they take a short walk before he fell off the bench. Steve, however, valiantly declined the offer and fought drowsiness, even though every once in a while, his eyes appeared to roll up under his heavy eyelids. Nevertheless, he tried to appear to intently listen to Mr. Somogyi's exposition of contemporary life in Hungary, spiced with the old man's home-brewed philosophy.

"You know, life in this country was once based on rigid attachment to the past. After the war, the country suffered such drastic changes, such violent social upheaval, that the people could no longer accommodate. Even now the future is uncertain and undefined. These country folk, independent and headstrong people, refuse to be pressed into some universal communist mold. With the ties to the past severed, the present some people find intolerable, and the future they consider uncertain at best. No wonder there is discontent, bitterness, and universal escape from reality. Suicide and divorce rates are among the highest anywhere, alcoholism is rampant among people of all ages. There are no leaders to look up to, no role models for the young to emulate. I don't know what this will lead to. Because of this hopelessness, mothers refuse to bear children, the birthrate has been negative for who knows how long; given the chance, the talented and educated leave the country. I tell you, things may look wonderful from atop this hill, but you can't see the pain buried in the hearts of people, you can only see the beauty of nature. Nature is always calm and beautiful. This place looked like this when we fought the Turks three or four hundred years ago, it looked the same during the world wars. Only people come and go, one unfortunate generation after another." He sighed deeply, his painful concern for the welfare of his fellow countrymen weighing heavily on his mind. Afraid that someone would cut him off, he quickly resumed again.

"I wish Hungarians would, for once in their history, be free to decide their own destiny. They may not be successful even then, but they would have only themselves to blame. You Americans are the lucky ones. I hope you appreciate that wonderful freedom your forefathers bestowed upon you. You, as a second-generation immigrant to that great country, I am sure you appreciate this more than most others. Am I correct?"

Steve had to think for a moment for a number of reasons. For one, in Hungary one could still get into trouble with the law for overstepping the limits of social criticism. A certain level of criticism was permitted, even encouraged, but to only a select few, certainly not to foreigners. Second, he had an important mission to accomplish. He had to act diplomatically whether he agreed with these views or not. He avoided a direct response. "My country certainly provides opportunities few other countries are able to. But some limits in the social system of other countries are self-imposed by necessity. Some cultures would not be comfortable with our form of democracy, our less stringent limits on personal freedom. There is a cost to be paid on all liberties, a cost not all people may be willing to pay at any given time in their history. Take a simple example, like crime, for instance. The high rate of crime in the United States is much talked about everywhere, as it is here, I am sure. You probably consider us uncivilized on account of that. You say, why not crack down on criminals ruthlessly and eradicate crime by increasing the number of police, stiffening the laws, or whatever. But our people are so afraid of turning more power over to the police or the military or the government in general that they would rather put up with the menace of crime. To them the uncertainty posed by crime is preferable to the certainty of a police state, no matter how many services that state is willing to offer for the protection of its citizens. Does that make sense to you?"

Lenke pitched in. "I think Hungarians would welcome your form of democracy even though the transition to it would be slow and perhaps painful at times. I think they are mature enough to handle it. Our history is one continuous struggle, a series of bloody revolutions for freedom and self-expression. Hungary's literature is a testimony to that. This country's greatest heroes are not politicians or generals, they are poets and writers and composers. You may recall some of these from your own readings. Have you heard of Petőfy, Vörösmarty, Kazinczy, Ady, Móricz, Bartók, Kodály? There is no end to the list. Their statues dot the city squares all over the country. Just ask any schoolchild and he will quote you a verse or sing you a stanza from one of them, or that's the way it used to be." Mrs. Somogyi put her arm around her daughter's shoulder to calm her.

Steve answered. "Yes. I know some of them. Geniuses. Real patriots. A vanishing breed here and everywhere. Let me assure you that their ideals carried across the Atlantic and have helped shape some of our own. Many of your best freedom fighters fought for American independence. Without these valiant men, whether from Hungary or from other countries, America would not be the free country it is today. I hope you will continue to send more of these high-caliber people to our side in the future."

Ildikó looked at Steve with wide-open eyes and her heart was beating faster with every word he said. She was deeply impressed with his answer, knowing that he'd been put on the spot.

Mrs. Somogyi squirmed in her seat. "Aren't we getting a little too deep into this? On a beautiful afternoon such as this? You know, Mr. Buday, Hungarians love two things in life: food and politics. They are insatiable and incorrigible. I am certain you will experience this during your stay here with our people. Women cook, men talk politics. It'll be coming out your elbows, before long!"

Steve laughed. "It beats talking about cars and sports. For me, anyhow."

Ildikó smiled. She had been listening all this time, happy at the fact that Steve seemed to be enjoying himself among her friends. She was glad that they accepted him and welcomed him among them as well. But she became concerned about Steve's getting too tired for the return trip.

"We should not overstay our welcome. Not to mention the fact that Mr. Buday has not slept in over twenty-four hours. Maybe we can continue this some other day?"

"You're not going to take him away from us already?" Mr. Somogyi protested.

"We have been here four hours straight, consumed some wonderful food, countless bottles of wine, covered a lot of political and historical territory," laughed Ildikó. "I promise we will return again for more of the same, soon."

"Naughty girls," complained Mrs. Somogyi. "Come here, Ábel!" she called out for the halt-witted, half-tongued handyman whose half-shot-off face showed the terrors of the last war. "Prepare a basket of goodies for these hungry kids. I can't let them leave hungry, for goodness sake."

Ábel not only returned with a picnic basket loaded with samplings of the hostess's creations and three bottles of wine, one for each of them, but in his unintelligible grunts made a request to Steve to have his picture taken with him. He insisted that he prove to his village buddies that he had influential friends in America. Steve complied with good humor and Ildikó snapped the picture. Ábel smiled happily and repeatedly slapped Steve on the back. "Don't forget to send me a copy now!"

Saying good bye took a while, as was customary among hospitable folks in the wine country. By five o'clock they were finally back on the road to Budapest.

"Your parents are wonderful people, Miss Somogyi. I really appreciate their generous hospitality. They are like a ray of sunshine, a very lovely couple."

"I hope you can visit them again, Mr. Buday. I can't tell you how much it means to them to meet a visitor from outside their little world. Forgive my father's inquisitiveness. He means no harm. He just loves to learn and exchange ideas."

Ildikó interjected. "What are your plans for tomorrow?"

"To tell you the truth, I really don't know. I am totally beat right now and probably ready for a good nap. I tell you what, I will call you in the morning and we'll make plans then. I don't mean to be unsociable, I just think I am a little tired now. And above all, I wish to be up to our visit to Attila's grave," Steve answered.

"You are a teaser. There is no such thing, at least not yet", Lenke said as she watched from the back seat with great interest and prayed that something would develop between her friend and Steve.

It was past seven when Steve dropped them off and headed back to his hotel. His eyes were dry and burning from fatigue and he could hardly find the way to his room. Once in bed, ironically, he found it extremely difficult to fall asleep, a common symptom of over-exhaustion that often plagues world travelers.

Chapter 16:
The Unfriendly Side of Budapest

It must have been almost midnight when Steve awoke already from his short and fitful sleep feeling like he had been hit by a truck. The long flight from New York to Frankfurt and then on to Budapest, which was about eight hours, and the time difference, another six hours, were taking their toll. The outing to the wine country had not helped either. His system was really messed up and he felt sort of disoriented. He sat at the window of his room overlooking the Danube and the massive building of the Parliament on the opposite side and tried to sort out the day's happenings. His senses returned slowly and his mind began to accept meanings as well as images. He noticed that the whole city was brilliantly illuminated.

The view was like fairyland out there. Myriad lights were strung along the graceful arches of majestic bridges across the river and along the boulevards, outlining church steeples and housetops and the jagged domed and spired structure of the Parliament. The effect was multiplied a hundredfold by the reflection of the lights in the mirror-like surface of the Danube. The picture reminded Steve of films he'd seen long ago of the turn-of-the-century Austro-Hungarian empire's glittering ballrooms with waltzing beautiful damsels and dashing soldiers in colorful uniforms, all sparkling with dazzling jewelry.

He quickly showered, and, feeling refreshed and hungry, be decided to have a late dinner on the terrace of the Bastion with the majestic Danube below.

"What's going on today?" he inquired from the young waiter, gesturing broadly toward the spectacle of lights.

"It's one of those days today. We have a visitor of state. I guess he must he important or else they wouldn't waste all this pomp and energy. I think he is the president of, I think, Sri Lanka."

"Sri Lanka?"

"You wouldn't think he is such an important person, would you? But who am I to say who is important! It's up to those guys across the river to decide who deserves the royal treatment!" He moved his head in the direction of the Parliament as he said that. He seemed like a talkative fellow, so Steve pressed him for more.

"Do they do this for all heads of state? When was the last time they did this?"

"Ah, I can't remember. It must not have been too long ago, but I don't know who it was for. Maybe somebody from Zimbabwe, or Cuba or something. Those guys get the royal treatment around here every time. They won't do this for everybody, let me tell you that. You know, a couple of years ago Liz Taylor and Richard Burton were here on one of their honeymoons or birthdays, or making a picture or something. Did you know that they actually asked the authorities to light up the city in their honor? The gall those people have!" he lamented indignantly.

"You're kidding, and did they do it? Light up the city, I mean?"

"No, they did not! And if you don't mind my saying so, I am glad they did not. Just who do they think they are? Now don't get me wrong. I've seen them in the movies and they are mighty fine people, really great actors. And she is a knockout at her age! But to illuminate a whole city for a couple of screen actors? I ask you," he said, shaking his head in disbelief.

Steve slapped his knees and wiped his tears from laughing so hard. "My friend, you are absolutely right. Just who do they think they are? Here is a toast to the president of Sri Lanka. I'm certain he deserves all the respect he gets tonight." He raised his glass in salute to the man who was enjoying all this honor and respect not befitting the stars of the silver screen.

Finishing his meal, Steve left the talkative waiter a sizeable tip. The night was still young and he wanted a taste of it. Enticing sounds of the city floated up the hill on the wings of an unseasonably warm breeze, tempting all but the most insensitive and tired of tourists to a fling on the town. Steve was neither.

Strolling around the building to the front entrance, he noticed taxi after taxi arriving and unloading guests, many of whom were women who quickly checked their hair and makeup before stepping out of the cabs. He found it curious and kept watching for a while. Finally, it dawned on him.

Prostitutes! Multitudes of prostitutes. Young and not so young, pretty and not so pretty, but mostly gaudily dressed women, arriving to provide a service to the international business traveler from all parts of the globe, demanding even behind the iron curtain the service that has no interest in politics, has no ideology or language barrier, only interested in business.

Steve could not resist feeling a tinge of sarcasm. Although he never felt anything but contempt for the trade on the street and pity for its victims, nor a desire to partake in its offerings - but to find it here, a vestige of capitalistic decadence tearing at the very foundations of communist ideology. Shocking!

He wondered if Marx and Lenin were turning over in their graves seeing the unadulterated greed and seeking of pleasure manifesting itself in the imitation of decadent Western values - prostitution, gambling, black-market currency exchange, alcoholism and drugs - all the vices that the workers' paradise was supposed to have been delivered from. But it was all here, in spite of Engels's prophecy that predicted that with the elimination of private property as the underlying cause, prostitution would also disappear. Well, it had not, yet. It was all here, not overtly obvious, or flashy, but it was apparent, and furthermore, it was selective. The Reds' way of extending the hangman's noose to their Western adversaries - for none of the above was accessible to the natives, only to the tourists. The gambling casino in one of the hotel wings was open for the locals to visit and mill around and perhaps quietly and unobtrusively observe, but not to take part of. The exquisite pleasures of gambling and prostitution were reserved for those in possession of hard currency. Dollars and Swiss marks, franks and pounds would get you anywhere; but not forints or other nonconvertible currencies.

Not that the locals desired, even if in possession of a few bills of foreign currencies acquired at outrageous exchange rates on the black market, to spend them on anything as extravagant as gambling. No, those precious bills were reserved for Western goods available only in so-called "dollar" stores, or for a long-awaited visit to a Western country. The system was designed to encourage tourist spending, not local spending, to feed the economy's insatiable hunger for hard currency.

Steve hailed the next available cab just vacated by a shapely brunette, and told the driver to take him for a spin about town. The pungent smell of cheap perfume lingered in the car, reminding him of a quote from Alexandra Kollontai, a Soviet champion and chief ideologist for the cause of free love, according to whom sexual contact between two adults should be as natural and simple as drinking a glass of water. He rolled down the window for fresh air.

"Stop here and wait for me," he called to the chauffeur after a few miles, and stepped out for a stroll down to the edge of the water near the majestic and old Chain Bridge, once one of the wonders of bridge construction architecture. He followed the stone steps down to the water and stooped down to feel it. It was cool but not cold, apparently not swelled by autumn rains in the Alps. The water level was quite low, about ten or fifteen steps below the spring-level watermark visible on the upper steps.

In the warmth of the gentle breeze and the gloriously illuminated lights of the city reflected in the calm dark water, scores of lovers strolled arm in arm, stopping briefly to embrace and kiss as if stung by the frivolity and eternal hope of spring. The more adventurous among them sat on the steps on the bank, huddled together closely, clutching one another with a passionate confession of mutual attraction.

Steve felt envious and for the first time became aware of a deeply buried need for a mate, a companion. This feeling surfaced above his adventurous, fun-seeking, and perhaps rather shallow lifestyle. Usually he fought these temptations, claiming that the inherent dangers of his assignments offered a perfectly valid excuse to avoid serious attachment and long-term relationships.

"Perhaps I am ready to settle down." The sight of a pair of lovers gazing into each other's eyes inspired him to quickly review his past affairs and romances. Insistently, his attention returned to Miss Vértes.

"This is crazy!" he mumbled and hastily called his cab.

"Follow me in ten to fifteen minutes," he called out. "I want to cross the bridge on foot."

The walk up to the deck of the bridge included climbing a great many steps carved into the massive stone abutment. At the top, he found himself standing at the foot of a giant sculpted lion adorning the entrance. A small bronze plaque at eye level told of the bridge's architect, Adam Clark, an Englishman, who about a hundred and thirty years ago dove into the waves from atop his creation to abruptly end his successful career. According to legend, he built the perfect classic suspension bridge, soaring high above the water. Or so he believed, until an observant spectator pointed out to the crowd's amazement during the dedication ceremonies that none of the four lions guarding the two ends of the bridge had tongues in their open mouths. A mere oversight for anyone but the master builder of Europe's finest bridges. Too late to save his life, the tongues that were invisible from below were later found on closer inspection.

Steve's reaction to the story was characteristic of him. Human nature continually amazed him with its unending variety of emotional reactions to life's surprises. To him suicide, committed for whatever reason, was nonsensical, unless in the extreme justified by hopelessly ill health. He shrugged and walked on.

Later he stopped to run his fingers over the carved stones of the suspension tower and stood for a moment in amazement, straining his neck to see the huge steel-chain suspenders hanging above in mute testimony to the enormous undertaking, the expenditure of materials and manpower on an immense scale, probably claiming numerous human lives as sacrifice to fate until its successful completion. He walked along the sidewalk, stopping at various points to take it all in, enjoying the view on and from the bridge. He agreed with the justifiable claims that this was one of the most ornate and sophisticated bridges built in its time. As he strolled along, he could feel the rumble of cars speeding in both directions and the gentle sway of the superstructure beneath.

The midpoint seemed like a good place to stop and look north at the view offered by the Parliament on the right and the Castle on top of the hill on the left. Undeniably, a thousand years of history and culture, combined with the strikingly natural setting of the twin cities of Buda and Pest, would have impressed anyone much less sensitive to such things as he. Steve could not help but feel slightly jealous when comparing the added dimension of accumulated centuries with the comparably illuminated, never-the-less one-dimensional, atmosphere of young and modern downtowns in the States, boxy black skyscrapers and all. Sadly, the same shapes were cropping up here too, destroying the harmony of random, ornate and unsymmetrical architecture of previous generations. He thought it a crying shame to see the rectangular outlines of the plate-glass-walled Hilton Hotel crammed into the midst of a twelfth-century monastery and cathedral.

Suddenly he felt a sharp pain in his back and grabbed for the spot, thinking that he'd leaned against a sharp protruding object.

"Don't move or I'll stick it in all the way!" he heard a gruff voice say, and felt the pain increase.

"Is this the new way to exchange your forints?" he tried to joke, but the sharp point of the stiletto pierced his skin and he froze motionless.

"Shut up! See if he's got a gun on him!" From behind, a pair of powerful meaty hands frisked him up and down, feeling for a hidden weapon. He had none, as usual. In a tight situation, he preferred to rely on his well-developed muscles and lightning-quick reactions to get out of trouble. The judgment of a gun was final, in his opinion; it left no room for error or time for a change of mind. "No gun!" the voice belonging to the hands grunted.

"Put your hands in your trouser pockets and keep them there! Turn around very slowly and don't make any moves unless you want to die!"

Steve cautiously followed the man's instructions, and as he turned he saw a big foreign car pull away from the curb in a hurry and disappear in the traffic flowing toward Castle Hill. His unexpected visitors must have been let out here and crept up on him while he was absorbed in sightseeing. On a closer look, the man holding the knife looked vaguely familiar.

"My American friend. Don't you think it dangerous to be walking out at night, especially on a bridge? All alone in the dark?" The tall one looked over the railing into the dark abyss below and shuddered. "What a sad and abrupt finale to an otherwise pleasant excursion, don't you think?" The man chuckled in a strange, almost maniacal manner as he struggled with his English in a horrible accent.

"Who in the hell are you, and what do you want?" Steve demanded, his mind racing to find a way out of his predicament. The heavy-set fellow came up behind him and suddenly he found himself locked in a chokehold with a gun in his back and a knife ready to be plunged into his stomach. He knew they had him and all he could do was to stall for time or an opportunity to shake his abductors.

"I'll ask the questions, if you don't mind!" The skinny one grimaced, flashing a pair of gold front teeth. Pictures of gypsies attacking innocent travelers flashed into Steve's mind. He recalled the intense prejudice his parents harbored against these dark-skinned people, who were a fairly sizeable minority in Hungary and were unjustly but popularly accused to be the alleged perpetrators of many minor crimes. They also had the habit of sporting gold teeth, the more visible the better. The fine suits his attackers wore and the expensive foreign-made wristwatch on the fat one's arm argued against this theory. He could not identify the accent, but felt that it was not local. He waited.

"Hey, Sahir! Why don't we just throw him over the railing. We know what he's after; the fewer people looking for the same thing, the better!" the fat one growled, tightening up on Steve's neck, threatening to break it.

"Shut up, you idiot! Maybe he knows more than we do. Until we beat it out of him, that is." The man called Sahir pressed the blade against Steve's belly with such force that he groaned in agony and jerked his knee up in reflex to protect himself. "Jumpy little fellow, isn't he?" Sahir laughed.

"What the hell do you want from me? If it's money, you'll find it in my wallet. Ten thousand dollars! Take it and leave me alone!" Steve whispered, playing for time and waiting for a wrong move on the part of the fat one.

Sahir flashed his gold teeth again with something he might have considered a friendly smile.

"No, mister! Not your money. Not right away in any case. You tell us what you know about the hidden uranium, then maybe we'll let you go. And don't tell me you don't know or I'll perform corrective surgery on your ulcers with this thing!" he threatened, bluffing. In reality, all he could do was hope that he and Hassan had grabbed the right guy on the bridge. Their instructions mentioned an American to be sent by the CIA. How in the world WOILA could sniff out such sensitive information so far in advance Sahir could never understand, but he'd learned to stop questioning and to follow instructions. Steve was the only American aboard their flight, and the special treatment he received from the Secret Police at the airport terminal made him a prime suspect in his mind. He and Hassan had tracked the American and his female companion the previous afternoon and followed her to her apartment thinking that he too would be there. Today, they'd finally found him again at the Hilton just when he was getting into a taxi.

Steve squirmed under the chokehold and was turning limp for the lack of air. His captor was strong as an ox and held him so tight that any attempt to break loose from his grip seemed utterly hopeless. He could hardly speak anymore.

"I can't tell you anything about the uranium, unless you let me breathe."

"Let up on him, stupid!" Sahir commanded. "Let's hear what the man has to say. It had better be good!"

Steve sensed the vise grip loosen around his neck momentarily and knew the time had come to act with lightning speed. Simultaneously, he kicked Sahir in the groin and lurched forward, arching so that Hassan's heavy muscular body flung through the air, crashing into Sahir, who was doubled over in agony, clutching his stomach. But his freedom was only short-lived, because his well-trained attackers recovered instantly and renewed their pursuit of him. It came to punches and Steve tried every trick in the book to knock one of them out. He was unsuccessful and tried to run away, but Hassan dove after him and grabbed his legs, trying to pull him to the ground. Sahir staggered to his feet and grabbed the gun up from the ground, where it had fallen during the tussle, and lifted it to shoot Steve.

The moment for a quick decision had come. There seemed to be no possible way to escape certain death at the hands of these assassins. In desperation Steve chose the next best alternative.

With one reckless move, he freed his foot from Hassan's grip and with the same continuous motion he dove over the high railing and disappeared head first into the dark black hole below.

Sahir and Hassan, both seasoned assassins, gasped in horror, for even they recoiled at the mere thought of someone voluntarily choosing this horrible, painful, and certain death. Both jumped to the railing and leaned over, straining their eyes and ears to see or hear some sign of the vanished American. But the great dark height and the noise of traffic on the bridge swallowed all signs of him. All they could see were occasional snatches of moonlight illuminating the dark waves below. There was no doubt in their minds that the American was killed instantly. No one could survive the impact of the fall from such great height.

"SHIIIIT!!!" Sahir screamed, his face contorting with rage and his fist pounding the iron railing, clutching with his other hand his groin still aching unbearably from the terrific kick he had received. Hassan stood dumbfounded and intently inspected a great tear along the seam of his coat sleeve, as if that were the most significant matter for the moment. He was shaken to the depths of his being and wobbled back from the railing dizzy and nauseated.

He threw up.

Chapter 17:
An Unpleasant Visitor

They were both startled by insistent loud knocking at the door. She stood up to investigate.

"Just a minute, Árpád. Let me see who it is. I never have visitors here, especially at noon. Maybe it is the mailman, though he never bangs on the door. This is odd."

Outside stood Captain Kutas of the Secret Police in full uniform, striking a theatrical pose and evidently extremely agitated. Unquestionably, he had come on official business. Without a word of greeting or an invitation to enter, he stormed right through the door, straight into her combination bedroom-living room. Ildikó left the door open and hurried after him.

"What is the meaning of this, Captain?! How dare you burst into my apartment like this?"

Kutas ignored the question and, turning on his heel, glanced around the room, his gaze finally resting on Árpád, who was sitting at the coffee table by the window. The shades were partly drawn and the room was only dimly lit. "Who is he?" he demanded arrogantly, giving Árpád a disdainful look. "I want to speak with you in private!"

"He is my brother, if you must know. Please explain yourself."

Árpád remained seated at the table and nonchalantly greeted the captain.

"Halló. What a distinct pleasure to meet you, Captain Kutas. Heard so much about you lately. Pray tell, what brings you to my sister's once private apartment with such aplomb?" he asked derisively.

"Never mind the sarcasm, boy! Your sister here is in deep trouble. Perhaps you can help her explain Mr. Buday's sudden and unexpected disappearance. Hmm? Do you realize, comrade Vértes," he said, directing himself now to Ildikó, his small piggish eyes frowning with obvious malice, "you know that your American spy-turned-archeologist friend is gone? Vanished into thin air? Most likely sunk to the bottom of the Danube, while you are having a leisurely tête-à-tête with your yet juvenile, but already very impertinent brother?" Kutas gesticulated wildly and lit up a cigarette in one minute, then put it out in Ildikó's half-finished coffee the next.

Ildikó turned pale. "Mr. Buday disappeared? That's utterly ridiculous. He dropped me off at my apartment last night and he returned to his hotel directly. He was totally exhausted and wanted to rest. I have a witness...no, I don't believe you!" she protested feebly.

Kutas lost the last remnant of his already thin patience. He began to shout. "You mean to tell me he went back to his hotel later? And how long do you think he stayed there? An hour? Two hours? Did you ever bother to check up on him? Did you know that close to midnight he left the hotel and took a taxi and walked across the Chain Bridge where he was attacked by strangers and thrown into the river? What do you say to that? And what do you say to your failure to keep an eye on him like you were supposed to? And what about the report you were supposed to give me last night? What happened to that?" Kutas shook his index finger into Ildikó's face. "Let me inform you, my little ignorant informant, that if it were not for the observant taxi driver who faithfully followed Buday, I would have no idea of his whereabouts! Come to think of it, I still don't.

For all I know, he is dead! In fact, what else could he be? When was the last time you've heard about someone surviving a fall from that bridge?"

Kutas moved toward Ildikó threateningly. "It's all your fault. You will take full responsibility for it, I assure you. I'll let you and that dumb Fehér take the blame. I told that SOB that I will not work with amateurs!" He yelled at Ildikó with uncontrolled rage, getting so close to her that she backed into the wall for fear of being attacked.

His insolent and brutish attack on his sister was more than Árpád could stomach. He jumped out of his chair and yanked the officer with full force away from Ildikó. It was his turn to vent his rage and start yelling.

"Listen here, you filthy miserable swine! Who do you think you are, bursting into a person's private residence like this? Do you have a warrant? Or a court order, or something? Because if you don't, and if you don't stop shouting and shaking your finger at my sister, I'll throw your fat butt out of here." Árpád's hatred of the system began to surface. "You rotten dog. You servile bastard! Get out of here before I kill you!" And he lifted his tightly clenched fist to strike him.

Ildikó screamed and jumped between them, restraining Árpád's uplifted arm. Not to save Kutas, but to protect her brother from the terrible consequences of his irresponsible behavior.

"No! Árpi, stop for God's sake! Don't get involved. Remember your father." And she started to cry.

Kutas jerked his jacket straight. Red-faced and with vile hatred, he pointed his finger at Árpád.

"You little bastard. You little nothing! I'll see you rot in jail for this, attacking an officer of the HSR! You know what you get for this? And for you, Miss Vértes. You may as well forget your little stint as detective and your career as well. As far as I am concerned, you can go back to your digging until they bury you too there!"

With that he stormed out of the apartment and slammed the door behind him so hard that large pieces of plaster fell off the ceiling. Ildikó's next-door neighbor, who was listening to all the commotion, quickly locked her door and hid in her closet.

Ildikó leaned her head against the wall to cool her burning temples.

"Oh, my God! What did I get you into? Árpád, what are we to do? You just attacked an officer of the Secret Police! You'll get arrested without a doubt. What will we do?" she kept asking. "Father will die if they take you away. You have no choice but to leave and hide somewhere! God! What is happening to us?" she sobbed, embracing her brother.

"Ildikó. Listen to me. Calm down, please. That's exactly what I came to talk to you about," Árpád appealed, leading her to her chair and gently forcing her to sit down. He remained standing and nervously fidgeted with the buttons on his jacket. He looked pale and thin, and had difficulty concealing the intensity of his passions. He was such a loveable character, so preposterously young and yet so painfully adult. Ildikó felt a surge of love and pity for him and attempted to stand up and caress his boyish face.

Árpád protested. "Ildikó, please sit down. This is very important. There is no one besides you whom I can confide in about this." He stopped and paused, searching for the right words, looking around to make certain no one could hear what he was about to say. At times like this even the walls grew ears in Budapest.

Slowly and quietly and emphasizing every word, he spoke.

"Sister! I am going to defect!"

He turned even paler, as if finally realizing the weight of his decision. Not that the idea was new to him. No, he'd agonized over it for months, turning it over and over in his mind and keeping it all to himself, afraid that someone would report his nervous and strange behavior and foil his attempt to leave the country. His friends at the university knew of his application for an exit visa to take a guided tour vacation in Austria. Anything out of the ordinary, any odd behavior, would certainly arouse suspicion and would only result in the denial of his permit to leave the country.

He had saved every penny he earned as a waiter in his spare time, spending on himself only what was absolutely necessary to live on, and buying any amount of hard currency he could afford at every chance he got meeting foreign tourists. The money did not amount to much, only about a hundred dollars worth of mixed currencies. But he treasured it dearly, hiding the bills in his mattress, counting them nightly, hoping against hope that the amount would somehow miraculously multiply. He knew he needed more to survive the first few weeks in a refugee camp until he could make contact with friends and distant relatives who had defected earlier and lived in Germany and the United States, already well established.

But now there was no more time to wait and plan. The tour would leave tomorrow and he had his permit in his pocket. All he needed to do was to arrange his affairs so that it would seem like he left the Capital for a remote location in eastern Hungary to visit a friend or acquaintance. He must concoct a credible scheme to mislead the police into thinking that he was hiding in the countryside. No one must realize that he was to leave for Austria tomorrow. Not until he crossed the border. Not even his parents. And especially not that bastard Kutas.

Ildikó nodded, her eyes reflecting infinite sadness. "I see you have made up your mind. After what happened here today I can't say that I blame you. Are you certain it is the only way?"

"I am certain. I have thought it over a thousand times. I have considered it from every angle forever. Believe me, I would leave anyway, even if today had not happened."

Árpád's face and the distant look in his eyes reflected a multitude of emotions raging within him. A mixture of hope and resignation, of rebellion and surrender to the inevitable. He'd suffered greatly and made his decision as though made by an ill person choosing between corrective surgery and confinement in a wheelchair for life. Either alternative hurt plenty, but the former was so much better, so much more promising toward total recovery. In his mind, he'd already accepted the lifelong pain of separation from his loved ones. But his soaring spirit had not been created for a caged-in existence under a dictatorial regime that conspired to confine his every move, every ambition, even his very thoughts and dreams. No matter what the cost, he had to be free. Free to learn, to experiment, to grow and understand, to make mistakes and recover, and to plan for the future unhampered by ideologies, slogans, and the fear of police.

His sister completely understood and appreciated his motives. Often, they had discussed these things, sometimes in jest as a wild but impossible dream, sometimes very seriously. But always careful not to slip in front of their parents. Especially their father, whose weak heart could not stand the strain of worry and anxiety over the uncertainty of his children's fate. Though he should not have concerned himself with Ildikó, for she never entertained the thought of leaving. To her life was much simpler than to her brother. A satisfying career, good friends, some valuable privacy, and good health. What else could life offer, regardless of where it was spent?

"What do you wish me to do?" she asked quietly.

Árpád pulled a much worn and carefully folded list from his pocket and unfolded it to read all the instructions he had for her. Slowly, item by item, he went down the list, meticulously reviewing each detail and accenting here and there, where special attention was required. It was a good plan and he was certain that by the time Kutas's henchmen would start looking for him he would be free and happy across the border.

"Don't forget to destroy the list. Memorize the details today, then burn it."

He now embraced Ildikó warmly and kissed her on both cheeks. They held each other tight for a long time.

"I will send notice as soon as I can. Kiss Mom and Dad for me, and tell them how much I love them. But not until you receive word from me. Goodbye, sister. I love you. I will miss you very, very much. God bless you forever."

Ildikó hugged him one more time. "Goodbye, Árpikám. Be very careful. And send word immediately."

Árpád's thin and haggard frame disappeared in the doorway as he gently closed the door behind him. Ildikó was once again left alone with her thoughts and fears. Surprising even herself, she did not cry. Deep within the recesses of her heart she knew that Árpád would be safe. He had to be safe. "God will protect him," she assured herself, and then thought of Kutas's visit. Just then she realized what he'd said about the American. She had lost two people out of her life today. Though she hardly knew Buday, she felt a great sense of loss over his disappearance. She felt cheated, cheated out of a bit of sunshine, a ray of hope Steve had brought into her lonely and unappreciated existence.

"Thrown from the bridge?" she shuddered. "Dear God. How awful! Please save him, wherever he is."

With that she unfolded Árpád's list and studied it carefully.

Chapter 18:
A Falling Angel

Once he was over the railing, second thoughts about the soundness of his judgment were of no consequence. Steve was committed. In the dark shadows under the bridge he had no way of judging the distance to the water, and to protect himself from being torn apart by the impact he pulled in his arms and legs into a tucked position. As he did, he began to tumble. Holding one last deep breath, he waited for the impact. The wind whistled by his ear increasingly loudly.

SPLASH!!!

Steve hit the water with such momentous force that he blacked out immediately, feeling no pain at all at the instant of impact. His momentum carried him at least thirty feet below the surface before he stopped sinking. The water was icy cold near the bottom and he was brought back to consciousness by excruciating pain all over his entire body. He wanted to scream out in agony as he flailed his arms to find his sense of direction in the total darkness and push himself to the surface, which he instinctively knew was infinitely far away. The weight of the water above almost popped his eardrums and his lungs were about to burst under the pressure of his breath withheld, it seemed, forever.

He was on the verge of drowning when at the last fraction of a second before drawing water into his lungs his head broke the surface.

Like a steam locomotive, he exhaled and inhaled, sputtering, choking, sucking. The air whistled in and out of his oxygen-starved lungs with lifesaving force. Gathering his last ounce of remaining strength, he flung his jacket into the air and wrapped it about his neck, trapping an air bubble to support his head above water. Survival training in the Navy had finally paid off. Before blacking out again, his eyes glimpsed the pearly outline of the bridge's illuminated arches fading away in the distance as he was carried downstream.

He was awakened from his stupor hours later by excited shouts and chatter and a sharp stab of pain in his back caused by a great metal chain tugging him toward a large flat barge of some kind. A half dozen or so men gathered, leaning and stretching over the side, towing and lifting his rigid body out of the murky water. His eyelids fluttered briefly, but a blast of blinding sunlight brought tears into his eyes to mix with the dirty water that streamed down his face and he saw nothing except sparkly blotches of light and faded shadows bending over him with curiosity and concern.

Someone brought a heavy blanket and wrapped him tight. Another lifted his head to force some fiery liquid through his clenched teeth, causing him to cough and spit and reexperience all the pain in his body he'd felt when he first surfaced. He fell back completely exhausted and too weak to even keep his eyes open. A protective shade was placed over his head and the rays of the sun began slowly to raise his already dangerously low body temperature.

To the crew on deck Steve was indeed a sorry sight to behold. All visible parts of his body, his face and neck especially, were puffed up and covered with great spots of every color of the rainbow. Blood was seeping through the surface of his skin over large areas and collected into large watery purple drops. Evidently, when he'd hit the water, he hit it spinning, face and neck first, damaging the capillaries under the skin, and the tremendous force of the impact caused the blood to ooze through as if by osmosis. In spite of his battered appearance, however, all the damage was fortunately superficial, and his total exhaustion came more as a result of hypothermia than internal injuries.

The barge's crew held a hurried conference to assess the situation. Various theories were rapidly advanced, most of them popularly rejected as being too outlandish. The theory proposed by the barge's captain, Frankie, gained the widest acceptance, according to which Steve was victimized by a barroom brawl following a local soccer championship game in which, of course, the home team lost, and he had the misfortune of being a visitor, or even worse, the referee. And to destroy the evidence of their heinous crime of beating up the referee, the local fans proceeded under the cover of night to the river and dumped him in. Anyone could see that this was logical.

Stories of such events abounded along the river and were swapped in earnest among the crews of riverboats cruising between Austria and the Black Sea. Having been avid soccer fans and partakers of post-match skirmishes themselves, no one aboard doubted the feasibility of such an occurrence. Besides, it was usually inadvisable to disagree with the captain. One look at his size explained why.

They all sighed with relief, glancing at Steve sleeping peacefully, and passed the bottle of white lightning around for the second time. The clear, vodka-like liquid was a distillate of ripe apricots, often reaching a hundred and forty proof. The stuff, called pálinka, had very little taste, if any, and only its pleasant aroma lingering in the nose hinted at the fruit from which it was distilled. Popular among all groups, at times it was claimed to be the national drink of Hungary.

Frankie, alias Frank Orbán, was the captain of the barge, as his huge size would have immediately suggested. An immensely muscular man with balding head, he was in his early fifties, and commanded his men with the unflinching self-assurance of a leader who never asked for a subordinate's opinion unless he beat it out of him. Under his command were the chef, Teri, who was also his common-law wife; a quiet and shifty-eyed prison guard called Zeb, who filled the post of steersman and pilot; a young man in his late teens who'd escaped from juvenile hall – his second home when not drifting on the river - who was the general deckhand in charge of washing the deck and running errands to shore, especially if the errand required the agility of a thief. There was also a gruff middle-aged man called Dino, who spoke very little, mainly because he did not speak a word of Hungarian. He was the resident stowaway, wanted by the Yugoslavian police for beating his wife. Were it not for an unfortunate twist of fate that she'd later died of a deep gash in her skull, inflicted by a woodchopper's axe, he would now be a free man.

All in all, they were an average crew for these parts, except perhaps for Frankie, a captain's captain, a larger-than-life figure who was a legend in his own lifetime.

In spite of his brutish appearance and reputation as a ferocious fighter, Frankie Orbán was a peace-loving, gentle, and sensitive man. Too bad that but for his drinking, he could have become anything in life he wanted. Maybe even a stoker on a great steamship, a prestigious position he once applied for but was rejected on the grounds that he tried to feed the first mate into the boiler instead of coal.

As legends went, Frankie frequented the village taverns adjacent to local soccer fields with religious regularity. To him the routine was as solemn as going to mass. After one beer, he was the friendliest of patrons, given to elaborate recounts of past barroom escapades. After three beers, he became belligerent and dared anyone to dispute the validity of his stories. After six beers, he was alone. Except perhaps for a few bodies strewn about the tavern. He would weep bitterly into his twelfth beer about his inability to form lasting friendships.

The barge floated quietly down the sunlit river pushed by the powerful square-bowed tug behind, a method more energy-efficient than pulling the tows through the propeller wash. All hands on deck busied themselves with daily chores of general cleanup and maintenance, navigating between the buoys and sandbars in the shallower bends, and keeping the powerful diesels running smoothly. The big engines churned away quietly and efficiently. Tony, the young deckhand, was in the process of washing and scrubbing down the deck with buckets of water lifted from the river, something he loathed to do, but Frankie was a frugal man; he had no intentions of buying a pump for him.

Steve moaned loudly and Teri the chef gently stroked his bruised forehead, washing the bloodstained spots with linen soaked in pálinka. It burned like fire and her patient came to in a hurry. He looked up into the round, leathery face of the ex-farmgirl tractor driver, whose features hinted at better and prettier days many years ago. Teri wiped the bloody spots with expertise, demonstrating a gentle concern reminiscent of middle-aged spinsters who always desired to have children but never dared or had the opportunity to.

A few years after the communist takeover Teri joined a collective farm as a proud tractor driver, one of thousands of young farmgirls lured to the task by colorful posters and resounding slogans. In her pretty polka-dot dress and a red kerchief covering the mischievous locks of her chestnut-brown hair tied in pigtails, she soon became poster girl for the collective's tractor brigade. Her brigade was called Red Star, and it became the number-one brigade in the socialist truckers' competition.

Interestingly, a brand of manure sold in the United States under the same brand name also became the number-one seller. Years passed and Teri worked as hard as six men. Eventually she was being treated as six men. One day she became disgusted with the whole affair and joined the river crew on Frankie's boat. Life on the river was hardly easier, however, and at times she fondly remembered the romance of her early days on the collective. In her vocabulary, the word collective usually meant that the male members of her brigade would collectively carry her behind the haystack only to leave her there exhausted but satisfied. Those were the days. The glorious days of a new society where socialism was built and strengthened by dedicated people like Teri.

Frankie turned the command over to Zeb, the pilot, and snuck upon the two of them, casting suspicious glances at Teri bending over Steve with motherly concern.

"Well, mate. How do you feel?" he growled.

"I feel like I just fell off a bridge," said Steve, forcing himself to smile but only succeeding at wrinkling his multicolored and swollen face into something resembling hickory-smoked Easter ham. Frankie averted his gaze with disgust.

"Leave him alone!" snapped Teri, pushing aside Frankie with protective maternal fury.

"I just want to talk to the man. I want to know who he is? All right?" Frankie shoved back, sending Teri reeling against the bulkhead.

"Later. I said leave him alone! Can't you see he is barely alive? Stupid!"

"I give up! You win. See you later, fella!" Frankie said, turning away, leaving Teri to satisfy her frustrated maternal instincts and trying to recall whether any of his own victims ever appeared as awful as his new passenger. Regrettably, they did not.

Chapter 19:
Unpleasant but Necessary

Kutas's world had suddenly turned topsy-turvy. Up until a couple of days ago, he had nothing to do except plan out his retirement in painstaking detail. In the absence of career-advancement opportunities, there was nothing to do but daydream about a cottage on the lake Balaton, fishing in the bright sunshine, sampling the wines of the region, and maybe even writing his memoirs. Yes, a man with his vast experience and fascinating background should certainly write his memoirs. Wasn't everyone writing memoirs nowadays? The next generation could learn so much from those experienced older fellows.

Then lightning struck.

All at once he had nothing but problems on his hands. Major ones. Take for instance the case of this American. He showed up one day, probably sent by the CIA on a secret mission. What else could it be? No ex-navy commander was going to waste his time searching for scraps of rotten bones buried under layers of dirt. No way! Then the next day he was gone. Vanished. Attacked by strangers and - can you stand it? - dumped into the drink. What strangers? Why? How in the hell did they know about him? Was there something big happening here? Questions, questions, but no answers.

He shook his head in desperation.

Captain Kutas reflected on the peace and quiet of the past few days. Maybe he should turn in his resignation before he got fired. He could blame it on failing health, or something. He had to find a good excuse.

As if it were not enough, Colonel Fehér read him a secret dispatch from the Hungarian Ambassador in West Germany, advising them of the presence of a cache of radioactive uranium lost somewhere in the Tisza by the Germans during the war - had they never set foot on this soil, the damn krauts - which was now being sought after by a bunch of desperados, international terrorists.

When it rains, it pours. Feast or famine.

As much as he wanted to upstage his boss, Fehér, and wanted it so badly he could taste it, Captain Kutas found his situation overwhelming. He was scared. This seemed to be a case for the big timers. And at this moment he did not consider himself to be a member of that distinguished and exclusive club. He really wanted out, except Fehér would not hear of it. That sly son of a baker was waiting for bumbling idiot Kutas to hang himself this time.

Well, he was not going to hang himself. But if he had to go down, he would go down fighting. And he would take that bloodthirsty Fehér down with him!

These impossible tasks at hand called for some clear and logical thinking. In-depth planning and organization required for a full search for the missing American - he wanted to see his dead body to be convinced that he was out of the picture for good - and for those pests, the terrorists, may they rot in hell. Sadly, he had very little information to go on. Almost nothing, in fact. All he had was the confused testimony of an excited and scared cabbie who'd seen the tussle on the bridge. He said he saw someone fly over the railing and into the water, and it must have been the American because he never showed up at the other end of the bridge. He saw the brawl while driving across the bridge in the opposite direction and by the time he was able to turn around and at top speed rush back to the scene, everybody was gone. Nothing but motorized traffic, no pedestrians anywhere. No sign of the victim or the assailants. Vanished, all of them vanished.

The only other lead he had was that amateurish, naïve Miss Vértes. His bloodhound instincts told him that a mutual attraction between these young and handsome people was not out of the question, and that Buday might, just might, look her up again, if he was still alive. Got to keep an eye on her. The thought of Miss Vértes suddenly reminded him of her brother and he cursed. He wanted to see that wisecracking, insolent kid punished, jailed if he could help it. But it had to wait until tomorrow. He had more important things to do today.

On top of his list was organizing a search for Buday. On land as well as water. Kutas called in his lieutenant and gave him instructions to search all river-going vessels on the Danube, and call on all police precincts and mortuaries in towns and villages along the river. From border to border. Buday's photo was to be dispatched to all local agencies. He wanted to see him dead or alive. And he had to hurry. A body in the relatively warm waters could decompose beyond recognition in only a few days.

As for Buday's assailants, well, all he could do was hope that some stroke of luck would reveal their identity and purpose.

For now, the bigger problem seemed to be the tracking of the terrorists and the forming of a task team for the search of the uranium. Fortunately, the Germans were able to provide a fair description of the events and sent an approximate map of the general area where the fateful battle supposedly took place. At least on one account he had a starting point.

"Lieutenant!" Kutas snapped. "I want a complete review of the entire list of recent arrivals into Hungary from Germany, Austria, and the US. Report to me any characters with the slightest suspicion. Contact the German police for further clues as to the identities of these crooks. Search for nationalities other than German as well. Where else would you think these sonsabitches could have come from? Bulgaria?" he mused, directing the question to himself rather than to his subordinate.

"Well, sir, I don't know, sir. Reading the papers, you know, I would not discount anyone from the Middle East. Libya, Syria, Palestine are strong contenders. Maybe Bulgaria and Turkey. Yeah, them too. Hell, they could have come from anywhere!"

"All right, do as I tell you!"

Kutas thought for a moment and decided that he would personally pay a visit to the Hilton and search Buday's room for clues. Maybe he would find something among his belongings or from the hotel personnel that would help solve the puzzle of his mysterious assailants.

While Kutas fumbled around in the darkness of uncertainty, Colonel Fehér did a little planning of his own. He called on the River Patrol to start cruising the Danube in search of fugitives and scan the Tisza's riverbed with metal detectors for large metallic objects, keeping an eye out for unusual activities in the area indicated by the German maps. He called for aerial reconnaissance as well.

"Never trust to some bumbling idiot anything you can do yourself" was his motto. His sharply rising career in the MSP was living proof that it was a good rule of thumb to live by. On an afterthought, he ordered his second in command to fly down to the site with the German tanks showing on the bank of the Tisza and post a radiation warning sign nearby to keep the curious idiots from trying to steal something.

Chapter 20:
A Gift from Attila

"Sándor, it is so good to be out here again. How are you? You know, I'll never go back to the city again. Not if I can help it. Every time I go back to Budapest all I get into is trouble. This is where I like it. This is my home. Never any trouble, just honest and hard work, peace and quiet." Ildikó gave Sándor a quick hug and her eyes surveyed the site. Her face reflected the strain of the last few days, but also showed gladness and renewed energy now that she had returned to her favorite place.

Sándor removed his hat and his suntanned face beamed with earnest gladness. "It is good to have you back again, Miss Ildikó. We all sure missed you. Somehow this place is never the same when you are gone."

Ildikó looked around, shading her eyes from the sun with the palm of her hand. She grabbed him by the arm and tugged at him. "Come on, Sándor, tell me how the excavation has progressed. Come, show me and tell me in the meanwhile what has happened since I left."

The pair walked about the partially opened and cordoned-off areas, carefully stepping around the grey-and-brown skeletons, some of which were already fully exposed, showing the unnatural manner in which their owners had met their demise. Sándor animatedly pointed out the progress the diggers had made. The workers stopped as she passed by and raised their black narrow-brimmed hats in greeting, which she smilingly returned, calling out to each of them by name. The monotonous clanking of the tools stopped briefly as she walked by the workers leaning on their picks and shovels. The usually somber expressions softened on the sweaty and leathery faces. Undoubtedly, Ildikó was their favorite archeologist team leader, and they missed her delightful chatter and concerned inquiry about family, children, the womenfolk at home, all the little matters these private and quiet peasant folks were too shy to talk about but glad to be asked about anyway. Amidst the dull beige of sand and dust, she was a cheerfully colored wildflower, her radiant red blouse shining like a giant red poppy, a pleasant stimulant for their tired eyes to behold.

The assistant archeologist, a young man with thick glasses and impeccable credentials, stood up to greet Ildikó, brush and scraping knife in hand. He'd been working on his knees all morning, clearing off the fine layers of dust from a number of skeletons intertwined in a seemingly haphazardly formed heap of bones, making it extremely difficult and time-consuming to separate and identify them as to which skeleton they belonged. Higher up from them, on top of the mound, a photographer and a number of assistants were preparing to lift the cameraman into position above the mass grave with a platform supported by a crane. Shots taken from at least thirty feet above the grave yielded especially realistic photos which then could be enlarged and scaled in the laboratory for accurate recording and measurement of relative positions and sizes of skeletons and artifacts.

An assortment of iron helmets and weapons, mostly bows and arrows, were mixed in among the bodies, suggesting that a terrible massacre had taken place here for some unknown reason. Ildikó was elated. The yield of the site was superb, better than any other Hunnic site she'd ever worked on. The progress of the work was excellent and the scheduled completion of the major portion of the grave seemed to be assured before the onset of the rainy season.

"Halló there. Nice to see you again, Miss Vértes."

The assistant wiped his hand on his dusty trousers and extended it out for a handshake.

"Hi...good to be back, John. I see you've been busy." She smiled happily. "Keep it up and we will have this pile of old bones mapped and transported to the museum by the end of the month. I cannot tell you how glad I am the work is progressing so well."

"Hey, when you have a good crew and an excellent foreman, how can you miss?" John replied, patting Sándor on the back.

"I know. They are good! I wish I could take them everywhere I dig," Ildikó laughed, and Sándor smiled sheepishly but acknowledging their heartfelt compliments gladly.

"It's a hard-working bunch out there. All I have to do is keep them from shoveling the bones out with the sand." He laughed and gestured to the workers nearby, who upon hearing his remark were ready as ever with a retort.

"Better be careful, Sándor, or we'll mix your bones with the pile. See if John can sort them out again." They howled loudly.

Ildikó continued her inspection tour with John while Sándor attempted to restore order. After roughly an hour she returned to her tent to review the daily logs and inspect the artifacts that were readied for shipment, having been removed from their original places after recording and photography. There were a half dozen boxes waiting for careful packaging and transportation. When completed, the museum would have years of work to clean and catalogue the hundreds of items unearthed here.

Her frizzled nerves were slowly returning to normal from the therapeutic effect of the atmosphere within the camp. She was more relaxed now. Just before her departure from Budapest, she'd received a brief but very happy phone message from Vienna: "I am OK, sis. Will write soon and tell you more." Evidently, her brother had made it across the border with the tour and was able to call, apparently already separated from the group. He was obviously still careful not to alert the operator by a lengthy and ecstatic telephone conversation, knowing that too soon his sister and parents would be subjected to police searches and lengthy questioning. The message was the happiest she had ever received and now she relaxed, her mind finally at peace. She planned to wait for a few days before breaking the news to her parents, as she did not feel quite strong enough for another emotional scene.

She decided to forget the past weekend and busy herself with the work piled up in her absence. With as many as fifty-plus items removed from the grave each day, she had the seemingly never-ending task of identifying each bone, each fragment of a bow or arrow, each piece of jewelry, knives, helmets, all sorts of ancient and delicate and wonderful things. Every item had to be carefully identified by a number relative to the exact location from which it was removed. The number assigned was a grid number, identifying the location and referencing an artist's sketch or a photograph – most likely the latter. The referencing system enabled the reconstruction team at the museum to assemble scenes in their entirety, to the most exacting detail. Only then could the historians and archeologists interpret and analyze the data for the benefit of historical record or future research.

The work was tedious, menial, and sometimes very tiring, if not outright boring. But it had to be done and she welcomed the chance and the old routine to take her mind off her brother, that pig Kutas, and maybe even that wonderful American. Deep inside she hung on to a tiny glimmer of hope that he would reappear someday.

Among the items on top of the sorting table her eyes caught a particularly finely decorated bow, with handsome handiwork on the multilayered wood construction inlaid with intricate designs of ivory showing battle scenes, archers, horsemen, and warriors giving chase. The intricacy of the inlays was really impressive, reminding her of gold and ivory work she had seen from Scythian and Greek artisans. The outlines of the characters were graceful and reflected the level of refinement of sculptural details one would only expect from the best Greek artisans. This particular bow had an inscription on the inside surface of the thick section where the archer's left hand would hold it, a usual place for inscriptions. Evidently, it was written in cuneiform. She was very familiar with this form of writing, since it was used by the Hungarians as late as the ninth century, at the time of their occupation of present-day Hungary.

Interestingly, once the Hungarian cuneiform was deciphered from an identical text in Latin - sort of a Hungarian Rosetta Stone - it was later used to aid in the deciphering of the Sumerian cuneiform which was found on thousands of clay tablets buried in the ancient cities of Ur and Kish and others. This gave rise to speculation among some in the scientific circles that perhaps the Hungarians were descendants of or related to the earth's earliest known civilization.

Just for the challenge of it, Ildikó decided to read the inscription, reading as she wrote the equivalent sounds down with the letters of the Hungarian alphabet. There were usually a variety of sounds that could match some of the Hunnic symbols, so it took a while to guess at the proper ones. This became a relaxing game of a crossword puzzle, something she really enjoyed toying with. The letters appeared on her notepad one at a time.

RUGILA, the letters spelled. The name was similar to some she had seen previously. Like Tuldila or Attila, both of which were given to well-known leaders of the Huns. The name Tuldila belonged to one of the lesser-known tribal chiefs under the king. She reflected on the possibility that the name Rugila perhaps belonged to another tribal chief not yet discovered. The fact that he would be found in a mass grave with a bunch of others, buried without special distinction, bothered her. At the moment the name meant nothing, though it had a familiar ring. She shrugged and continued with the examination of the other artifacts.

Her favorite Hunnic jewelry was worn by women. Large gold pendants suspended on long heavy gold chains at about breast level. These pendants were wrought of pure gold; their color was deep yellow when polished, indicating that the metal was not alloyed. Their size varied from about two by five centimeters to about six by ten centimeters in area, anywhere from one to three millimeters thick. The largest among them weighed as much as five ounces, a pretty heavy clump of metal to be worn about the neck. It was tempting to speculate their value on the open market; surely any one of them would have brought a handsome price, not even considering their intrinsic historical value. She had never been tempted to pursue this line of thought any further, but some of the workers had, and she'd recently increased the security around the compound and had a metal detector installed at the gate to screen personnel leaving the area. During breaks, or whenever weather temporarily halted the work, she gave impromptu lectures to the diggers about the historical significance of the excavation and stressed the immense value of all that was unearthed, irrespective of whether it was a mere fragment of a bone or a large gold coin. She felt that most of the workers, especially the older ones, were trustworthy honest men, too proud to steal. But it made good sense to take some precautions with the younger ones. Not all of them were above taking possession of something they felt had a fighting chance of being sold for a few forints on the black market. Gold objects were the popular favorites, as shown by police records on recovered stolen property, but that was logical, since gold always had a steady demand and could be sold untraceably when melted down.

The tent was becoming too dark to continue working and she finally bothered to check the time. Ten past five. To her surprise she did not hear the usual clamor of the workers preparing to leave and stand in line at the gate and wait for the bell. Listening, she became aware of faint sounds of excited shouts in the distance and looked out of the tent to see what was happening. Most of the workers were crowded around the dig, staring intently down at something in the pit. Ildikó grabbed her jacket and walked hurriedly to join them, curious herself to see what the excitement was all about.

"Ildikó, hurry up!" someone shouted. "Come and see...God, it is beautiful!"

"Look at the size of that thing!"

All of them gathered around with mouths agape, obviously impressed by something unusual, something even these veteran diggers had not seen before. Ildikó finally reached the top of the mound, panting heavily, and the bystanders opened a path for her to get below. As she reached the bottom of the excavated area she noticed John directing the photographer to stand closer to a shiny object and take additional closeup shots.

John looked up. "Come here, Ildikó. Do you see this beauty?" She inched closer and suddenly saw before her eyes the largest and most beautiful gold pendant she had ever seen. It was still lying on top of a warrior's skeleton, hanging on a heavy gold chain wrapped about his neck. Between the strands of the chain under his chin, the stem of a broken arrow protruded out of his chest. Another arrow penetrated straight through the heart. His death must have been quick. In spite of the dirt and dust covering the jewelry, the orange-yellow of the gold shone through, glittering in the setting rays of the sun. Ildikó leaned forward to inspect the object closer and tried to brush away the last fine layer of dust when without warning she was overcome by the shock of unexpected discovery.

"Good Lord! I don't believe this," she muttered faintly. "This is mine! I gave it to him. The Enchanted Stag! My poor, dear old friend, Rugila."

John had to grab her to keep her from falling. Her muscles went limp and she nearly fainted. John called for a blanket and someone dashed off to get it. She was surrounded by concerned and curious onlookers. All the blood ran out of her cheeks and she appeared ghostly white. Cold beads of perspiration formed on her forehead.

"I am sorry, John..." she whispered. "I am OK. Don't worry. In the excitement to come back here I forgot to eat all day. Just give me your hand." She breathed deeply and stood up, still wobbling on her weak knees. She returned to get another view at the wonderful discovery.

The crowd was too excited to notice a pair of big teardrops roll down her alabaster face.

The small, twenty-five-watt light bulb just did not do it no matter how hard the diesel generator worked to keep it burning. Ildikó lifted the kerosene lamp out and lit it. She waited patiently until the thick black smoke disappeared and adjusted the flame until it shined brilliantly. Between the two lamps, products of two different generations, both necessary to provide adequate light, she could finally see all she needed.

Her shadow, as she paced the floor of her room-sized tent, jumped about on the walls in a frantic hurry, trying to keep up with her. Outside, the camp nestled among the mounds and the valleys of the excavation in peace and quiet. The full moon cast a silvery hue on the motionless sandy waves and the half dozen or so tents standing within the fenced-off area. The tents' occupants were sound asleep, except for Ildikó and Sándor, both of whom for reasons of their own nursed their worries into the late hours of the night. The purring of the small diesel generator could be heard faintly in the distance, working steadily and faithfully to provide the only light and warmth to be found for miles around in this godforsaken, lonely land.

Ildikó stopped to check the items displayed on top of her desk: the golden stag, the chain, the bow, all once the property of Rugila the faithful warrior. She lovingly ran her fingers over the smooth cold surface of the golden stag, feeling the gentle hills and valleys of the perfectly molded shape, over the graceful body and limbs, the neck and the head and the gorgeous antlers crowning this handsome and proud creature. Its touch seemed so strangely familiar, her fingertips vaguely recalling a feeling they'd experienced before. She noticed a slight imperfection, a slight scratch on the back of the animal apparently caused by the deadly arrow that pierced poor Rugila's heart.

She glanced over to the corner of her desk where she'd placed Rugila's skull. Small and round with high cheekbones, it reminded her of the many Hunnic and Mongoloid skulls she had often seen before. Except for a missing plate in the back, the bones of the skull were perfectly preserved by the dry sands of the region. The shiny bone surfaces gently reflected the friendly amber light suffusing the tent. The flame of the kerosene lamp that was suspended from the ceiling seemed to line up with the hole in the skull and the flickering light shone through the eye sockets, giving her the strange feeling that it was alive and wished to speak to her.

She stopped her pacing and sat down on her cot and faced the skull. She felt an intense desire to get to the bottom of all this weird, unexplainable, and bothersome phenomena. The nightmares and occasional flashbacks scared and confused her greatly, but she now felt more strongly than ever that she stood at the threshold of some infinitely immense and important discovery. She fixed her eyes at the light emanating from Rugila's skull and waited for an explanation. "Tell me, good friend and faithful servant. I know you want to tell me something I want to know!"

She waited. There was no answer. She felt frustrated.

Turning her head, she noticed the light from Rugila's eyes falling on a book lying on a shelf. She impulsively picked it up to get her attention away from all this nonsense. The book was titled *Old Hungarian Legends* and had been published only recently by Dénes Lengyel. She'd bought it soon after publication on a friend's recommendation that it was the best available compilation of legends dating back to pre-Hunnic times. She'd never had time to even look beyond its cover, which was decorated by the picture of a beautiful golden stag. Paging through the book in a sort of absent-minded way, and looking for nothing in particular, she was startled by a plate on the eleventh page. It was a photo of the Golden Stag. The Enchanted Stag of the Scythians, unearthed at Zöldhalompuszta. It was unmistakably the twin of the one in her possession, with a forward-leaning posture, the right foreleg bent under the belly to indicate jumping, the head turned backward, eyes wide open. The animal was obviously fleeing, in flight from a terrible and unseen pursuer.

She read on excitedly, her heart beating in her throat.

It happened once that Hunor and Magyar wandered far while hunting and were lost among the marshes of Meotis. All of a sudden, a great stag popped out of the bushes and the brothers pursued it immediately. The stag ran with great speed and suddenly disappeared without a trace. They looked for him at length, but without success.

As they kept looking for the stag, searching throughout the entire marshland, they found the area very suitable for grazing.

Returning to their father, they asked his permission, and obtaining it, they moved with all their cattle into the marshlands.

The province of Meotis bordered Persia. It was surrounded by sea on all sides, except for a narrow strip of shallows. There were no rivers there, but the land was rich in grasslands, trees, birds, fishes and all kinds of wild animals. It was difficult to access or exit the area.

The people of Hunor and Magyar entered the marshlands of Meotis and stayed there for five years. On the sixth year they ventured out and wandered towards the plains where they ran into the wives of the sons of King Bélár, who were in their tents in the absence of their husbands. When Hunor and Magyar found them, the women were celebrating the feast of the trumpet, and were dancing to the tunes.

Hunor and Magyar captured them with all their cattle and took them back into the marshlands of Meotis. They also captured the two daughters of the prince of Alan, whom they married. Hunor married one, Magyar the other. All the

people of the Huns and the Magyars are descendants of these
women.

She sat in silence for a while, trying to comprehend the meaning behind this simple ancient legend. She searched her mind desperately for some clue, any clue, that would give her the key to the riddle, as it were. She remembered waking up from her recurring nightmare, soaking wet and shivering and terrified to death, but she could never recall the substance of her dream. Sometimes she would recall small fragments, minute flashes. Like today, when she thought she recognized the old warrior and the golden pendant. But she intuitively felt that there was more to this whole thing than just that, something infinitely more significant. But what was it? The key must lie here somewhere. For instance, why was she so fascinated by the figure, the shape of the stag? Ever since she could remember she'd been enchanted by it. She saved pictures of stags, would beg her parents to take her to the zoo, where she would stand for hours studying the magnificent animals, until her parents dragged her away, shaking their heads in bewilderment. There must be something significant about the golden stag, and it was right here, in her very hands; she was holding the key to her dreams right now!

She stood and picked up the pendant again and held it tightly, pressing her hand against her breast.

Suddenly, as if on command, the whole picture became clear. The very thing her mind could not recall, her fingers did. She saw herself standing before a wonderful, handsome, commanding figure of a man, a king, who had just given her a gift, a small but wonderful gift, and she was standing before him, shy and trembling, holding in her hand the gift, a golden pendant in the form of a beautiful stag...and she was clutching it dearly, squeezing it against her chest, just like this, just like now!

"Dear Jesus! I've got it! I've found him! This is his grave!" She flung the door open and ran out into the night, lantern in hand and calling for Sándor. She was hysterical. "Sándor, for God's sake! Come here! Hurry. Please hurry. I've found it. I've found him." She cried loudly and ran toward the mound, swaying the lantern in her hand, stumbling over rocks, falling and getting up again and running wildly toward the burial mound where her beloved king and lover Attila lay, waiting.

Bewildered by the sudden cries, Sándor darted out of his tent only to see Ildikó running in the moonlight toward the excavation. He took off running after her.

Chapter 21:
Down, Then Up the Creek

Lonely and deserted. Nothing but water and shallow sandy shores as far as the eye could see. And hot. Sizzling hot.

Steve stroked his hair, only to find that his head was covered by a giant handkerchief tied at the corners and serving as a makeshift hat against the stinging rays of the midday sun. Teri's doing, without a doubt. In his heart, he silently thanked his newly acquired guardian angel.

The great barge, loaded with mounds of shining black coal, drifted almost imperceptibly. As it neared the shore at one point Steve could make out the lonely figure of a young girl dressed in white, twitching a stripped branch in her hand, unhurriedly driving a flock of geese along the muddy bank. Now and then the gander halted and squawked loudly, as if in protest, flapping his giant wings until prompted by the stick into motion again. The geese followed, squawking and gossiping, accepting his lead with willing submission. Male chauvinist pig, or gander, rang a familiar slogan in Steve's ears, and he smiled. The honking of the big white birds carried far above the surface of the water and sounded like a friendly message of welcome from the countryside.

Soon a young woman came into view. She stood up, trying awkwardly to straighten her back strained by hours of bending over her wash in the river. Her skirt, folded up and fastened at her waist, showed shapely white legs and thighs. She waved a friendly greeting with a white cloth. Steve waved back. His eyes scanned the horizon. Nothing else but the vista of the great river, easily a mile wide at this point. The view of the women on shore faded over his shoulder, then out of sight. Not a sound on the water or in the distance, except perhaps the faint ringing of a faraway church bell. A heavenly admonition adopted for mundane and early routines. A reminder that it was noon. The images of the women on the beach, wet colorful fabrics, the white spots of the geese against the grey mud of the bank burned into his memory. Images that came from nowhere and returned in silence into the recesses of his mind for future recollection. Nothing significant, just beautiful.

On the wings of a gentle breeze the enticing aroma of food cooking somewhere nearby floated in his direction and tickled his nose. His stomach growled in response and he tried to stand up to investigate. His muscles ached sharply and he faltered.

"Hold it! Careful, old buddy. Careful. Wouldn't want to take another swim, would you?" A pair of strong hands grabbed him from behind and steadied him before letting him go. Steve wobbled dangerously close to the side of the barge and could have fallen in again. As he turned, the friendly face of a giant, a head-to-toe soiled version of Mr. Clean without the earrings, appeared within his view.

"Hi, I must be hungry." Steve said, pointing to his noisy stomach.

"That's good. That means you'll make it. It seemed touch and go for a while, judging from your color." The deep voice reverberated like thunder into the all-pervasive silence.

"Teri! Get lunch ready. We're hungry, for God's sake!" the giant yelled in the direction of the barge's cabin, situated in the rear, partly hidden by the mountain of coal. Out of the stovepipe protruding from the roof a friendly column of smoke rose skyward, suggesting that something was cooking. Someone rang a bell, evidently the call for a meal, because the previously unseen inhabitants of the barge appeared one at a time and headed straightaway for the cabin.

The tiny room, which served as dining room, game room, and conference room, depending on the specific need of the moment, became crowded with the five of them. Zeb, the steersman, remained at his post. He stood steadfastly on the bridge, one hand into the food, another on the wheel, his eyes on the water.

Teri seemed to be in her element, buzzing back and forth with great zeal like a mother hen. Especially around Steve, casting unbashful and admiring glances at the newcomer. The table was set as usual for the regulars. Aluminum mess kits consisting of a flat pan, a cup, and a fork. No knives, since river folk preferred to use their own. Much sharper and handier than dull kitchen utensils to be sure. No tablecloth, no napkins - what was a shirtsleeve good for anyway? That was all.

Except for Steve. Teri must have sensed that behind the black-and-blue exterior, the wrinkled and river-soiled clothing, was a man much more refined than appeared on the surface. She dug into her prized collection, her dowry, and came up with a porcelain plate, real crystal glass, stainless fork and knife, all set upon a clean, hand-embroidered flowery placemat. First class!

Not exactly a democratic arrangement, Steve noted wryly, watching the others for signs of annoyance or resentment. He did not notice any. Only restrained curiosity filled the weathered, soiled, and wrinkled faces. Teri quickly wiped the greasy bench before Steve sat down. Then, before serving the others, she measured out for him a giant portion of roast goose – Tony had made a quick trip ashore - and pan-fried potatoes. She filled his glass with ruby-red wine. Her enthusiasm knew no bounds and she was about to slice the meat for him when Frankie finally got fed up.

"Leave him be, damn it!" he snarled. "He can take care of himself. Now get!"

Feelings hurt, Teri withdrew into a dim corner of the room and sat down, never taking her eyes off Steve. She crouched like a cat, ever ready to spring into action in the wink of an eye, should the exalted guest be in need of something.

Having consumed lunch in perfect silence, save for a few loud belches, they put on tap a small barrel of wine Tony had carried up from the ship's cooler belly.

"Well, dear sir. We've already said enough," the captain greeted Steve somberly. "It is your turn to speak. Briefly and to the point then, please tell us what you are up to and why you have chosen to swim the length of the Danube in evening attire." The question demanded an answer and Steve felt he owed his rescuers nothing less than an honest, adequate, and detailed explanation. The time had come to solicit help, since he needed partners to accomplish his purpose. And better help than these illustrious characters he could not ask for. Thinking for a moment, he decided to tell them the honest-to-goodness truth, word for word, as it had really happened... With that he raised his glass and cleared his throat. His lower lip was still swollen and he lisped. He had the undivided attention of his company.

"Honorable Captain, ladies and gentlemen," he started and looked around, casting a knowing glance in Teri's direction. "I shall be forever indebted to you, kind people, for saving my life and pulling me out of this cursed river just when I was to draw my last breath. Who knows how my aquatic adventure would have ended had you not stumbled across me before my corpse would have become feed for the hungry sharks of the Black Sea.

"Before I tell you my story, please kindly allow me to express my gratitude for the most delectable and plentiful meal that I ever had. I must tell you truthfully that this was the best dinner I can recall. God keep you around for a long time, lovely Miss Teri!"

Teri's color turned a shade deeper, as far as her already dark skin and the dimly lit corner allowed it to be noticed. With her apron, she wiped a telling tear from the corner of her eye. She was absolutely taken by the courteous stranger.

Steve continued. "The story of how I fell among you is very brief and simple." He stood up as if searching for heavenly inspiration to continue with a boring tale. "I have been commissioned by an American firm - you should know that I happen to be an American of Hungarian descent – to search out an insignificant package lost in these parts some years ago by another firm, German I believe. My task is that upon recovering said package I dispose of it before our competitors get their greedy little hands on it. You know how we Americans love competition. I am personally quite excited about this little adventure." Steve breathed deepl, before resuming.

"Other firms, our many determined competitors no doubt, have gotten wind of the existence of this little package. Why I suspect this may be the case is because I have actually encountered two representatives of one of these mysterious competitors. Yes, it happened late yesterday evening while I was peacefully strolling across the Chain Bridge admiring the lovely sights of your very attractive capital. These kind and helpful but curious representatives approached me with such fervor and treated me with such convincing persuasion that I had no choice but to avoid them by jumping from that delightful architectural masterpiece. Unhappily, as my face and hands attest to the unalterable fact, in the dark I had no idea of the height I was about to measure by my fall." He showed his hands and face to all, causing them to recoil in horror. "Believe me, I have since bitterly regretted the consequences of my ill-fated decision. Ordinarily, I am not one given to act with such carelessness. In this case, however, I must really blame it on the single-mindedness these gentlemen exhibited to question me at length. After that, all I can recall is you, kind people, trying to fish me out. Briefly, then, that is all that happened."

Frankie shook his head with deep disappointment. His pet theory about the soccer game and the postgame attack on the referee had just evaporated. "Not even close..." he thought. He grunted, still incredulous.

"Ah, come on! This is the stupidest story I've ever heard. That a guy would jump off the Chain Bridge just to avoid a couple of jerks who want to find out about a lousy package? Whoever heard of such horse manure? If I had been there your so-called competitors would now be floating gently downriver. And, my dear friend, just how do you propose to prove your fairytale is true? Huh?" Frankie looked around triumphantly, challenging his guest to further explanation.

Tony agreed with his boss enthusiastically and repeatedly slammed his palm on the table. He preferred to take Frankie's side in all arguments; the few times he had not were recorded in indelible black-and-blue spots on his butt. Dino stayed impartial. He did not comprehend a word that had been said. Teri, however, soaked it all up, believing every word and living through the tale as if it were her own personal experience. She gasped out loud when Steve recounted the pain of hitting the water.

Steve remembered his trump card he'd used very successfully many times in similar situations. He knew he could always rely on it to disperse any lingering doubts about the validity of his statements. With considerable effort, for his arms still hurt like hell each time he moved, he reached into his hind pocket and pulled out his wallet, from which he fished out a stack of neatly folded and completely soaked but still recognizable green bills. Ten thousand dollars in ten increments, needing a little patience and drying, but perfectly useable. He moved slowly and deliberately, unfolding and smoothing the bills individually, so that none of the intent onlookers would harbor any doubts about his intentions to be nothing less than completely honest.

"Holy smokes! Get a load of that stuff!" Tony suppressed a scream as Frankie kicked him under the table. Undaunted, Steve continued with the operation of delicately stretching each of the wrinkled thousand-dollar bills. He spoke:

"Gentlemen. To prove to you beyond a shadow of a doubt that I have frankly and confidentially recounted all I know and withheld nothing from you, I am willing to divide this token amount of money you see in my hands fairly and squarely among you, with only one small, entirely reasonable request: that you cooperate with me in my endeavor to find and dispose of the aforementioned package. My employer will be eternally grateful to you for your assistance."

At this point he halted and at a snail's pace scanned the attentive faces and squinting eyes glued to the money in his hands. Large beads of perspiration formed on Dino's forehead. He was considering the case of a small bribe to certain authorities to put off his sentencing indefinitely. Steve picked up his glass and drank, smacking his lips in enjoyment.

"In my judgment, we are traveling at this very moment in the general direction of the hidden merchandise. I shall show it to you on the map in good time. We should not be very far from the most likely spot where it is hidden. I can also state with certainty that with trifling effort we should be able to successfully retrieve it together, something I would never be able to accomplish alone. How about it, gentlemen?"

Tony groaned heavily, his breathing noticeably labored.

The sight of the greenbacks accomplished what no arguments, however eloquent, could have. The crew, sitting in this dark and dirty little room, had never in their entire lives seen this much money, not even collectively, let alone individually. Converting at black market rates, the sum of ten thousand dollars amounted to half a million forints. Easily sufficient for early retirement for each of them, starting right now.

Sensing the resistance to his arguments was rapidly evaporating, Steve moved in for the kill.

"I must beg your forgiveness that momentarily this is all I have at my disposal. I assure you, however, that upon successful conclusion of our joint enterprise, I will have at my further disposal for distribution among you a sum equal to this one."

One million forints! Staggering! The transfixed minds of the already dizzy crew began to spin at the speed of light. One million forints divided fairly - Frankie figured on taking half, the others split the rest - was enough for a comfortable retirement and then some. The friendly little tavern situated next to the soccer field flashed before Frankie's eyes with amazing clarity. He could dedicate his remaining days to the cultivation of warm and lasting friendships. He leaned over and whispered something into the ear of Dino, whose eyes grew appreciably larger with rapt attention.

Teri risked a comment. "Won't the gentleman have need for some of that money? Must he give all of it away, right now?" She worried for Steve's sake.

The others looked upon her as if she had lost her mind or at least spent too much time in the sun. "Shut your trap, woman, or I'll shut it for you. Keep out of men's business if you know what's good for you! Sir, we are in total agreement with you." Frankie turned from Teri to Steve with amazing affability. "How can we be of service to you?"

Knowing that the captain's friendship was foremost in his dealings with the crew, Steve peeled off two bills and ceremoniously placed them before Frankie, answering almost apologetically.

"Bear with me, dear Captain, for a short while until I am able to increase the amount of the down payment. As soon as I see that we have reached an understanding about our cooperation in this business venture, I shall make good on further installments. What I need in return right now – and I am making the assumption that my firm's Hungarian competitors will make every attempt to stop me, though I would rather avoid them for the time being - is as follows: a set of identification papers and some new clothes. I presume that this request will not cause you gentlemen undue hardship."

"Oh no, not at all!" enthused Tony, moving rapidly out of Frankie's reach to avoid another kick he expected was coming. It was, but missed its target and almost overturned the table.

"Pardon me, sir," Steve continued, "I shall also need transportation to the location, and your help with digging it up, and its proper disposal. It is possible that the task will require participation on the part of each and every one of you; furthermore, an armed exchange with the competition is not out of the realm of possibility. Competitors of my firm have been known to resort to violence."

"It shall be done as you wish. Your stupid competitors don't scare us a bit. If we could handle the second string of the World's Proletariat United soccer team, we can handle them! When do we start?" Frankie asked, raising his glass high for sealing the agreement. His eyes glowed with unrestrained excitement.

"Why not now?" Steve laughed. "Bottoms up!"

They all emptied their cups and Teri rushed to the table to refill them without delay. As a lark is happy slicing the crisp clear air, singing the wonders of nature and praising the glory of its Creator, so is a man fished out of cold and murky waters, bathing himself once again in the sunlight of friendship and in the warm waters of trusted companionship. Steve was happy as a lark. He spent his third day aboard the barge, already, resting and exercising, sunning and making plans for the upcoming trek. He did as he pleased. Though he did not want to cultivate his status as resident deity in Teri's eyes, he did secretly enjoy all the attention he got, even if undeserved. More than once he tried to warn her to restrain herself a little for fear of upsetting Frankie, who after all was his most valuable companion. Frankie apparently had done some simple figuring himself and weighed his tarnished reputation as the world's greatest lover against the lure of ten thousand dollars. His reputation lost. He decided to be pragmatic about his wife's temporary insanity and tried not to put a stop to it. He did not think that Steve would be desperate enough to take a liking to Teri, and he himself felt a tiny bit of fatherly sentiment toward the young American. Besides, Teri's motherly antics often amused rather than upset him.

They were a big happy family, prepared to tear apart anyone who would dare come between them and the friendly stranger, especially as their feelings of mutual attraction were more than a little tainted with the prospect of instant wealth lying within their grasp, or just a few days away in any case.

Steve's looks had improved dramatically over the past two days. The swelling decreased measurably and the natural color of his skin returned as the black-and-blue spots were gradually absorbed by his body. The rest and the excellent food helped. Tony made daily trips ashore to restock the pantry and continually amazed Steve with the variety of merchandise he returned with. They lacked nothing. Duck, geese, suckling pig was their daily fare. Steve never questioned the source of Tony's bargains, though he suspected that the fox population of the surrounding countryside might be severely accused of wrongdoing as the number of poultry steadily decreased.

On deck Steve and Frankie were immersed in quiet discussion, looking at a map spread out before them. Steve's replacement clothing, faded blue jeans, Made in Hungary under license by Levi Strauss - won't the spread of capitalism ever stop? - a dark-grey military shirt, and Yugoslavian military boots, once the property of Dino, who graciously turned them over to Steve for his share in the money. The new identification papers, forged on board by Zeb the pilot, expert in such things, showed one Anthony Budica, a migrant Yugoslavian worker temporarily hired by the Amalgamated Coal Transports, which owned and operated the barge and employed the crew. Steve pointed to a spot on the map. "Here it is, Captain. Right here, within this half-mile circle. When we get closer I'll get better bearings."

"That's about a hundred kilometers from here," Steve estimated. "Tomorrow we start. I will take Tony and Zeb with me, you and Teri stay with the boat until you drop off your cargo, then join us in a couple of days on the Tisza side, over here...Let's see...a hundred kilometers is about sixty miles...or about two days hard walking."

"I've got a better idea." Frankie furrowed his brow, thinking real hard. "It would take us a day and a half just to reach Titel with the barge. That's where the Tisza and the Danube join. A day to unload and a full two days to sail back on the Tisza again. That's a total of three and a half, maybe four days. Plus, a half day to catch up with you at the location. Too damn long. You could be in a heap of trouble long before we get there."

"You may be right. I figure on two days to cross the Puszta on foot, unless we really push it or if we get some kind of transportation," Steve said.

"Not likely." Frankie shook his head. "There is nothing in these parts except maybe wild burro. But just try and catch one. I'll send Tony to scout around for something. If he can't come up with something, nobody can. But listen, what I think we should do is to tie up here tomorrow, right at this point, keep Zeb on board to cover for us and keep an eye on the barge. And if anyone would decide to look for us he could tell them that Teri fell ill and we had to rush her to a hospital. There are no hospitals within fifty kilometers of here and they would not expect us to return in less than a couple of days. That's enough to get where we're heading and see what we could find."

"How long do you think Zeb can stall before they would get suspicious?" asked Steve.

"No more than three days. The coal is normally expected within a week of departure, but nobody is in that much of a hurry around here. If it takes three days longer than usual, so what. The building of socialism takes time, everybody knows that!"

Steve agreed. "All right, you know better than I. Do we have the equipment? Let's lay it out for final inspection."

Frankie seemed impatient. "I told Tony to start doing that. I don't know what's taking him so goddamn long. I tell you, young people take this socialism shit too seriously!"

"You did say you guys had guns, didn't you? Tell me, how in hell do you get guns in a country where possession of weapons is severely punished by law?" said Steve, shaking his head.

Frankie chuckled. "Are you kidding? Haven't you heard about 1956, our revolution? Enough weapons appeared overnight to hold off the

Hungarian secret police and the Russian army. Don't worry, we've got them. You just make sure you know where we're going and that we find something when we get there."

"Well, I tell you, Captain." Steve gazed at the sky. "There are people up there watching us even now. They can see things from there you and I can't from down here. Trust me, those guys know what they're up to."

"From up there? Are you crazy?" Frankie perked up in amazement. "Are you sure you didn't hurt yourself by falling off that bridge?" Then he shrugged in resignation. "But what do I know? You Americans know everything."

But in the next second his face lit up and he grinned broadly. "Wait a minute! It isn't just you Americans. We had a guy up there with the Russkies not too long ago. Teri read about it in the *Peoples' Freedom*. Berti...Bertalan Farkas. That was his name. A Hungarian. You heard of him?"

"Yeah, I heard of him, The Russian cosmonauts gave him a ride, didn't they?"

"They sure did. We are really proud of that son of a gun. He came from among us, simple folks. Great guy, he is," Frankie said, standing up from the map and searching for Tony to see if he deserved a stiff kick in the butt to get him moving.

"Damn! Here they come!" he snarled.

"Who is they?" asked Steve, getting up quickly himself. He did not like the tone of Frankie's voice.

"Your competition. The River Patrol. The bastards. They must be up to something, they are really in a hurry. Just look at the wake behind that boat! Better get off the deck! Move!"

Steve ducked quickly out of sight, behind the pile of coal, and flew down the stairs, heading for his hiding place below. The last thing he heard was the buzzer Frankie used to warn the crew of impending danger, and the echo of feet running on deck.

Chapter 22:
Not the Damn Police Again

The swift gunboat of the River Patrol planed on the smooth surface of the water and fell upon them in a flash. Uniformed guards with submachine guns hanging from their necks stood at the stern, feet spread apart. The man in charge, a young second lieutenant, yelled into the bullhorn.

"Stop! Stop your engines, we're coming aboard!"

Frankie shouted to Zeb to obey the order and the big diesels died down. The exhausts gurgled and belched one last time and after that only the splashing of the waves against the hulls could be heard in the sudden tense silence. The red flag on the gunboat hung limp in the breezeless air.

Bang! The patrol boat bumped against the side of the barge. Frankie cringed, thinking of the damage to the smaller boat, but he figured the stupid son of a bitch deserved it. A couple of soldiers in the dark-blue uniform of the River Patrol jumped across the narrow gap and climbed the ladder lowered by Tony. Eventually, they secured their boat against the barge. Ceremoniously and in full realization of his importance, the young officer stepped aboard and was followed by three other soldiers equipped with Russian-made submachine guns. Russki guitars, they were called in Hungary. Lightweight weapons with lousy accuracy, but useable under all weather and battle conditions. Hot or cold, soiled or not, they worked. The five soldiers in shiny boots and smartly pressed uniforms first flanked the officer, then, as if on command, spread out running in all directions and began their search over the barge, poking their guns into every nook and cranny they could find.

"Your permit, Captain!" snapped the officer as he crisply saluted, then stretched out his hand and impatiently snapped his fingers. Frankie and the rest of the crew lined up along the side and stood in stiff attention. In their blackened and sooted faces only the white of their eyes shone with the fury of anger and undisguised hatred against the cocky intruders.

"Your papers, I said."

Frankie handed them over without a word. The pokerfaced officer inspected them carefully.

"You are Captain Orbán, I take it," he said finally, looking Frankie over from head to toe, not without some apprehension about his huge size and threateningly muscular appearance.

"Yes, sir. I am the shipmaster."

"Four, including myself. This is my wife here." He pointed to Teri.

"What is your cargo and your destination?"

"Coal, as you can see for yourself. We are on our way to Titel. That's in Yugoslavia, just south of here, in case you did not know, sir."

"Just answer my questions. No wisecracks. Do you have any unauthorized persons on board? Or have you seen any strangers along your way, dead or alive? If you do not tell the truth, steps will be taken!"

"No, sir. Neither. No one on board that we know of. Haven't seen any dead bodies either, and as far as strangers go, everybody I see is a stranger to me in these parts. If I may ask, who or what are you looking for?"

The officer's face reddened with angry embarrassment. "No, you may not ask. According to my orders I must search your vessel. If you have any objections you may take them to the Ministry of Waterways. I must warn you, however, that harboring of criminals, stowaways, and illegal aliens is strictly prohibited by law and violators are punished severely. Any unauthorized person on your ship will be arrested immediately and you and your crew will he summoned to appear in court within ten days. Your ship and cargo will be impounded until the court releases them to your employer. You have the right to appeal, of course." He smiled sarcastically, taking his cap off to wipe his brow.

While this exchange was going on between Frankie and the officer, the soldiers proceeded to search the deck from bow to stern. Two of them stayed on deck to continue their inspection of the cabin, poking the pile of coal with long pointed steel rods to see if anyone was buried under it. The other three cautiously made their way down the narrow staircase to the engine compartment, the sleeping quarters, and the various storage rooms.

Nothing.

They angrily banged on the walls and the floor, listening for the echo of empty spaces. In some places it echoed, others it did not. The walls and floors showed no visible gaps to suggest that any of the echoing spaces were accessible. All welded construction, smooth large metal sheets welded to heavy beams, forming solid and impenetrable barriers.

Steve's hiding place was ingeniously built into the sidewall such that from the inside it looked flush with the rest of the wall. The bulge required to hide the fugitive ran on the outside, visible only from an external vantage point. It was a tiny compartment, housing the engine exhaust ducts. There was just enough room for an average person to stand straight up, arms beside the body, hands folded in the lap. Like a stand-up coffin. No room to move, to crouch or stretch. The residual heat from the exhaust ducts of the big engines just turned off made the dark hole incredibly stifling and hot. The sweat was pouring off him in great streams. His clothes were drenched and the salty sweat stung his eyes unbearably. He was unable to wipe himself and he toyed with the idea of laughing hysterically.

He could hear the shouts of the soldiers running up and down the metal floors of the narrow corridors, striking the walls like unemployed maniacs. One stopped just short of his hiding place and probed the thin slot in the metal wall first with his fingernails, then with his pocketknife. Next to his ear Steve heard the sickening screeching of metal against metal, causing goosepimples to run up and down his arms. The soldier breathed heavily as he strained to open the crack.

Snap! The hardened blade of the pocketknife snapped and it flew into Steve's face, just missing his eye, and slashing him slightly. He held his breath to keep from hissing in pain. The obstinate soldier cursed loudly and whacked the wall angrily with the butt of his weapon. The heavily constructed solid-steel door, held tightly with internal sliding locks, suggested a solid wall. The frustrated young man, anxious to impress his demanding superior, kicked the wall again, spat noisily, then moved on.

Suddenly, from further down the corridor, echoes of excited shouts and the heavy thuds of running boots ricocheted between the steel walls, which magnified the noise level greatly.

"They found something," Steve thought and tried to remember where they stored the weapons. Good thing Tony took his time, he mused; they could have been caught red-handed right on deck. After a deep breath and a sigh of relief, he considered passing out from heat prostration.

Teri was first to deduce what had happened. She kicked Frankie's foot and whispered, "They got Dino! Look, his face is bleeding." One of the soldiers kept shoving Dino in front of him, hitting him from behind with his rifle butt. Dino stumbled, almost falling, all without a word.

"Aha!" the lieutenant exclaimed. "So, there are no strangers on this ship? Only the four of you, and who in the hell is this one?"

Silence.

"I said, who is this man?" shouted the officer, beside himself. "Answer or I'll arrest every one of you!"

Dino cursed long and steady at the officer and spat, just missing his boot. He swore again until the soldier behind him hit him with such force that he fell to the floor. Frankie jumped to his help and knocked the soldier in the chest, sending him tumbling right over the railing into the water. The sharp clicking of the safety clips stopped him from pursuing the matter any further.

"Stop or I'll shoot!" a soldier cried.

"All right. Calm down, don't shoot. I will tell you who he is."

"You'd better start explaining then," the officer advised.

Frankie proceeded to tell a complicated and seemingly never-ending sob story about penniless dirt farmer Dino who left his farm and hungry wife and kids and asked permission to hide on the barge and work odds and ends and difficult chores that no one else would perform so he could save up some money and return to his family and move them off the farm into the city so he could send his illiterate children to school and his sick wife to the hospital, etcetera, etcetera.

The officer lost his patience. "That's enough! Save your wind for the judge. I am locking him up. As I told you, you have ten days to appear. I suggest you dock this monstrosity at the nearest facility before you get to the border and the whole bunch of you head for Mohács and report without delay!"

He was about to order his troops to transfer back to the gunboat when, unnoticed by all, another gunboat pulled up alongside them with some soldiers in khaki army uniforms standing in threatening positions and Captain Kutas at the bow.

"Ahoy there! Comrade Lieutenant! What have you there?"

"None of your damn business!" the lieutenant shouted back.

The remark ticked Kutas off to no end, as he had spent the whole day running up and down the river without finding as much as a dead fish. He was running out of time. He knew he had no authority over the River Patrol and it infuriated him to suspect that Fehér might be behind all this.

"Don't get smart with me, kid! I have my orders from the highest authorities!"

"So have I. So buzz off."

There followed a series of verbal volleys unworthy of print - except perhaps in cheap paperbacks - and shortly Kutas made an abrupt withdrawal and departed with high-speed fury.

In the proceeding commotion, with all the waves created by Kutas's boat, the lieutenant's gunboat neatly untied itself from the barge and floated away from them. The officer became hysterical and ordered his men to dive after it and bring it back, and when they refused commandeered Frankie to start the barge's engines and race after it.

"This is not a racing boat," Frankie reminded the jumpy officer, smiling a little as he said it, driving the man into a frenzy.

Twenty minutes passed before the barge finally caught up with the gunboat, and even then, the only way to catch it was to pass by it and turn ninety degrees into its path. Soon a sickening crunch indicated that they'd successfully captured the boat. With the crew transferred, Frankie and his crew waved good bye. Dino stood among the soldiers with a sad look on his face.

"One of these days I'm gonna get me a lieutenant and punch him until he turns inside out," growled Frankie, gnashing his teeth in helpless fury.

"Oh, my Lord! He'll suffocate down there!" Teri dashed off to release Steve.

Totally exhausted and weak, he fell out of his confinement into Teri's strong arms.

"Thank God you came. I was about to drown in my own sweat."

Back on the deck they searched for the gunboat. To their great surprise and delight, the gunboat disappeared into the waves and the crew was frantically swimming for shore. Zeb shoved the throttles forward and the great barge accelerated, away from the enemy.

Early next morning the little caravan started off hastily. In three days, their objective had to be accomplished. Frankie led the pack, the others following single-file; sort of like geese following the gander, Steve recalled. He found the parallel amusing and was tempted to even squawk once but changed his mind. He adjusted the heavy pack on his back and chuckled aloud. The four figures slowly made their way into the saffron haze suspended like a mysterious oriental veil before them and slowly swallowing them. The lonely figure of Zeb stayed behind, standing atop the bridge of the bulky grey barge.

Chapter 23:
A Cropduster Will Do

Hungary is not a country where unlimited opportunities for private aviation abound. The closest one can get to flying an airplane is by joining a club for soaring or signing up as a crop-duster. Soaring claims a wider membership than the latter.

Sailplanes were not what Sahir had in mind when he tried in vain to explain to the obtuse and obstinate Hungarian contact he met with in Budaörs, a suburb of Budapest hidden among the hills of Buda.

"Tell this stupid idiot" – Sahir turned to his interpreter impatiently – "that I have no time to ride the thermals above the plains in sunny southern Hungary; what I want is a plane capable of carrying a three- or four-hundred-pound payload in addition to the pilot and two passengers, a plane that can land and take off on water and fly five hundred kilometers at treetop level without refueling!"

"And then he will wake up from his dream!" murmured the Hungarian agent, not intending the comment to be translated. "Ask your boss," he finally said," if he has any ideas where such a wonderful plane would miraculously appear from? In this country, you just don't find such a plane in our friendly skies. And even if one existed, it would be owned by the government."

"I don't give a damn who owns the planes, steal one if you must." Sahir put his hand on his forehead and rolled his eyes skyward. "Don't these fools have any imagination? Obviously, not one of them received his training in Palestine!" he commented to Hassan, who as usual stayed in the background.

"Tell this nincompoop that in two days he'd better deliver a plane that meets my specifications with a pilot who will land it right here" – he pointed to a spot on a map – "and who will take off from the same spot with the load and with me and Hassan. And tell him that I want the pilot to fly us below radar all the way to Orekhova in Bulgaria. That's all!"

"But...that's impossible," groaned the Hungarian, raising his hands in protest. "Even if I could find a plane, and the best I can do is a crop-duster, which has very little room for passengers by the way, it won't have the desired range to get there. Is your boss out of his mind?" he asked, totally annoyed with Sahir's unreasonable demands.

"Use your head, stupid," shouted Sahir. "Convert the duster to an amphibian, and use the storage tanks intended for chemicals for the extra fuel. Simple! Five hundred kilometers is nothing. Now get moving. You've already used up a half a day arguing!"

The Hungarian agent left amidst heavy shaking of his head and clearly discernible curses hissed between his clenched teeth. Had Sahir understood Hungarian, he would have heard numerous reference to his mother and all his close relations up and down his respectable and sizeable nomadic family tree.

As it turned out, getting his hands on a crop-duster wasn't all that difficult. Converting it to an amphibian and using the chemical tanks for fuel — well, not easy, but not impossible, either. With money, he could get anything done. The hard part was to find a desperate pilot, a heroically fixated being who'd exhibited suicidal tendencies within the last few months, who wanted to join the ranks of a vanishing species. The Hungarian was beside himself.

"To fly it into Bulgaria? Undetected by border patrol in four countries? Hungary, Yugoslavia, Rumania, and Bulgaria? Five hundred kilometers under the radar? Asinine. Idiotic! The guy is off his rocker!" he mumbled as he went down the narrow staircase from the stifling-hot second-story apartment where the meeting had taken place. He thought of the news he'd recently seen in the papers about the unsuccessful assassination attempt on the Pope and about the alleged plans to get rid of the head of the Polish Solidarity Union. He chuckled to himself as he reached downstairs and looked around carefully before stepping out on the street. "Those goddamn Bulgarians, they bit off more than they can chew, didn't they? I wonder how long they'll get away with it!" He knew he was working with the impossible WOILA, but if there was a subgroup he could not stand to work with, it was the Bulgarians.

Chapter 24:
Yes, There is a Desert in Hungary

Steve's happy mood soon evaporated with the morning dew. The little caravan of four made slow headway against the rising sun into the flat and desert-like country. Able to keep up a lively pace only in the cool morning hours, they found the higher the sun rose above the horizon the slower their pace became. The light backpacks, containing only the bare necessities for a three-day excursion, soon weighed upon their shoulders as heavily as a load of coal.

Steve led the pack now, with Teri and Tony following close behind, and last, about a hundred yards behind them, ambled along Frankie. After the first ten miles Frankie was no longer on speaking terms with anyone. His big face was red as paprika and his eyes flashed furiously if someone called to him to hurry up. Sometimes he talked to himself to keep himself company and trudged along as well as he could. This day of all days the heat and the humidity both shot up, indicating a possible coming change in the weather. Rain perhaps, though the sky was still clear, no clouds visible anywhere on the horizon. They sweated profusely and stopped to drink often, too often actually, running their reserves dangerously low. They hoped to reach a settlement indicated on their map about halfway between the two rivers. Any place that deserved to be shown on a map should at least have water and shade, they reasoned. But that was another five hours away.

The countryside they were crossing was the last remnant of what was a totally undeveloped area subject to unpredictable and destructive floods by both rivers, but especially the Tisza, which did not get regulated at all until the latter part of the last century. As a result, progress was slow in these parts. For years the area was only used for grazing of sheep and cattle, a practice which further deteriorated the land, causing the sands to slowly encroach on the pastures and turning them into Sahara-like sand dunes. In the olden days, the desert-like region was difficult to travel and it provided a haven for outlaws whose lives in some cases even became legendary. Not unlike the Old West, in Steve's mind, as he listened to tales told by his companions. In modern times, however, technology gradually reclaimed much of the land for agriculture, but the population was still extremely sparse, settlements few and far in between. By necessity, the route Steve selected was the most difficult one, but it offered the best protection against being discovered by the Hungarian police or militia.

Passing around a bend along the trail, they came upon a small grassy knoll spread between sandy mounds. Teri decided to follow the trail behind one of the mounds to take care of some business that had weighed heavily on her mind for the last few miles. Her eyes searched the area for a bush or a large rock to provide the opportunity for a much-needed relief, but the choices were few. Under normal circumstances the lack of topography would not have presented any insurmountable problem to her, but with Steve here...well, it was different. She walked away leisurely, her steps somewhat restrained by what might have been pain.

Her scream unexpectedly pierced the silence, startling the men who looked up in surprise to see her leap into the air with the grace of a gazelle and after landing run frantically up the side of the mound. They dropped their gear and raced after her only to be stopped dead in their track by a viper coiled up in the way. Regaining her composure and drawn by curiosity, Teri inched back carefully and let loose a string of curses at the innocent and frightened snake. Her legs were visibly shaking from the shock.

Steve calmly took the rifle from Frankie and aimed carefully. The snake, surprised by the sudden commotion, froze and held its head high, watching Steve motionlessly. Its tongue flickered in and out of its mouth and it emitted a sharp hissing sound that sent chills up one's spine. They all watched in expectant silence.

Steve fired and the beast leaped up into the air in a cloud of sand, splattering its blood and its entrails, bird feathers and bones and all, all over the tall dry grass.

"Yeaccchhh!!" Teri concluded the revolting affair, unaware of the dark streaks forming on the legs of her jeans. She turned and resumed her trek behind the mound. Upon returning, her cheeks were noticeably flushed and her eyes carefully avoided Steve's.

"I spilled my stupid drink," she muttered in embarrassment and fell back to last position as they resumed walking.

Fatigue and heat soon overcame them and they sat down again to rest. To keep cool, they used their drinking water to wet their handkerchiefs to wipe their faces and necks. But that used too much water. Frankie was getting restless. He could tolerate the heat to a degree, but he was definitely unprepared for the long hike. His leg muscles ached unbearably. He cursed loudly and tried to spit on the ground except his mouth was too dry. He felt totally miserable and could not stand to keep quiet any longer.

"All I can say that this better be worth it. This is no joke. This is the desert. Hell, we're running out of water. My tongue is stuck to the roof of my mouth and my lips are chapped raw. How far is that blasted settlement? Show me your map!" He yanked the map out of Steve's hands and looked at it intently. "I say, we've got to know where we're going in this furnace!"

"Knowing it won't make it any cooler and easier," commented Tony quietly, careful so Frankie would not hear.

"What? What did you say?" Frankie hollered. "Keep your mouth shut! Nobody asked you!"

"He said that hollering about it won't make it any cooler, stupid!" Teri came to Tony's help, turning carefully into the sun to dry her pants as quickly as possible. "If I can stand it, you can."

Steve remained silent. To him the weather was nothing like the stuff he encountered in the deserts of California, though the humidity made it feel worse than it actually was. He estimated they would reach the settlement before sunset, hoping to find some supplies there. Things could go to hell in a hurry if they could not get restocked there and if the crew decided they were too tired to continue. He felt he was getting close to his target; the question was, once they found it, how to dispose of it. It seemed natural that Frankie's barge would be the best way to ship it into Yugoslavia, then down the Danube to the Black Sea where his contacts, some Greek shippers, would take it off his hands and get it back to the USA. He chuckled, thinking that his poor friends had no idea how much more they'd gotten than they'd bargained for. But everything in due time.

His mind drifted back to cool and breezy Monterey. Just the spot to be in, right now. He saw himself strolling the quaint streets in Carmel, arm in arm with Ildikó, the two of them enjoying the sweet little shops and art galleries, the variety of fabulous restaurants. The echo of her voice as she lectured him in the cool dark cathedral in Budapest rang in his ears still. "You are now in the Saint László chapel. One of our early kings who led a saintly life and according to legend brought forth water from the rock with his sword. This scene is depicted on the wonderful fresco overhead." Her voice sounded so sweet, so lovely, and so real that he opened his eyes to see if she was there. But he saw nothing but an ocean of sandy waves frozen into immobility by the curse of an evil spirit. He wished that King Saint László would have accompanied them on their journey, if for no other reason than to find water.

He shook off his momentary weakness and stood up. "Let's go! We have an agreement, remember? Not to mention the next installment, if we make it, that is. Do you guys want the money or not?"

The rest of them picked up their gear and fell into line with amazing obedience. There was no further discussion on the subject of heat. Steve seemed to have discovered the proper way to prod them into motion.

In spite of the humid heat and their previous exhaustion, they made good headway and about four in the afternoon Tony excitedly reported from atop a sand dune that the settlement was in sight.

"Phew! I thought we'd never make it," sighed Frankie. "Come to think of it, it wasn't so bad after all." They were all smiles.

Steve patted him on the back. He had to stretch to do it. "I bet someday you'll remember this outing as the best one you've ever had in your life."

"And the only one, I hope!" Frankie laughed.

They were still a quarter of a mile away from the settlement when out of a small dust cloud came a group of kids running out to meet them, most of them scantily dressed, if at all. Some were stark naked. And dirty! Their deep dark skin and shiny black hair suggested that it might be a settlement of gypsies. The filthy little rascals jumped all over them and begged to carry their backpacks. They willingly obliged but kept a wary eye on the stuff, just in case. The oldest, obviously their leader, showed off his skill at cracking his whip. It made such a loud crack that the visitors were forced to cover their ears. It was painful to hear it. The other kids did not seem to mind.

The village, if it could he called as much, consisted of a few houses, barns, a row of acacia trees, and a well. Yes, a beautiful, modern artesian well. Turned out that artesian wells were the only means to bring water to the surface from extreme depths. In spite of the sea of mud surrounding the well, our company of four soon found themselves right in the middle, washing and splashing and drinking merrily, unperturbed by the cheering flock of children and gawking members of the adult community driven out of the shade by curiosity. They made quite a spectacle of themselves. Teri's pants became soaking wet again but she only laughed when Tony made a passing remark regarding the color. The group's outlook improved measurably despite the discouraging mess that surrounded them. What they saw was quite depressing, however colorful. The scene of abject poverty these people suffered was reflected in the crumbling walls of the adobe houses, in housetops made of twigs and tall prairie grass, in fallen broken fences. Cats and dogs, pigs and goats, and all manner of poultry roamed the area and created a deafening noise each time the kids rushed them to chase them away. The animals seemed as curious as the humans. One muddy swine decided to scratch his back against Frankie's leg. He found this outpouring of welcoming affection too much to take and sent the pig along its way with a terrific kick in the ass. The friendly creature departed, objecting amidst earsplitting squeals.

Tony's sharp eye immediately caught a glimpse of a couple of horses tied up in the ramshackle stables and a great big hairy mule put out to the meager pasture. He approached an old man in the crowd, figuring from his long grey mustache and his long-stemmed pipe that he was the boss, the voivode. He was not mistaken.

"That's the oldest jackass I've ever seen," he observed phlegmatically.

"Old?" The voivode perked up indignantly. "Just what do you mean by old? Maybe you've never seen a mule before! If he is a day older than you, I'll give him to you. How old are you?"

"Eighteen," Tony exaggerated, looking around perplexed. He had not the faintest idea of the longevity of the long-eared animals.

"Like I said," teased the old man, calmly puffing on his weathered pipe, "he is not as old as you are. But you can still have him. All you have to do is ride him away from here."

"Me? You mean it?" Tony's eyes sparkled with the chance offered at riding the rest of the distance tomorrow. "Are you sure? I can really have him?"

"Yes, he is all yours. Go get him."

"Go ahead, ride him," the children yelled in unison, their faces beaming with anticipation of unexpected fun.

Tony began to have second doubts. The closest he'd ever gotten to riding was watching a Western in a movie house that sported American films once in a great while. There was no way to back out now without losing face. To be fair, Tony did have courage. The whole crowd closed tightly around him and cheered him on. The mule looked friendly enough as it nonchalantly continued grazing, paying no attention whatsoever to the commotion. Fearful of getting bitten, Tony approached the mule from behind. The crowd gasped.

Nothing.

He patted it on the back. "Good old mule, nice old mule." The children were laughing hysterically as he muttered under his breath. The animal totally ignored his advances. He grabbed the thick fur around the mule's neck and, straining, he put a leg over the animal, standing on his toes to reach high enough. Carefully, since the animal still did not move, he pulled himself onto the mule's back and sat up, squeezing hard with his knees, holding tight the fur with one hand, patting the animal with the other.

Still nothing.

The mule slowly picked up his big head and stopped munching and shook his head as if chasing the flies away. Tony relaxed and turned toward the crowd to give a triumphant smile. Nobody smiled back. Funny, he thought. He nudged the mule with his heels to get him moving.

Suddenly all hell broke loose. The mule dropped his head and bucked violently, kicking with his hind legs machine-gun fashion. Tony flew up in the air, then crashed back on the violently writhing animal's hard, bony back, not letting go of the fur and hanging on for life. The mule screamed and hee-hawed and kicked again and jumped wildly to unseat his rider, running in circles and heading for the crowd right through the mud puddles. Tony bounced at least four feet above the mule as it lurched forward, throwing his hind high up in the air, then fell back, except the mule did not care to wait for him. It took off right through the crowd, amidst screaming kids, squealing pigs, and squawking, screeching poultry.

Tony landed smack into the middle of the thickest mudhole, falling on his back, nearly disappearing in the disgusting sopping brownish muck.

The spectators laughed hysterically. Kids ran up to him and jumped into the mud, covering themselves also with the slimy stuff. Soon, the lot of them were wrestling and sliding and throwing big handfuls of mud into each other's face. The pigs joined happily into the free-for-all.

Needless to say that after considerable time spent under the water spout trying to clean up, Tony assiduously avoided the friendly villagers. He'd had his fun for the day.

While enjoying the spectacle at the well, Steve became aware that he was being watched. Soon he located a pair of shining black eyes peering at him from behind a group of young men. He could not resist looking back; the eyes burned the back of his neck and their owner was a gorgeous young gypsy girl with striking features who apparently tried hard to get a better view of him. As the herd of people scattered in panic to open the way for Tony's crazed mule galloping by at full speed, she managed to cross over to his side and drifted closer to him. With all the commotion, Steve was able to get only partial glimpses of her, but what he saw convinced him that she was the most shapely, exquisite desert flower he had ever seen. He stopped following Tony's hilarious escapades and paid more attention to search her out from among the milling crowd. Undoubtedly, she'd been created by Mother Nature in one of her most fickle and generous moods. Her coloring, her smooth olive skin touched by the flush of the excitement of the day, the long raven-black hair, great big expressive eyes, and full, luscious red lips. Steve attempted to take further inventory but was prevented from doing so by the cursed horde. She appeared anxious to get closer and communicate with him. But before they could reach each other she was forcefully dragged away by a young man in an obvious fit of anger.

The rowdy mood eventually abated and Frankie took advantage of the quiet moments to approach the voivode and bargain for the two horses he felt had a fighting chance to make it the rest of the way with an appreciable burden. He figured that he needed one of them, Steve and Teri could ride the other, and Tony, well, he had his own mule now. The bargaining process took less time than expected and Frankie developed an uneasy feeling about the bargain. In his mind, the old gypsy could have squeezed him a lot more than he did, but be it as it may, a hundred dollars bought the two horses. Since he had no means to break the several two-thousand-dollar bills into smaller denominations, he had to beg Steve to advance out of his own pocket the two hundred dollars. Steve reluctantly agreed, having looked the horses over and deciding that they were strong enough to carry the backpacks if not the riders.

As evening drew near the villagers settled down to the business of the evening meal, to which Steve's party was cordially invited. Sitting next to the voivode, Steve had his fill of barbecued goat meat and goat cheese and an earful of tales about the tribe. Steve questioned the old man at length about the desperate tank battle of 1944 and inquired whether he knew of any mysterious disease that might have spread among folks living in these parts. The voivode shook his head, not recalling anything unusual, though he did indicate that the general location of the battle was strictly avoided by his people since it was considered to be a place of death, haunted by evil spirits, filled with skeletons and terrible things. Only the demented went there to dig up the graves and skeletons and disturb the sleeping spirits. Steve suspected that the digging he referred to might have been due to cleanup efforts or archeological excavations, both of which the superstitious villagers avoided with fear.

Overall, the visitors were welcomed with genuine openness and without reservation by most of the villagers, except for a group of young thugs who cast suspicious and angry glances at the newcomers. Especially at Steve and Tony. The village machos appeared to resent the intruders on their turf. No different from the gangs in the big cities, Steve thought, recalling countless examples of gang-related articles in the Californian press. He ignored their dirty looks and impertinent remarks.

It became dark, the flames of the blazing campfire were shooting high in the air, and the party was on. No self-respecting gypsy would be caught dead at such a gathering without his violin, and here too there were a dozen of them. Soon the night resounded with fiery dances and heartbreaking melodies. No other people on earth can make their violins speak in tongues of birds or make their instruments cry like the gypsies. Steve's heart floated on the music.

She danced. In her graceful movements, he saw the flying swallow zigzag through the air, the palm trees sway with the breeze, the twirling dervish of the Far East spin with dizzying speed, it was all there, and all for him alone. She was saying something, calling, enticing, hypnotizing. His head began to swim in a pink cloud. Thirsty, he gulped down another cup of heady beer. It was in his heritage to fully enjoy this fiery display of enticing and fascinating insanity. This was not Las Vegas, this was not Monte Carlo. Her dance was unrehearsed. Her dance was an intoxicating and spontaneous expression of primitive sexual offering. And the music, the frantic rhythm, the haunting melody, these had been known to drive his ancestors into suicide with unflinching pleasure. His blood was racing in his veins, his heart pumping wildly, and he started to get up and join her in this crazy and beautiful dance.

The music stopped.

Steve looked around, his head swirling with all the emotions whipped up in him, and noted in amazement that he seemed to be the only person affected this way. The musicians rested, the noise of lively chatter suffused through the air, the magic was gone. He felt cheated and disappointed and wanted to shout, "Please don't stop, please continue, I've just began to enjoy it!" But he felt foolish and kept silent.

When he looked up he noticed the beautiful gypsy girl approaching him, her hips swaying seductively with rhythmic motion as old as creation, the female of the species stalking her male. Her crimson lips were half parted, showing perfect and sparkling white teeth; her big black eyes remained affixed on him with the concentration of a hypnotist mesmerizing her subject. The glowing fire behind her shone through her colorful chiffon skirt, revealing a silhouette of slender legs, perfectly shaped thighs, and round full hips. It occurred to him that she was wearing nothing underneath. Her large but firm round breasts were scantily covered by a red shawl tied in a knot in the middle, exposing more satin olive skin than his eyes could scan in a single glance. Reluctantly, he looked again, unwilling to take his eyes off her thighs. He felt the hair bristle on the back of his neck and a warm flush flooding his loins.

She spoke in a deep-throated voice and pronounced her words slowly. Even so, he had difficulty understanding her as she intermixed words with strange guttural sounds, words he had never heard before. He had to ask her repeatedly to forgo gypsy expressions.

Soon she came to the point. While speaking to him she stroked his arm with the softest hand imaginable and drew lines with her long fingernails on his chest through the opening of his unbuttoned shirt. It sent chills up his spine and he felt an overwhelming desire to grab her. He also felt angry, noticing her nervous glances cast over her shoulder in the direction of the same group of young men he'd seen before, now huddling and crouching around the blazing bonfire.

"My name is Zena. What's yours?" she purred.

"Steve."

"Do not look so eager, Steve. He is watching us."

"Who is?"

"My fiancé. The one that's leaning against the tree stump, playing with his knife."

"Oh! I see. Your fiancé, so, you're gonna get married?"

"The hell I will." Her eyes flashed. "That's what I want to talk to you about, it is my father's will that I marry him. I loathe him! I want to get away from here. I hate this place! I want to go to the city, become a model. Take me with you. I will repay you!"

"Repay me? How?" Steve inquired with increasing excitement, his eyes roaming over her curves hungrily, places where he wished his hands could be. He shook his head as his vision blurred and tasted a weird taste in his mouth.

She wooed him more. "I have ways; you look like you haven't seen a woman in a while. I can tell in your eyes," she snickered.

"I didn't know it is so obvious," Steve answered as a strong electric shock flashed through his body and it began to ache with unbearable desire. "Careful, if you touch me again, I won't be responsible for my actions."

She threw her head back wildly. "Oh? But I want to touch you again," she teased. "But not here. Meet me in my room tonight. See the candle in my window, near the big acacia tree? Come to that one. I will leave my door unlocked. I will tell that one that I have a headache. Be careful, though. Carry a weapon, gypsies always do. And keep a pair of eyes in the back of your head. Even shadows can be deadly around here. You could be killed, if they find out."

"Don't worry, just be there," Steve said, and his eyes followed her sumptuous figure outlined against the light of the fire. He became as aroused as he had ever been. The danger, the anticipation of the wild passionate embrace, drove him mad with desire. He lost his powers of reasoning, his common sense. He fell under the spell of the beautiful gypsy girl. Not the first time for a man in history.

He took another big swig from the tepid beer. He spat it out with disgust and wondered if it had been spiked. It tasted funny and he felt unusually woozy.

The young men, in their late teens or early twenties, sat around the fire motionless and seemingly uninterested, but there was tension on their expressionless faces and their eyes stared into the dancing flames. Zena's fiancé stood up with a black stare on his youthful face. In the dim light, a huge white scar across his face showed that he had already proved his manhood. When Zena reached him, he turned away abruptly and with a flash of his arm threw his knife against the tree stump. The six-inch blade penetrated the wood deeply and its handle vibrated noisily for several seconds. His friends looked up briefly only to look away again as if nothing had happened. Zena and her fiancé spoke briefly and she tore herself out of his restraining grip and ran into the house.

Steve felt for the handle of his own knife and ran his finger along the razor-sharp blade. Appearing completely uninterested, he turned and walked into the darkness. Only Teri sensed that he was in big trouble.

Later, after the fire burnt itself out, she crept up to Steve and whispered in his ear. Her voice quivered with concern.

"Don't go near her. She is certain death for you. You don't know these people. They are as wild as the Puszta. They have their own rules, they are macho men. They must kill you to protect their honor. I beg you, listen to me." Steve pushed her away without a word. Her protective behavior really bugged him now. What did she think she was anyway? His babysitter? She withdrew sobbing.

Soon the candle in Zena's room was snuffed out and Steve stood up. He almost filled his britches as he bumped into Frankie in the dark. His frame loomed large over him. "I wouldn't do it, if I were you!" he said and put a fatherly hand on Steve's shoulder, buckling his knees a little.

"Leave me alone, for God's sake." Steve jerked his shoulder out of Frankie's grip and disappeared, leaving in a direction opposite the house. Frankie sighed, relieved. Steve, however, took a turn after some distance and headed back toward the house on a semicircular path. He would walk twenty paces, then halt and listen intently. Each crackle of the still-smoldering fire startled him repeatedly. His heart was beating audibly. Finally, he reached the door. Pushing down the handle, he carefully tried to open it but the damn thing creaked loudly. He stopped and held the door motionless, wondering what the hell to do next. He whispered: "Zena, it is I!" There was no reply. Minutes passed and sweat poured down his face and for an instant he wished he would have stayed far away from this place. But he was committed. He could not let go of the handle for fear that the door would creak, so he held his breath and shoved it ajar forcefully, careful not to bang it into the wall. The door moved silently and obediently. He exhaled and called for Zena again, but still no answer. "I must be crazy to do this," he thought, but entered the room and tiptoed toward the back of the room, where he expected to find the bed. After bumping into several pieces of furniture he finally reached it. She lay on top, unclothed, silent. His hand caressed her leg, her thigh, and followed her gentle curves up to her warm round breasts. As his hand ventured further up toward her face it bumped into something cold and wet protruding out of her chest. He shuddered violently and cursed involuntarily.

"That son of a..."

He could not finish, and as soon as he said it he knew he was dead. He wanted to straighten up quietly but suddenly a blinding beam of light flashed into his face and went out again. In the split second the light was there he saw the shape of a man flying toward him. In utter panic, he yanked the knife out of Zena's chest and thrust it blindly into the darkness. He felt the blade penetrate something hard, nevertheless yielding, and heard a groan and the dull thump of a body on the dirt floor. He listened for further sounds of motion. Nothing. Suddenly, he felt very tired and dragged himself toward the faint light coming through the open door. He stopped briefly outside and sighed deeply. His hand was sticky wet and he tried to rub it off on his pants but it would not come off. He left in the direction he'd come from.

His friends were already waiting for him.

"I think we'd better leave right now. I think I killed him. He murdered Zena, the rotten bastard! I am so sorry," Steve stammered.

Teri quickly put her arms around his shoulder and helped him along the dark path to follow the others into the protective cape of the black night. Wild geese honked high overhead and dogs barked in the distance.

Steve kept muttering as he walked. "I am so sorry, I am so sorry, I should have listened to you."

"I understand, she was very beautiful," Teri reassured him. "But I think she deserved her fate. She was an evil woman and caused the death of many a man. She drugged your drink!"

The caravan was back on the road again. This time their transportation was waiting ahead of them, two horses and a mule. Tony had triumphed after all.

The matter of the uranium lost on the banks of the Tisza was ever on Steve's mind. After all, his mission was to recover it without delay; Attila's sword was only a side interest, an adventure, or so he wanted to believe. He was given strict orders to find it, recover it, or determine that it was no longer of use to anyone, especially WOILA. After the escapade with the gypsy girl, he experienced pangs of guilt; after all, he was on an assignment. For all he, or anyone else, knew, the Uranium would still be useable for building one or more dirty bombs. The Arabs, Sahir and

Hassan, would not chase him all over Hungary for nothing, even making attempts to kill him. Certainly, Ildikó was an important distraction, no matter how beautiful and desirable, no matter how much he began to have feelings for her that he had not experienced before. He had to admit, he was in a terrible mess, more confused than at any time before.

Steve shook off his wandering thoughts and decided to reconfirm with the on-orbit crew the coordinates of the suspected location of the tanks and the uranium. He sent a message to Baumgarten asking for a reaffirmation of the coordinates, his message indicating that he was very close and now he needed to get serious step-by-step directions. To his frustration, the message was not received for some reason; there was zero response from Baumy. "Damn," he muttered. He decided to proceed with his friends in the general direction his map indicated, hoping that when he got to the spot, there would be enough distance between the tanks and the dig to not confuse and endanger either mission.

Thanking his good fortune, he arrived near the tanks, half submerged in water and half in sand. Amazingly visible to all from below or above. A pure wonder that they were still there and exposed to both people and the elements. Perhaps the location, desert-like and far from all civilization, possibly safe from the superstitious gypsies. Ildikó's dig was some distance further upstream, so Steve and his friends could crawl to the rusted behemoths under the shadow of the thickets and stay out of sight of Ildikó and the diggers, who were obviously quite busy with their own work. Steve and his friends snuck upon the giant Tiger tank and climbed on top of it and tried to pry open the access hatch, which, to their good fortune, was rusted through and through and could be easily dislodged to gain access to the inside. The access was made extremely difficult by the burned skeletons of the German crew who'd tried to escape their fiery death. With a shove or two, the skeletons crumbled to the floor, opening a view to a big metal box, black, charred, but closed and mainly undamaged. Images of the Radiation Danger signs were still visible, giving Steve a reason to remain optimistic. Just how to get it out and hide it from archeologists, Arabs, and the Hungarian Secret Police?

Steve decided to wait for nightfall, while Frankie, Teri, and the others worked to clear the inside of the tank and dig a shallow temporary hole for the box in the wet sand. Steve noted some equipment, weapons and sundry items that were still recognizable, even after forty years of having been buried in sand, occasionally in water. The big gun was still in position and pointed in the direction of the dig. He thought that it might even fire, but this was no time to try it. He also had his doubts about the condition of the uranium, but hell, he was no expert; all he knew was that it probably had a half-life of a couple of centuries. Nightfall came, his crew collapsed on their tarps among the bushes, and Steve decided that he could not resist paying a surprise visit to Ildikó, who probably badly needed him to solve her own problems. He started to walk to her still-slightly-illuminated tent.

Chapter 25:
A Clash of Cultures

Ever since her new discovery, she'd become tense and extremely irritable. Very impatient and, as a matter of fact, her assistant found it increasingly difficult to tolerate her demands any longer. Even the workers complained to Sándor that her demands on them were unreasonable and certainly damaging to their morale. Sándor tried as best as he could to smooth the ruffles and offered no other explanation to them than "It must be that time of the month, hang in there, guys, it won't last forever."

The night Ildikó suggested to Sándor that she'd discovered Attila's tomb was not one he was likely to soon forget. He just did not understand her emotional outbreaks, the horrible nightmares, her delirious torrent of words at the grave, claiming that, somehow, she actually knew that the king of the Huns was really buried there. He had to swear on his honor not to tell a soul about anything she said or did at the time and pretend as if nothing had happened. Sándor could sense the tremendous strain that she was under and actually feared for her sanity. He contemplated various ways to suggest to her to take a break and relax her nerves for a while. He heard from Ildikó about her brother defecting to Austria and assumed that most of her strange behavior could be attributed to her concern over his future.

Attila's spirit hovers over the DIG

John, the assistant, on the other hand, was fed up with her irrational insistence to hurry the work. She knew as well as he that this type of work was best done patiently and unhurriedly to avoid the many costly and irreversible mistakes bound to happen when the crew worked haphazardly. Besides, the rains were at least two weeks away, so what was her problem anyway?

Just this morning she'd made such a temperamental scene at the grave that he decided to wire her superiors to recall her at once. He offered no detailed explanations but indicated that her behavior damaged the morale of the workers. He knew that the office wouldn't act without an investigation, but at least one of the superiors would visit the site and have a talk with her. He felt more than a little guilty for having done this behind her back, but he was sure that it would be in her best interest to be relieved of her responsibilities for a short time. On the other hand, John viewed himself as a perfect replacement for the job and figured he had enough seniority for a promotion long overdue. The change would do some good for both of them.

Ildikó spent a terrible night, incessantly pacing the confines of her tent like a lioness, at once angry and racked with pain and frustration. She wanted to reach out and touch that casket she knew was there, separated from her by no more than a few inches of dirt. She acknowledged to herself that by now her recent behavior must have irritated and alienated all her coworkers, and she was hurt by the rejection she felt radiating from those she loved. But she could not help becoming enslaved by the overwhelming desire to be the first to unearth the world's greatest archeological find since the tomb of Tutankhamun. A find which, in light of the scant information existing on the Huns and their leader Attila, might in a sense be even more significant, if not as glamorous. Legends about the mighty warrior and leader were told for centuries, whetting the appetites of archeologists and fortune hunters alike. Perhaps she would be the lucky one; yes, she knew she was.

Consistently she fought the strange thoughts and premonitions that her subconscious forced upon her, and resisted the notion that in another life she personally knew Attila. What a macabre suggestion, what a horrible thought to dig up her lover's bones from under fifteen centuries of dust and dirt. Besides, if her nightmare was accurate, she should find her own bones nearby as well. The bones of the girl in the wooden cage...if this was Attila's grave it must also be hers. Stupid...she shuddered and shook it off. But it did not let her rest and she resumed the cataloguing of a pile of bones in her tent. By the time she realized it was quite late and the sun was already setting below the horizon and her dark tent was becoming intolerably hot. She got up and opened the flaps on the door and the windows to get some breeze through. She heard steps just outside.

"Hi, Miss Vértes, I presume?" she heard a familiar voice say, and she flew out the door into the arms of the man she had missed so much lately.

Embarrassed by her sudden outburst of ecstasy – after all, he was still a stranger whom she'd met only twice – she quickly withdrew and blurted out, blushing and smiling broadly, "I thought you were drowned and dead!"

"Well, do I look like a corpse to you? You've been seeing too many skeletons lately. Maybe I really appear like one. Do you have a mirror I could borrow?" Steve teased in his usual manner, and she thoroughly enjoyed it.

"No, no, I didn't mean that, you look just fine, just fine!" she grinned, her eyes sparkling with delight. "I am so glad to see you. I'd just about given you up for dead."

"May I come in?"

"Please do, and don't mind the mess. I just finished work. It's not that I am lazy. I had a terrible night, not to mention work. Can I get you something?"

"Water. Lots of water. The colder the better. It was a long ride. I don't think I will ever cool down. Say! I didn't realize that I would find you here, what a coincidence. I must say I am glad. Is this where you dig for your Huns?"

"Yes, this is the place. I must show you around. I think you said that you were interested in Hunnic relics. You should be delighted with what we have here. But here, a glass of water. I am afraid I have no ice."

"Thanks." Steve drank heartily, the water streaming down on both sides if his mouth. He was dehydrated. He returned the bottle and looked at her. She seemed a little worn since he'd seen her. She returned his gaze, poorly disguising the joy she felt.

"We have a lot to talk about," she laughed. "I was not much of a guide to you, was I?"

"Well, you can't hardly blame yourself for my sudden disappearance. Please accept my sincere apologies. I hope I didn't get you into any trouble?"

"No, don't mention it. All my troubles were of my own, nothing to do with you. I was actually glad to come back to work here. But it's good of you to drop in."

It was like opening the floodgates. She simply could not stop talking. About everything. About things she would have considered too personal to share with someone she hardly knew. Without consciously considering it even for a moment, she felt completely at ease to confide in Steve and she poured out all the bottled-up emotions, her concerns about her brother, her parents, about Kutas, who would show up any time to question her, about the pressures of her job, the workers' resentment of her behavior and short temper; and on and on she went, venting off the pressures and nagging little doubts within her that threatened her very sanity.

The one subject she very carefully avoided was her nightmares and any references to Attila's grave. She was just too embarrassed about that part of her life. It seemed so unreal, so confusing – how could anyone understand it? She had kept it a secret, even from Steve.

The time went by almost unnoticed. At dawn, she gave Steve a tour of the excavation, chattering without a stop, introducing him to everybody. Admittedly, the workers immediately took a liking to him, if for no other reason that he kept her off their back for the best part of the day.

Steve attempted unsuccessfully and at numerous occasions to interrupt her and to interject a comment or an observation, but to no avail. Only toward noon did she finally realize that she had done all the talking, and, asking for his forgiveness, inquired about his own experiences for the past few days. Steve, however, declined, saying that there wasn't that much to talk about and that there would be other opportunities to do so, he hoped. Ildikó assured him that there would be.

She was so busy talking and showing Steve the interesting points of the excavation that she failed to notice him taking a few notes on a small notepad, as if he were measuring up the area. What she did not know was that Steve found that the NASA-provided coordinates matched up exactly with the fenced-off area. He began to worry about the possibility of the archeologists finding the uranium and having been exposed to the harmful radiation. He tried to make several skewed references to a large metal container but Ildikó only gave him a blank stare, obviously not knowing what he was talking about.

Steve begged off for a short period and prepared himself for something he should have already done earlier. In his little notepad, he had the mission timeline for the space shuttle *Discovery*, from which he knew that in the next few minutes the ship would be directly overhead, ready to communicate. He wanted the exact coordinates of the container. As instructed by Baumgarten, he lay on his back and spread his legs to get maximum exposure to the incoming signals.

He waited.

In a little while he felt a tiny electric shock tickle his left wrist, just under the black plastic watch he had been wearing. He pushed the code on the tiny buttons, acknowledging the signal. He reset the watch again for receiving and waited, intently watching the blank display on the wristwatch. Occasionally, scrambled symbols flashed through the screen, indicating that the ship was trying to transmit. He rotated his position slightly to get a better alignment with the spacecraft's flight direction and acknowledged the signal.

All of a sudden legible and comprehensible letters and words appeared on the tiny display.

"DISCO..RY .O.G.OUND. ACK.OWLE.DGE MESS.GE."

He punched in the reply. "GROUND TO DISCOVERY. TRANSMIT."

The words appeared again. "COORDI.NA.ES VERIF.ED. DON.T MOVE. SITT.NG RIGHT .N TOP OF T.RGET. G..D LUCK. OUT. BY THE WAY, WH.T'S ALL THE OT.ER STUFF?"

"Holy smokes, I am sitting right on top of it? Good God, what is she digging up here?"

He sat up as Ildikó approached.

"What were you doing? You must have been looking at your watch for five minutes. Is something wrong?"

"No, I wanted to stretch out a bit. It's a technique I learned in Yoga. I must show it to you sometime. No better way to relax. Have you ever practiced Yoga?"

"No, I am afraid I haven't." She looked at him strangely.

During the course of the day Steve had had a brief opportunity to introduce his friends as well. He received more than a few raised eyebrows at the colorful appearance of the soiled barge crew. The emaciated horses and the long-haired mule elicited more than just a few laughs and comments. At evening meal, when they were invited by Sándor to join for dinner, the few workers who remained at the site to work some overtime complained to the foreman that they were not about to sit at the table with these questionable characters. Frankie made sincere efforts to befriend the stuffy peasants and for the time being it seemed that a relative congeniality, however strained, had been achieved. It was like East-West relations, a cold war on a personal scale.

When Teri had a glimpse of Ildikó and Steve together she knew her secret love affair was really in trouble. Last night she'd feared for Steve's life; today she feared for her own. She knew it was hopeless; Ildikó was the one for him. "All he wanted to do was find the bitch!" she grumbled and kicked Frankie in the shin, causing him to hiccup in surprise.

"What the hell do you want?" he hissed. "Get ahold of yourself, you'll ruin the whole thing yet. Stay away from him and remember, I am your husband." He beat his hairy chest. Teri turned and spat.

From then on Teri became morose and refused to eat or talk and acted extremely unsociable with everyone. Even the teasing she got from the younger workers failed to cheer her up, even though they reminded her so much of the tractor brigade. She sat on top of a dirtpile and watched with envy Steve and Ildikó walk together, immersed in lively conversation. They were such a lovely pair, matching each other so well. So smart and sensitive, both of them. She knew instinctively that no gypsy beauty would be a match for the pretty archeologist.

During the day, Steve had enough of the Huns for a while and suggested they take a rest. "I am tired, how about you?" he sighed, lying back and closing his eyes. In reality, he wanted a chance to stop her from talking archeology and get down to a more personal level. But he was tired, travelling all night and till late morning, and his conscience would not let him forget the incident with Zena. He knew he had been tricked and felt very fortunate to have escaped with his life. But the thought of the beautiful girl killed in cold blood bothered him greatly.

Ildikó felt that something was troubling him and she wished she could help, but did not know how to go about doing it. She watched his tired face, still bearing the telltale signs of his accident and the adventures of the past few days. She wondered if he'd suffered much and leaned closer to his face to get more familiar with the features she'd come to like so much. She carefully adjusted the tarp above them to keep the sun out of his face and sat up and watched the work going on around them in the distance.

Over the work area of the dig, there hung a huge dark-orange dust cloud, a very painful nuisance, but an indication that progress was being made. She gently put her hand on his and leaned her head against his shoulder briefly, to let him know she cared. That insignificant contact, that inconsequential human touch, was to her like getting her batteries recharged. It was like a human filling station for her emotionally drained self. She stayed that way, frozen still until he moved.

"Please don't move. It feels so good," she said.

"All right. Put your head back where it was."

"I am so glad you're here, Steve. Don't leave me, I need you very much." She turned pensive and hung her head down.

Steve stroked her hair. "What are you doing?"

"Just sitting here, thinking."

"About what?"

"Lots of things. Árpád, me, you."

"Me?"

"Yes, you too." She smiled. "Not all bad, I hope."

"No. Not all bad. But" – she changed the subject – "I still am worried to death about this police officer. I think Kutas really is an evil person. I think he wants to hurt people. For some reason, he did not arrest my brother that day, but I am sure it wasn't because he did not want to."

"Arrest him? For what?" Steve asked.

She proceeded to tell him about Kutas's visit to her apartment. It was obvious that the memory of that morning still weighed heavily on her mind. She became quite agitated as she spoke.

"That police man, that captain in his neatly tailored uniform and shiny boots! He looked so awfully confident. So cocky and smug in his attitude. God, I'd like to see him just once under different circumstances, out of his uniform, out of his element. And see if he could keep his cool. That parasite! I hate his kind!" Ildikó's cheeks were crimson with anger. Her black eyes darted to and fro and finally came to rest on Steve.

He answered thoughtfully, sensing the pain and fear in her.

"Of course he is smug. He is no different from the rest of the damned bureaucrats. They all get that way given enough time. It is a natural progression in our society for a man to start out lean and hungry, ready for change and sacrifice. He is full of drive and desire to improve his lot, maybe the lot of others, to alter the way of things. He may go to extremes to reach his goal and, having achieved it, he himself becomes unchangeable.

"Visualize the avalanche, for instance. Once it starts sliding there is no way to stop it. It falls and rolls and slides, moving toward its unalterable goal, that of reaching the bottom. It moves boulders, destroys forests, plows mercilessly through anything in its way. But once it comes to a stop, having done its work, it becomes completely complacent, frozen in place, as in dead weight; like a wounded elephant falling on top of the unfortunate hunter who was not agile enough to move out of its way. Such is the way with men, with individuals and societies alike. As with the hungry visionary, with the lean revolutionary - your friend the captain finally reaches the top and he finds his niche in the newly created hierarchy, he now has something to fear and to protect, something to keep from changing. Status, income, a nagging wife, insatiable youngsters, you name it. He looks back on the long hard road behind him, paved with sacrifice, sweat, pain, and guilt. He sees the countless men lining up to remove him and destroy him, if necessary. No! He does not want to go through it again. He has arrived. The system he helped create will protect him for a while and gives him the necessary assurance and confidence and inertia. He knows he is safe for a time and knows things will not change overnight. He also knows that if and when they do, he is finished. Kaputt! Therefore, the former instigator of change begins to resist change. He assumes an air of confidence and authority. As the avalanche, he has reached bottom, he has become dead weight."

Steve was getting heated up. He just loved to expound on this subject. It also gave him the chance to do the talking for a change.

"But you see, it is fortunate for the world that there are so many others standing in line behind this type to shove him aside, driving just as madly as he once was to affect change. This is a continuous and unending process. Not that change for its own sake is necessarily desirable or beneficial in all cases. But look at the alternative. Is complacency better? Is stagnation better? No! I think not. Constant controlled and non-violent change is healthy and necessary. No individual or class of individuals should ever become so desperate as to resort to violence and force to affect change on account of short-sighted leadership. On the other hand, no person or class should become so smug in their beliefs to think that they have achieved the best, the optimum, and therefore there is no further need for change and improvement.

"Oh, yes, the captain. I agree, I hate his kind too. Mostly because he represents more than just himself. He represents a system that has tremendous inertia. But there is always hope. Forces are building up unceasingly to move him. There is the next wave of revolutionaries behind him that want their chance to bask in the sun for just a little while and receive the praise and adulation of their peers, unaware that with each coming winter a new avalanche is being formed at the top.

"Your Captain is nothing more than a little man on stilts. One day someone will kick the stilts out from under him and he will be just a little man again."

Later, in the darker hours, Steve joined his friends for a few minutes. He pulled Frankie aside and told him that he had reasons to suspect that they were within reach of their target. On impulse, Steve thought he better keep the location of the target to himself for now.

"Just stay cool. Let's not do anything rash. Wait for me to give the word. I have to locate the damn thing first. But I know it's here. Tomorrow we will look for it, and please keep Teri from screwing things up, OK? By the way, did you see how much junk is scattered all around this place? All war equipment. Finding the stuff I am looking for will not be easy. Hell, it may be impossible!"

Frankie promised to keep himself and the others quiet and reminded Steve that they were not in America and that he had the right medicine to keep Teri in line, if necessary. He showed his hand to him, which in the moonlight looked as big as a stoker's shovel.

Steve and Ildikó joined the others already gathered around the fire. Everyone seemed to be in a pensive mood this evening, perhaps due to the strange reddish coloring of the sky. "Portent of significant things to come," whispered the peasants, who were knowledgeable about such things. Someone brought out a flute, the instrument of the Puszta, and began to play the haunting and bittersweet melodies of the wide-open spaces. Melodies that told of lonely shepherds tending their flock, yearning after their sweethearts; of rowdy outlaws who robbed only the rich to redistribute their wealth among the poor; of love and nature and the swift passage of time. Some of the men joined in with the flute and sang in deep masculine voices songs that brought tears to Ildikó's eyes and reignited in Steve childhood memories with his parents and friends doing the same around their campfire, except one that was eight thousand miles away and many years ago. The songs were reminiscent of the captive Jews singing their famous chorus in Verdi's *Nabucco*.

As the last of the workers disappeared and the last snatches of the songs dissolved into the night, the two of them remained by the fire, still under the influence of the fiery wine and pálinka and sad songs. The fire still glowed, casting long shadows on the ground behind them. Looking down, she drew figures in the sand. One of the figures was that of a stag. Thinking of the Huns and wanting to break the silence, she finally spoke:

"Have you ever wondered what made the Huns into the fierce warriors they were? I have. Was it their social structure? Their ability to freely roam the plains? To run with the wind and not be confined by walls built by men, inhibited by customs and bureaucratic laws? These people only answered to their own immediate leaders. They lacked the complicated hierarchy of the Roman system of government. Perhaps that was to become their downfall. Without structure and walls and buildings there was no permanence. Their short-lived glory, however enviable, was just that; short-lived. But I believe the Huns possessed a quality only free men can possess. Can you recall what Hippocrates said about this quality? It went something like this, and I am quoting loosely: Where there are kings there are great cowards because the souls of subjects are enslaved and they refuse to take risks readily and recklessly in order to increase the power of whom they serve. Independent people, on the other hand, take risks on their own behalf and not on behalf of others, and are willing to go into dangers because the price of victory is all their own."

Steve's eyes followed Ildikó's stick poking the sand. He thought it curious that she kept drawing the same figure. His thoughts ran deep as well while she spoke, but he did not answer. He drew an unconscious parallel between the Huns and the American Indians. Both a fiercely proud and free-spirited people. Neither group particularly adept at the art of survival within the confines of civilization. They both loved their independence too much. Both were consumed by love for nature, their horses, the freedom to move about with the wind, to worship Gods having their roots in nature and in freedom and courage. Both peoples were destined to wither away in a short time after they had been surrounded by fences erected by more complacent men who preferred the security of walls and tradition to open spaces and new horizons. Who was right? Fortunate for mankind, he reflected, that fate produced a blend of both. It would be a terrible world to do without the Huns and Indians of history, but would mankind be capable of surviving without the consistency of sedentary civilizations? Is it not the Hun in our blood that prompts us to explore the deep recesses of space, to roam among the planets and the stars in our mechanical stallions, shooting off our laser beams as arrows in our quest to conquer strange new worlds?

The night sparkled with stars. Occasionally a shooting star streaked across the black expanse broken only by the faint haze of the Milky Way. Ildikó pondered legends she'd heard from her grandmother in her childhood. Legends that were handed down through generations by other fiercely independent people who also had their roots among the people of Attila. In particular, she thought of Csaba, the Prince of the Székely nation, leading his horsemen in charge along the Milky Way, kicking up stardust in their wake.

It felt good for both of them to sit by the warmth of the fire, in the dark of the night, at once united in spirit with one another and with nature and the past. Both were intelligent and sensitive and well educated, dedicated to knowledge, heritage, and self-fulfillment. Neither desired to speak any longer. Words would have only broken the magic that permeated the whole atmosphere. They were in the company of kings, warriors, and each other. "I would that this would last forever," thought Ildikó, and she glanced over to see Steve's profile etched against the night sky. She inched closer and leaned her head against his chest. She felt as secure as never before, as if her destiny were about to be fulfilled here and now, with a person whom she somehow knew and loved before.

Steve reached over and gently pulled the blanket over her shoulders. The night had grown chilly. He bent down to her face bathed by the soft colors of the low-burning fire. Her cheeks appeared flushed and her eyes shone like diamonds.

He lowered his lips to hers and they kissed long and tender.

As their dry lips became wet with the moisture of desire, they kissed harder and harder, biting, nibbling, then biting hard with their teeth, desperately trying to make up for the hunger and unfulfilled passions of what seemed to her like millennia.

Chapter 26:
A Convention of Unlikely
Characters

"**D**on't touch me! Get away from me, you brute!"

"Come on, baby. What's the matter with you? Give Daddy a kiss."

"I said leave me alone! I don't wanna kiss you."

"Hey, this is me, your big daddy. Here, let me hold you. That's it, baby, yeah. Ah HELL!" Frankie screamed. "To hell with you, stupid broad!"

BANG!!!

"Ouch!" Teri yelled as she flew off the cot after Frankie gave her a good shove.

"That'll teach you to kick me in the – ooohhh! Bitch!"

CRASH!!!

A metal bucket flew across the tent and landed on Frankie's head with great noise, spraying cold water everywhere, knocking over and snuffing out the small oil lamp he'd just lit.

"God damn it! I'll get you, just wait!" Frankie jumped up, soaking wet, water streaming down his face, blinding him even more in the already pitch-dark tent. "Don't touch me or I'll scratch your eyes out!" She let out a bloodcurdling primordial scream.

All the others sleeping in their tents sat upright in their beds, their hair standing on end, saying things like, "Oh my God! It must be true. Skeletons do come alive" and "From the wrath of the Huns deliver us, oh Lord!"

CRUNCH!!!

The tent toppled over noisily as Frankie yanked out the centerpost to teach her a lesson in marital obedience.

"Hey, you guys. Keep it down! We're trying to sleep!"

"Stupid grease monkeys. Don't they know it's not even morning yet?"

"Shut up or I'll smash your face!" came the lion-like roar from underneath the violently heaving collapsed mass of heavy canvass.

"Get your hands off my foot. OUCH! I'll kill the ape! So help me God, I will!"

As Steve flicked on his flashlight, the dirty and soiled face of a snarling aborigine gone berserk poked out from under the tarp.

"Teri!" he gasped in horror. "Is that you?"

"Who the hell do you think it is? The witch of Szeged?"

Steve could hear the ending, on account of how she bit her tongue as she struggled to pry off a pair of huge hands closing around her throat.

"What should I do?" Steve shifted his weight to his left foot.

"Just a family squabble, don't pay any attention to them," Tony responded, tugging at Steve's elbow. "Leave them alone. They love each other. They really do."

"They could have fooled me!" Steve said, reluctantly yielding to Tony dragging him away.

"Besides, interfering could cost your life," Tony advised. "I know, I've seen them before. You should've seen the barge. We spent a week rebuilding the cabin."

"Well, the sun is coming up anyway," Steve said, looking around to see the disheveled and disgruntled faces popping out of tents all around them.

"Gentlemen!" he shouted. "It is all right. Just a minor disagreement. Go back to bed. Good night."

"Who the hell is he kidding?" "It's OK, he says!"

"Why don't they get the hell out of here, those bums! Now I'll never get back to sleep."

Comments like this and worse were flying around, loaded with meaning and specific suggestions as the future welfare of the unwelcome intruders. It took a few minutes for things to settle down and for the camp to become quiet again.

"Well, it's a heck of a start," mumbled Sándor, who eyed the dimly lit horizon in the east where the sun's red rays struggled to break through enormous, towering black clouds.

A slight breeze swept through the open campground, picking up scraps of paper and blowing them against the chain link fence where they fluttered and wiggled desperately to break loose.

Just about the time when those awakened by the untimely ruckus had dozed off into that gentle dreamland, the wakeup alarm sounded, unmercifully dragging them back into stark and miserable reality.

Gradually the camp came alive with a lively clatter. Nearby, water was being poured into the common wooden washbasin, previously used for watering cattle, a bucket at a time carried from the river. Those disposed toward personal hygiene vigorously splashed the icy-cold water on innocent bystanders as they gingerly dipped their fingers into it and wetted the corner of their eyes. Others stood around idly, sneezing and clearing their throats loudly. Real men pulled out their palinka flasks and took giant swigs, just to get the day started, so they said.

Further away others were building a fire while the cook rattled his pots and pans, trying to decide whether to improve on yesterday's fare, since his very life had been threatened if he dared to serve it again; but being a brave soul and used to much abuse, he decided to risk it just one more time. "You can't please all the people, well, never" was his motto. Amazingly, he was still alive.

Sándor fiddled with the dials on his battery-powered transistor radio, trying to get an update on the weather forecast. When he finally tuned it in, he was not exactly elated with the results. The weatherman reported an unseasonably early weather front swooping down the plains from the north, pushing destructive squalls ahead of it. He reported it to Ildikó, who just about panicked upon hearing it and issued orders to resume the work immediately, and sent some of the diggers to erect tarps over critical working areas. Her instructions included digging a channel directing any waterflow away from the lower levels of the dig. She was especially concerned with high water that might be coming from the river itself, waves pushed higher by gusty winds.

The wind from the east picked up a little and the lights suspended on wires between posts swung back and forth, the posts squeaking in pain. From the north, a twirling-dervish-like dust cloud approached with great speed, indicating a car or a group of cars heading in this direction.

Steve and his party occupied the high spot on a sand dune covered by trees, and he used his binoculars to survey the riverbank where all the activity took place. He noted that there were two areas visible: one was the dig, the other the rusty skeletons of military equipment a little further away, also along the riverbank.

Steve calculated that his coordinates he'd verified yesterday corresponded exactly with the center of the excavation activity. He surveyed the rusted-out trucks and tanks and wondered how in the world the astronauts picked the one spot over the others.

On the dune, Frankie and Teri were busy trying to erect their tent in the ever-stronger breeze. Their eyes avoided each other's and the dark stares of the rest of the tenants.

Tony tied up the horses and the apathetic mule after feeding and watering them. He placed them right outside the gate, just in case his friends decided on a hasty departure. Amazingly, with the blowing sand, no one noticed them.

Diggers feverishly removed layer after layer of dirt in the center of the mass grave, accompanied by shouts of concern and unguarded curses from John, standing on one side of the mound, and sharp words of exhortation from Ildikó on the other.

A sudden gust of wind toppled a tent and its canvas flapped in the wind with irritating noise. Sándor had some workers put large rocks on the edges to keep it from blowing away.

Out of the dust cloud a big sedan, possibly originally green in color, pulled up at the gate. Five men got out and one of them, apparently an interpreter, animatedly requested permission to enter the premises and inspect the excavation. Sándor reluctantly complied, though it was not his usual policy to permit visitors unless previously authorized by the museum or the resident archeologist at the site.

Damn it. He'd never had such bad premonitions. Why did all these people have to come today? His eyes searched the sky. The wind began to blow steadier but stronger now. Behind it rolled a giant black front. Flashes of lightning could be seen zigzagging between the clouds. But they were still out of earshot.

Sahir, who was one of the passengers in the approaching amphibian-like crop-duster, could hardly believe his eyes. He leaned over to Hassan and shouted into his ear.

"What the hell is going on around here? Where have all these sonsabitches come from? Don't waste your time. After we find it, shoot all of them, if you have to!" He scanned around impatiently.

Ildikó left the grave and searched for Steve to ask for his advice. She could not find him.

Within minutes of her leaving, John rushed down from the mound to report to her that the corner of a rusty container had become exposed and that it was in poor condition and crumbling away. Ildikó wobbled on her feet momentarily and dashed off with John to supervise the progress. Her heart was beating wildly with excitement.

A new dust cloud, larger than the earlier one, appeared on the horizon, this time from the west, suggesting a caravan of sorts. To the north, a smaller cloud raced toward the camp, apparently kicked up by a single small passenger automobile.

The normally calm surface of the Tisza was whipped up into a froth. White caps on the crests of two-foot-high waves sprayed into the air, their droplets sometimes carried as far as the camp.

The small passenger car, a Moszkovics, won the race to the gate. It was the museum director, demanding to see John.

Steve gathered his comrades and gave them instructions to get ready for action. What the action was he did not specify. The situation became more and more clouded, and it wasn't just the weather to blame.

Out of nowhere a twirling dervish suddenly popped up and raced across the flat grounds, hopping between tents and knocking over tables laden with boxes of skeletons awaiting shipment. One wooden box fell off and broke into pieces, bones scattering all over the ground.

Ildikó put her hands to her temples to keep her head from exploding. She saw the director standing with John and arguing. She knew it was about her. And who were these strange creeps standing around the grave anyway? Who in hell let them in?

The metallic box became further exposed, showing about three feet of it sticking out of the ground. Ildikó yelled to the workers to hurry but to be careful as well not to damage it. Instead of acknowledging her instructions, one of them threw a shovelful of dirt up in the air and she got a mouthful of sand to chew on. She could hardly close her mouth without hearing the sickening crunch between her teeth. She spat convulsively.

The large dust cloud arrived at the gate too. Three jeeps loaded with soldiers. They stormed right through the gate, shoving aside Sándor, who was just about to ask if he could help. Ildikó saw the military troops and almost fainted. They were not going to arrest her now, just before her great discovery? She hid behind the mound.

Overhead, so low it almost hit one of the posts, a light plane buzzed the camp and disappeared into the foggy and dusty mist over the river. Hardly a minute passed before another plane flew by noisily in the opposite direction. It was an odd-looking amphibian.

Kutas, who came with the jeeps, shook his fist.

"I didn't order those damn planes, so where in hell did they come from?" His second-in-command shrugged and gave him a blank look. The soldiers raced up the mound and found a gaping hole cluttered with skeletons, old weapons, rocks, shovels, and wheelbarrows. In the center of the hole, sitting on top of a smaller mound, was a dirty, rusty, old, slender black box, maybe about six feet long. Kutas pointed toward the amphibian plane circling above the river, preparing to land.

"Everybody aside! In the name of the government I impound this site! Move carefully. No funny business or we will shoot!" Captain Kutas hollered his orders at the top of his lungs to overcome the increasing roar of the storm. He waved his arms like a madman. The crowd was taken aback by the sudden appearance of militia and they retreated slowly. Someone stepped on the chest of a skeleton behind him, crushing the ribcage into pieces with a disgusting crunch.

"Be careful, you idiots! Look what you have done! Get out of here, all of you!" Ildikó shrieked, her eyes rolling wildly in her eye sockets, her windblown hair totally disheveled. She appeared like a demented witch cursing the mortals.

Kutas stopped, unsure of what to do.

"Listen, young lady," he yelled back, "I have some unfinished business with you. You're in enough trouble already, so stay out of my way!"

The front was moving in and the wind became a steady howl. Sand and tumbleweeds flew everywhere. The sound of thunder was almost overhead. Big fat droplets of rain hit people in the face and on the head.

Steve moved about quietly and unobserved behind the crowd, spreading his troops out evenly, covering the middle from all sides. Each of them carried a weapon, except for Steve. All he had was a shovel. The rest were instructed not to use their weapon unless shot at first by the enemy.

Kutas ordered his men to proceed.

"All right, men, remove the box and carry it to the truck. Careful, don't drop it!"

The soldiers brought in a makeshift stretcher and carefully lifted the box off its earthen pedestal and gently placed it on the stretcher. Large pieces of rust and dirt flaked off where their hands touched it, exposing a black oxidized layer, under which another layer, a somewhat yellowish gleam, was visible.

Ildikó was becoming hysterical. She frantically tried to stop the soldiers from manhandling the box. They just shoved her aside. She fell against a pile of rocks. Her face contorted with pain and rage bordering on insanity.

"You uncivilized morons, you barbaric animals! You'll pay for this! Don't you know what you are doing?" she cried, but her words were swallowed by the deafening roar of the hurricane-like winds of the storm moving on top of them.

The soldiers picked up the stretcher and staggered in the wind toward the gate. A terrific crack temporarily blinded and deafened them all. The lightning hit one of the posts. It burned with bright orange flames, throwing sparks on all directions. The crowd panicked and started to run for cover.

Taking advantage of the mayhem, Sahir landed his plane in the water near the bank and waded ashore. He moved in and pulled out his submachine gun from under his jacket and fired a volley of shots into the air. The people froze in their tracks; some threw themselves on the ground and clawed their way toward the trenches, terrified out of their wits.

"Drop your weapons!" Sahir screamed in Turkish, his machine gun doing the translating. Amazingly, all understood his meaning. Soldiers slowly backed away from the stretcher, their hands held high in the air. Kutas was infuriated with his men.

"Cowards! Take cover and shoot the bastards! Don't let them out of here alive!"

"No! Please don't shoot!" Ildikó begged, throwing herself in front of Sahir. "You'll damage the coffin."

Not understanding, he just kicked her aside. She doubled over in pain.

Seeing Ildikó fall to the ground, Steve had had about as much as he could take. He lost his reasoning and ran up the mound to protect her. As he reached her he stumbled and fell against the casket, knocking it over. It tumbled off the stretcher and opened up. Something fell out of it.

"Oh God!" Ildikó prayed in agony. "I can't stand this anymore." She jumped off the ground and ferociously attacked Sahir.

Teri moved behind one of the soldiers, who took careful aim at Sahir. He was temporarily shielded by Ildikó and the soldier waited. Teri's heart pounded wildly as she for a split second considered the possibility of Ildikó being hit. Then she shook the evil thought from her mind and lifted the crooked legbone high in the air. It must have belonged to a German at one time, it was so big. She smashed the soldier in the head with it and the man slumped down quietly with a surprised look on his face. Teri glanced across to the other side and saw Frankie lifting another soldier high and throwing him into the pit. The unfortunate soul did not come back out. She waved to her husband joyfully.

Kutas's command rose above the noise.

"Shoot to kill!" A round of submachine-gun fire kicked up little pockets of dust around Sahir, who was still wrestling with Ildikó. She nearly scratched his eyes out. Steve stopped for a second to nod at her approvingly.

Hassan moved on Steve with his gun aimed at his belly at close range. Suddenly he recognized his victim and gasped in surprise, "It's you! You didn't drown?" and froze momentarily.

Steve retreated on his buttocks and hands, and as he did he felt a piece of metal behind him. It was a rusty sword. He picked it up to fend off Hassan, though no rusty sword was going to protect him against a hail of bullets from four feet away. He pointed it toward the Turk, who was just recovering from his shock and proceeding to pull the trigger with a sadistic smile on his fat face.

CRACK!!!

A tremendous blinding flash of light shot out of the old rusty sword, knocking Hassan back about twenty feet and splattering his brains all over the place.

Sahir panicked and put his finger on the trigger to finish both this wildcat of a woman and the American, whom he also now recognized. He thought Hassan had been killed by a lightning.

ZAP!!!

The gun fell out of Sahir's hands and his face twisted with excruciating pain as it slowly turned as black as charcoal. He staggered and fell into the dust, his charred hand visible.

The others crawled on their bellies to get away from this hellish place, most of them too afraid to even lift their heads out of the sand. Others watched horrified, driven by curiosity stronger than fear.

Steve moved back to the metal box, which by this time showed the gold on the inside; the silver lining had turned pitch black and the iron had just rusted away. Curiously, Steve wondered why there was no skeleton inside, just a pile of ash.

"Well, I'll be a monkey's uncle. She will be crushed."

Kutas jumped out of his trench and wildly began to fire at Steve. Bullets were hitting everywhere, sparks flying as they ricocheted off the casket.

Steve calmly pointed his magic wand at Kutas. BLAM!!!

Another bluish, lightning-like flash and Kutas's limp body went flying back into the trench.

"Stop! Drop your weapons!" Steve yelled. "Anyone who moves is dead!" He gazed at the thing in his hand.

"Jesus! What's going on? What in the world have I got?" he hollered to himself, his teeth chattering with excitement. He shrugged his shoulder and smiled sort of dumbly.

Overhead a military plane swooped down on them, spraying the area with machine-gun fire. It faltered and was brought down by the storm and headed toward the frothy water. Another flash. The plane exploded in a giant orange ball of flames, its pieces falling all over. The burning fuselage continued on its path until it fell into the river. Some militiamen were able to jump out and hit the water. On the water, several militia riverboats arrived and pulled up to the bank. It suddenly seemed like the whole world had converged on the site. The noise was almost unbearable.

Steve chuckled, "Baumy will never believe this!"

Ildikó sat up and started to laugh. She laughed hysterically, tears streaming down her cheeks.

"Thank you, God of the Scythians! Thank you! Blessed be your name. You have saved your faithful servant after all."

Steve let out a yell of victory and joy. "Yippieeee!!" And he threw the sword high into the air. Instead of falling back to the ground, it began emitting strange colored lights and generating weird humming sounds. Then, with earsplitting noise, it flashed one more time, this time piercing the black cloud overhead. With accelerating and deafening noise, it flew higher and higher until it disappeared in the thick darkness.

"Attila, my love," Ildikó crooned and snuggled up to Steve, kissing him on the lips, her own wet with her tears and the gently falling rain.

"What?... What did you call me? Are you all right?" he said, his face assuming the dumbest expression. She broke into laughter.

"Nothing, my love. Nothing. I am just happy. I love you!" They hugged and kissed passionately.

A tremendous cheer and applause rose from the crowd. Frankie and Teri and Tony were jumping up and down wildly. Sándor was wiping his eyes, deeply touched. He then muttered: "Somebody should really make a movie of this."

After giving up on Attila's sword, Sahir and other WOILA personnel turned their attention to their ultimate goal, the uranium in the tank. Badly hurt but not killed by the sword, he crawled in pain to the tank and commanded his Arabs to quickly surround it, and with some hesitation, and lots of assistance, he climbed in. They could not contain their excitement when the box came into view. Groaning, he tried to lift it off the floor, but found it to be too heavy and gave up to plan his next step. Sahir, ever the curious one, with his remaining hand, fiddled with the gun turret, peeking through the periscope, and to his surprise Steve and Ildikó at the dig came into view. Ever evil and mischievous, he put his finger on the trigger and mockingly pulled it to annihilate his bitter enemies. Nothing happened, so he tried again, this time squeezing much, much harder. Apparently, it was sufficient to trigger the bullet, firmly stuck in the turret. His expression turned to horror as he and the entire inside of the tank turned into an inferno, followed by a huge explosion, blowing the tank, the occupants, and the uranium into a giant fireball.

Unaware of what the activity was at the tank, Steve and Ildikó turned in shock to witness the explosion. Ildikó hugely surprised, Steve smiling broadly.

"What is funny about this, would you mind telling me?"

Steve just chuckled. "I will; after Uncle Sam, it will be your turn to hear. Excuse me for a minute; I have an important call to make. Actually, two calls, I have to tell them both I'll be late!"

Epilogue

"Frankie, old friend...you haven't changed a bit!" Steve shook the shovel-sized hands heartily.

"That's the advantage of growing old at an early age," Frankie replied, embracing both of them and squeezing them breathless.

"Air..." Ildikó gasped.

Frankie might not have turned much older since they'd lost sight of him after the eventful day, but he definitely showed signs of affluence. His once-muscular barrel-shaped chest was now overshadowed by an even more barrel-shaped belly. Surely the sign of the friendly conversations in his little tavern by the old soccer field.

"Hey, Teri! Look who is here!" he bellowed, and momentarily Teri appeared at the door, wiping her hands on her apron and smiling ear to ear with joy.

"My goodness, what a surprise! What are you doing in these parts?"

"We're on our honeymoon. And I bet you won't guess our mode of travel." Ildikó giggled.

"All right. Don't tease. Tell me!" Teri demanded.

"We are travelling the entire length of the Danube on a boat. On your boat. The barge. Isn't that wonderful?"

"My God, there she is!" Teri gasped, looking down the hill toward the Danube. There she was, the big grey whale, unchanged except for the small white honeymoon cabin in the bow.

"Tony!" Teri screamed. "Come here you big, big man. You've grown so much!" She slapped her hands together.

"I am the captain now." Tony showed his badge proudly. "What do you think of that?"

"Oh, I can't believe this is happening." Teri laughed. "Come, tell us everything. How have you been? When was the wedding? Come on, speak!"

Ildikó and Steve gave a detailed account of everything, hardly able to keep up with the questions. They expressed their disappointment at not seeing the crew at their wedding, which had been the event of the year, held at the Coronation Church with half the country present. Even Steve's boss, Baumgarten, was there, though he left his dark molehole only on the rarest of occasions.

"Well, there was this small matter with the police," Frankie muttered. "You know, Dino, and the abandoned barge. But I took care of everything," he chuckled, patting his bulging wallet. "But tell me, Steve – may I now call you Steve? Did you ever find what you were looking for?"

Steve smiled. "Well, as a matter of fact, I did not. Colonel Fehér did. It was still in the river. Rusted and inactive. Of no use to anybody. Oh well. But as far as I am concerned, yes, I have found what I have been looking for." And he put his arm around Ildikó and smiled broadly. They all did.

In the twilight of the evening Ildikó and Steve returned to their cabin and stood on its deck to watch the glorious sunset. They embraced warmly.

"You know, I am still bothered by what you said to me after I threw that junky old sword in the air." Steve inquired, "Why did you call me your Attila? And why did you think you found Attila's grave when actually there was no body in the coffin?"

"Some things simply cannot be explained," Ildikó mused, teasingly. "Perhaps someday we both will understand it. But now, my love, what will you do about our future family?"

"Family?" Steve blushed for the first time in his life. "Is that what you want, a family?"

"Yes. I want a son. And I want to call him Attila. I want that name to live on forever."

"Attila? Whatever you wish, dear." Steve smiled and kissed her passionately.

Ildikó's gaze slipped over the horizon to that great ball of orange fire sinking gently into darkness. She whispered to herself, almost inaudibly:

"Yes. My Attila. The Immortal Hun."

Appendix/Glossary

HUNS

Hunnic names – Ekhe, Attila, Utigur, Ildikó, Kursik, Mundzucus, Tuldila, Gudeoc.

Priscus – Greek traveler and historian at the time of Attila, around 450 AD. Reported extensively about Attila, whose castle in Hungary he personally visited.

Jordanes - Jordanes was a Goth who, although not a scholar, devoted himself to writing history in Latin. His first major work, *De origine actibusque Getarum* ("On the Origin and Deeds of the Getae"), now commonly referred to as the *Getica*, was completed in 551. Recorded Attila's burial in great detail. Wikipedia.

Mundiuch (Mundicus?) – Attila's father.

Theoderic – Father of Attila's bride, Ildikó.

Longobards - Ancient Germanic people. By the 1st cent. A.D. the Lombards were settled along the lower Elbe. After obscure migrations they were allowed (547) by Byzantine Emperor Justinian I to settle in Pannonia and Noricum (modern Hungary and East Austria).

Paleography - The study of ancient writing systems and the deciphering and dating of historical manuscripts.

Hunnic writing: It is possible that a written form of Hunnic existed and may yet be identified from artifacts. Priscus recorded that Hunnic secretaries read out names of fugitives from a written list.[32] Franz Altheim considered it was not Greek or Latin, but a script like the

Oguric Turkic of the Bulgars.[32] He argued that the runes were brought into Europe from Central Asia by the Huns... The runes were inscribed on wood stick like the original hungarian runes. Wikipedia.

GERMANS

Hitler Jugend – German youth who have joined the fight under Hitler near the end of WWII.

Stuka – A famous, fast, and agile German fighter bomber.

Teutonic – Of German origin people.

Tiger – Heavy German tank.

Ferdinand – Heavy German tank, designed by Porsche.

KRIMPOL – German – Criminal Police.

Interpol – International Police.

Ausgezeichnet – German – excellent.

Kaputt – German – dead.

HUNGARIANS

1956 Revolution – Popular uprising against Soviet Communist rule in October 1956. Crushed by Soviet tanks after two weeks of bloody fighting. Over two hundred thousand fled Hungary.

Óhegy – Small mining village in the mountains of North Eastern Hungary – fictitious source of uranium.

Merry Widow – World-famous operetta by composer Emery Kalman.

Árpád – Hungary's prince at the time of the occupation of Hungary by Hungarian people, 985 AD.

Klára Rothschild – Famous fashion designer in Budapest, prior to WWII.

Visegrád – Seat of Hungary's kings, just upstream of the Danube's southbound bend.

Balaton – Large inland lake in Hungary, located in the country's center west of the Danube.

Puli – An ancient breed of Hungarian sheepdog, smart, long-haired, mostly black.

Petőfy, Vörösmarty, Kazinczy, Ady, Móricz, Bartók, Kodály – Famous Hungarian poets and composers.

Fisherman's Bastion – Faces the Danube from the top of Castle Hill on the Buda side.

GYPSIES

The Romani (also spelled Romany; or Roma) – A traditionally nomadic ethnic group, living mostly in Europe and the Americas and originating from the northern regions of the Indian subcontinent. The Romani are widely known among English-speaking people by the exonym Gypsies (or Gipsies), which some people consider pejorative due to its connotations of illegality and irregularity. They are a dispersed people, but their most concentrated populations are located in Europe, especially Central, Eastern and Southern Europe. Wikipedia.

Vojvode (Polish) – Vajda (Hungarian) – Used to indicate the chieftain of a gypsy community. Also, a sort of judge dealing with internal affairs. Wikipedia

RUSSIANS

T-34 – Light Russian tank.

Moszkvics – A small Russian-made communist era car.

Marx - The political and economic theories of Karl Marx and Friedrich Engels, later developed by their followers to form the basis for the theory and practice of communism.

Lenin - Vladimir Ilyich Ulyanov, better known by the alias Lenin, was a Russian communist revolutionary, politician and political theorist. He served as head of government of the Russian Republic from 1917 to 1918, of the Russian Soviet Federative Socialist Republic from 1918 to 1924 and of the Soviet Union from 1922 to 1924. Wikipedia

TERRORISTS

WOILA - World Independent Liberation Armies. A fictitious modern-day terrorist organization consisting of Middle Eastern and German and other members intent on destroying American targets.

Dirty bomb – A bomb containing uranium or plutonium. A small suitcase-sized bomb. Upon explosion by a standard detonator can contaminate large areas and poison thousands of people

USA

CIA – Central Intelligence Agency.

NASA – The National Aeronautics and Space Administration, performed control of Apollo and Space Shuttle flights at Cape Kennedy and Houston sites.

CAPCOM – Capsule Communications Officer.

COMTEC – Communications Tech in a spacecraft monitoring control room.

EECOM – Emergency, Environmental and Consumables Management communicator

EVA – Extra Vehicular Activity; astronaut activity outside the space capsule.

Porifera - Sponges, the members of the phylum Porifera; meaning "pore bearer"), are the basalmost clade of animals. Porifera's innovation may be the most important the pharmaceutical industry has seen in the past 75 years.

MISCELLANEOUS

Tutankhamun – Famous Egyptian pharoah, 1300s BC.

Hippocrates – The Hippocratic Oath is an oath historically taken by physicians. It is one of the most widely known of Greek medical texts. In its original form, it requires a new physician to swear, by a number of healing Gods, to uphold specific ethical standards. Wikipedia.

Made in the USA
San Bernardino, CA
17 December 2018